W9-BZC-693

"It Doesn't Take a Man to Run a Business or Make a Home."

All the frustration of dealing with Ambrose and keeping secrets from Wade poured out of Lottie as she spoke. "It doesn't take a man to run a business or make a home. It takes someone who is willing to stick it out through good times and bad."

Wade held his hands up as if to surrender. "Now, I didn't mean to rile you up, Lottie."

"No, you meant to insult me and the way I provide for Jack and Rose."

"You've made a fine home for the three of you and you know it. But what would happen if you got sick or hurt? Who would harness the mules then?"

He was speaking to her worst fears, the kind she had nightmares about. She clenched the porch rail until her knuckles ached. "I pray very hard that doesn't happen."

"You can tell me to go to hell, but what happened to the children's father? Why isn't he here with you?"

Oh, lord, did he suspect? No, he couldn't know about Ambrose. "That is none of your business."

The color of Wade's eyes turned stormy with swirls of green and gray. "And if I want it to be?"

Somehow, he'd moved so close to her that she could feel the heat of his body. She tried to move away, but he stopped her. "Don't," she said.

He used the side of his finger to turn her face to his. "Don't what, Lottie? Don't ask questions? Don't do this?"

He brushed a kiss across her lips. Once, twice, and then his mouth settled over hers as if its whole purpose in life were to make her feel complete. . . .

Dear Romance Reader,

In July of 1999, we launched the Ballad line with four new series, and each month we present both new and continuing stories set everywhere from medieval England to the American West—the kind of passionate, romantic stories you love best, written by the most gifted authors. At the back of each book, we tell you when you can find subsequent books in the series that have captured your heart.

This month, rising star Cheryl Bolen offers the third installment of her atmospheric *Brides of Bath* series. What will happen when a man driven by honor loses his heart to **A Fallen Woman**? Next, the always talented Tracy Cozzens explores **A Dangerous Fancy** in the next entry of her *American Heiresses* series as a proper young woman, who has caught the eye of the Prince of Wales himself, discovers that a roguish commoner might be her unlikely savior— and the kind of man who could win her love.

The fabulous Pat Pritchard continues her *Gamblers* series with the second of her incredibly sexy heroes. A U.S. Marshal posing as a hardened cardplayer has no time for romance—until he meets a woman who makes him feel like the **King of Hearts.** Finally, promising newcomer Kate Silver whisks us back to the glittering French court of Louis XIV in her brand-new series . . . *And One for All*. When a Musketeer in the King's Guard learns that his comrade may not be all "he" seems, he must promise to keep her secret, **On My Lady's Honor**—unless passion sweeps them both away. Enjoy!

Kate Duffy
Editorial Director

The Gamblers

KING OF HEARTS

Pat Pritchard

ZEBRA BOOKS
Kensington Publishing Corp.
http://www.kensingtonbooks.com

To Jane Smith, the kind of aunt that everyone should have.
With love, Pat.

ZEBRA BOOKS are published by

Kensington Publishing Corp.
850 Third Avenue
New York, NY 10022

Copyright © 2002 by Patricia L. Pritchard

All rights reserved. No part of this book may be reproduced
in any form or by any means without the prior written con-
sent of the Publisher, excepting brief quotes used in reviews.

If you purchased this book without a cover you should be
aware that this book is stolen property. It was reported as
"unsold and destroyed" to the Publisher and neither the
Author nor the Publisher has received any payment for this
"stripped book."

All Kensington titles, imprints and distributed lines are available at special quantity discounts for bulk purchases for sales
promotion, premiums, fund-raising, educational or institu-
tional use.

Special book excerpts or customized printings can also be
created to fit specific needs. For details, write or phone the
office of the Kensington Special Sales Manager: Kensington
Publishing Corp., 850 Third Avenue, New York, NY 10022.
Attn. Special Sales Department. Phone: 1-800-221-2647.

Zebra and the Z logo Reg. U.S. Pat. & TM Off.

First Printing: August 2002
10 9 8 7 6 5 4 3 2 1

Printed in the United States of America

One

Damn and damn again! Wade fanned his cards out and then cursed some more. The only thing he hated more than playing poker was losing at poker. Even when he did so by choice.

And of all nights, Lady Luck had picked this one to show up. Making matters worse, she'd just offered him a gift, and he was going to throw it right back in her face. He could only hope that the lady in question didn't hold grudges—at least not for long. With no small regret, he plucked the pair of queens he'd been dealt and threw them facedown on the table.

"I'll take two."

Drawing a careful breath, Wade picked up their replacements and added them to the other three cards in his hand. When he slowly spread them out, two tens stared him in the face. Added to the pair of deuces that had escorted the queens, he could very well win the hand. *Shit.*

"I fold."

It wasn't hard to feign disgust as he tossed the small pile onto the table and waited for the others to play out the round. Ignoring Lady Luck's generosity was bound to cause him grief. Everyone, Wade included, knew she was both fickle and vengeful.

He'd learned that lesson firsthand years ago when he lost both his ranch and the woman he loved in a poker game. Cal Preston, the gambler who'd won them both, had forced him to learn how to court Lady Luck and win. He'd called it a matter of survival.

However, the price for this evening's work could very well be Wade's life. With grim determination, he set about losing every dime he had.

A few hours later, Wade staggered out of the saloon, deliberately stumbling into a couple of cowboys who were just arriving. They gave him a not-so-gentle shove to help him on his way. On the whole, his act was a convincing one, if he did say so himself. Hell, he even smelled like a drunk, down on his luck and reeking of cheap whiskey.

Whistling an off-key rendition of the song the piano player had been hammering out with enthusiasm but no real talent, Wade wandered in the direction of the local stage office. He didn't have the money for a ticket, but that wasn't going to stop him from catching a ride to his planned destination. He paused long enough to look up at the night sky and immediately wished he hadn't. A falling star flashed and burned out in a single breath. As his eyes followed its path, old memories immediately cluttered his thoughts, hurting as much as they always had. In his mind's eye, he pictured Lily standing on the front porch of their house.

She used to send her heart's wishes soaring with the stars as they flew across the night sky. With her dark eyes squeezed tightly shut, she'd murmur some small request. Afterwards, she always laughed at herself for being silly. But he'd never laughed.

He drew a calming breath. Considering how

happy Lily was these days, the old superstition had definitely worked for her. But wishing on a star of any kind hadn't helped Wade at all, not once, no matter how many times he'd tried. He knew that for a fact because if the stars had ever smiled down on him, he would be the one who Lily had married. And he would have been the one to give her the baby she was due to have in a few weeks.

It took some effort to shove that idea back into the shadowed corners of his mind. He'd been down that road too many times, and nothing ever changed. Seven years ago Lily had married Cal Preston, and Wade had lost everything that had ever mattered to him. Before that, it had been just Wade and Lily struggling together to build a life, but then a turn of a card changed everything for them both.

She'd begged and pleaded with him not to leave the ranch they owned jointly, but the friendship she offered him was worse than her not caring at all. It had been a long time since he'd let anyone close enough to cause him that kind of pain.

And it would be a cold day in hell before he would again. It was time to get moving again before anyone took too much notice of him. Staggering and mumbling to himself, he wended his way down the street. Once he'd made sure that no one was watching, he slipped off his drunk act as easily as he would shed a shirt. Moving quickly, he followed the shadows around to the back of the building, where the horses and stagecoaches were stabled. He already knew which coach would leave for the Oklahoma Territory at first light.

He'd hidden his saddlebags in a convenient pile of hay behind the barn the night before. After retrieving them, he checked the contents to make sure that nothing had been touched. Satisfied that his guns, spare shirts, and badge were right where they should be, he tossed his few belongings into the stagecoach and climbed in after them.

With luck, the driver wouldn't know how many people he was supposed to be taking with him in the morning. Wade's boss had promised that the right people would be bribed into turning a blind eye to an extra passenger. Even though the plan seemed sound, there was always the chance something would go wrong. If so, he'd deal with it.

Tomorrow and its problems would come soon enough. For now, he settled into the far corner of the backseat and willed himself to sleep. With luck, he wouldn't dream.

Wade roused himself long enough to make sure the coach was still in one piece. If it hit another pothole the size of that last one, he wouldn't bet on its lasting the distance to the stage station they were headed for. He elbowed his neighbor into moving over an inch or two to give him room enough to pull out his watch.

Given their current speed, they should reach the station right on schedule. In only a few minutes, he needed to start making his presence known.

So far, no one had paid him the slightest bit of attention, but that was about to change. He pulled out his flask and took a long pull off it. When he gave a contented belch, the woman sitting across from him sniffed loudly with disapproval. She tugged at her skirts, trying unsuccessfully to put some distance between them.

He winked at her and then took another drink. So far, he was being only mildly irritating. He figured on getting himself thrown off the stage before they reached their destination, but he had no desire to walk any farther than he had to. Another mile went by and then another.

Finally, he pulled out the stops. He downed the last of his drink, which was nowhere as strong as he pretended, and then launched into a bawdy song at the top of his lungs. The man on his right turned an angry frown in his direction.

"Sir, there are ladies present."

Wade shook his head sorrowfully. "I know. That's real disappointing to me. If they weren't so determined to hold onto their virtue, this trip wouldn't be half as dull." He leered at the matronly pair and gave them his most endearing smile.

"Maybe we can talk them into changing their ways." Ignoring their outraged gasps, he leaned forward and said, "Ma'am, you're a little old for my tastes, but you're still a fine-looking woman. You interested in a little fun?"

That did it.

The man next to him took a wild swing at Wade. He didn't bother to duck, figuring the crowded conditions would keep his adversary from putting much power behind his punch. He was wrong. His lower jaw snapped up, knocking his teeth against each other with a sickening sound and causing him to bite his tongue. That hurt like a son of a bitch.

He responded with an attack of his own, the pain giving his performance an edge he no longer had to fake. After a short scuffle, two of his companions had him pinned in the corner while another shouted for the driver to stop. The coach shuddered to a halt, tossing the passengers from one side of their seats to the other. Buck, the driver, let loose a stream of curse words as he climbed down and yanked open the door to the stage. He stuck his

head through the opening and glared at the occu-
pants. When he didn't see anyone dead or bleeding,
he muttered another series of words that had the
women blushing.

"What's the damn emergency?"

The older of the two women pointed an accusing
finger at Wade. "He has repeatedly insulted us, and
we want him removed."

The effect of her indignant words on Buck was
laughable, but Wade did his best to maintain his
belligerent expression. There would be time later
to enjoy a chuckle when he was alone. For now, he
needed to maintain the charade for a few minutes
longer.

The explosion wasn't long in coming. "You
stopped me because you don't like what he said?
Damn it, people, I've got a schedule to keep!"

One of the men joined in. "He's drunk and dirty.
Your company charges an outrageous amount of
money for this trip and then crams ten of us in here
like cattle. I expect better treatment for the money."

That got the driver's attention. "How many did
you say?"

"There are ten of us in here."

Buck climbed up on the step to look inside. Wade
could see him carefully counting heads as he
rubbed his unshaven jaw with a callused hand.
When he was done, he clearly didn't like the answer
he'd come up with. Jumping down, he ordered
everyone to climb out. Several people complained,
but it was clear that none of them were going any
farther until they did as Buck ordered. Wade was
the last one out.

"I need to see your tickets."

One after another, everyone held up a folded
piece of paper stamped with their various destina-

tions. Everyone, that is, except Wade. Buck noticed the omission immediately. He narrowed his eyes in accusation.

"Where's yours?"

Wade patted his pockets and came up empty. "I don't seem to have one with me."

"Well, hell," Buck complained. "The company finds out that I've been giving free rides, they'll have my hide." He spat a stream of tobacco juice onto the ground. "I don't know who you are, mister, or how you managed to get by me, but I can tell you this much. You're not going another inch unless you pay up now."

His fellow passengers were really enjoying the drama playing out in front of them. Their heads swiveled from side to side as they followed the conversation.

Wade backed up a step and offered Buck a nasty smile. "Well, you see, the fact is that if I had any money, I'd still be back in town playing poker instead of riding in this rattletrap wagon."

The insult did the trick. Buck's face turned red. "You won't be going anywhere in a hurry now. Start walking."

Wade protested, just as they all expected him to. "Walking where? There isn't a town within miles of here." Wade could only hope that he'd timed things correctly. If he was wrong, he could be walking for twenty miles instead of the few he was hoping for.

"You should have thought of that before you stowed away on my run." Buck spit again. "Hell, you're lucky I don't turn you over to the sheriff, or just plain shoot you myself."

Before Wade could protest again, Buck turned his anger on the others. "I'm already late. Anyone

not back in the coach before I get back on top will
be walking with this fool."

That had everyone scrambling. At least they had
the decency to toss Wade his saddlebags from the
window just as Buck slapped the reins and set the
coach back in motion.

Wade covered his mouth and nose with his bandanna until the dust kicked up by the horses and
wheels settled back down. He chose a nearby rock
to sit down on, looking dejected in case anyone
bothered to look back in his direction.

Once the coach was out of sight, he slung his bags
over his shoulder and started on the long walk to
the stage station. So far, everything was going as
planned.

Hours later, that was no longer the case. His feet
hurt and his stomach was making its demands
known. The sun was rapidly disappearing behind
the hills to the west, making him want to be done
with the whole damn day. Either he'd misjudged
the distance, or the station was farther from Springfield than he'd been told. Either way, the sun was
going to drop out of sight sometime in the next
thirty minutes or so, leaving him in the middle of
godforsaken nowhere with no food and very little
water.

Feeling the effects of the day's heat combined
with the lack of nourishment, he was finding it in-
creasingly difficult to keep going. He'd give himself
another twenty minutes. If there were no signs of
the stage station at that point, he'd find a place to
sleep for the night and start again in the morning.

A few minutes later, everything started spinning,
so he sat down to keep from falling down. Once he
hit the dirt, he made one feeble attempt to stand
and then gave up and let sleep overtake him.

* * *

Wade rolled over and glared up at the sky. Every sharp-pointed rock in southern Missouri was jabbing him in the back and had been all night long. He'd tried moving a couple of times, but the damn things followed him and picked up some of their friends along the way. Seeing the first streaks of light clearing the horizon to the east, he gave up on trying to sleep and sat up.

A hot cup of coffee and some breakfast would go a long way toward improving both his mood and the way he felt. However, considering he was out in the middle of nowhere with nothing in his packs, that wasn't likely to happen any time soon. He dragged himself to his feet and started walking. His new spurt of energy didn't last but a few minutes.

It couldn't have been more than half an hour later when he stood at the top of yet another Ozark hill. Once again, Wade cursed Lady Luck and her perverse sense of humor. Not half a mile from where he'd slept, nestled in a small valley, sat the stage station he'd been looking for. Had he kept going only a few more minutes the night before, he would have stumbled right into the place.

Smoke drifted up from the stone chimney, testifying to the presence of the stationmaster. And if there was any justice in the world, the man would have a pot of coffee already on the stove and be willing to share. That alone was enough to send Wade stumbling down the hillside, drawn by the promise of coffee and a comfortable place to sit.

He skidded the last few feet down the rocky slope and stopped. The sudden descent left him reeling with dizziness, no doubt aggravated by the fact that he hadn't eaten for a day and a half. He leaned against a tree, waiting for his head to clear enough to go the last distance. Since not many folks came calling at this hour, it wouldn't do to go rushing up to the door demanding entry.

Instead, he headed for the pump over near the barn and helped himself to some fresh water to drink. It took three cupfuls to quench his thirst and wash the dust out of his throat. Feeling somewhat better, he stripped off his jacket and shirt and tossed them aside.

Still feeling shaky, he splashed several handfuls of water over his face and hands, doing his best to wash off the stench of stale whiskey and trail dirt. It wasn't much as baths went, but for now it would do. He was about to search his saddlebags for a clean shirt when the sound of a trigger being cocked froze him in midmotion. Without being told to, he slowly raised his hands in the air and waited for directions.

"Turn around nice and easy."

The only surprise was that it was a feminine voice giving the orders. Wade didn't argue, knowing that a woman could kill him as easily as a man if provoked.

He didn't know what he expected as he slowly turned around, but it wasn't a woman almost tall enough to look him square in the eye. She had her gun trained right at his gut, where a shot would be guaranteed to drop him in his tracks. He made note of the fact that she looked right comfortable with the rifle cradled in her arms.

"Good morning, ma'am." His words sounded fuzzy to him. He shook his head to clear it.

"Pick up your things and move on along." She

gestured in the direction of the road with the barrel of the rifle.

"I was hoping for a meal."

"I only feed stage passengers, not drifters."

Her last words sounded as if they'd come from the bottom of a deep well. Wade tried really hard to figure out what she was saying, but his mind refused to cooperate. That was when he noticed he could no longer feel his hands and feet, and there was a peculiar buzzing in his ears. The last thing he saw was the ground coming up to meet him fast.

Lottie continued to keep her sights on her unwanted guest for several seconds, making sure that his sudden collapse wasn't a trick to put her off guard. If it was an act, it was a darn convincing one. He couldn't possibly be comfortable with his neck and head at such an angle.

Deciding that she was safe enough for the moment, she eased off the trigger and set her rifle down, making sure it was out of his reach. She knelt down by his side and lifted his eyelid. Sure enough, his eyes were rolled back and unfocused.

"Mister, you picked a heck of a place to keel over."

Whatever was wrong with him, she needed to get him inside and out of the sun. It wasn't too hot as yet, but it wouldn't take long for the temperature to rise to miserable levels. She lifted his head and neck high enough to get her arms around his chest. She ignored the strange sensation of touching a man's bare skin. Ignoring the blush that crept up her face, she dragged him a few feet at a time until she reached the front porch of the house.

She got him as far as the first step and had to

stop. She wiped the beads of sweat off her forehead with her sleeve and drew a couple of deep breaths. This time she managed to get him to the door. Kicking it with her foot, she called for help.

"Rose, Jack! Come here, please."

A few seconds later, Jack pulled the door open and stepped out onto the porch beside her. He stared down at the man who lay slumped across her feet. Perplexed, he looked out toward the barn and then back to Lottie.

"Where'd he come from? There's no stage due in."

The boy knew the schedule as well as she did. After all, their lives revolved around it. "I don't know, and I didn't get a chance to ask before he hit the ground." She drew a deep breath and sighed. It was no good avoiding the inevitable. "Why don't we get him inside? Once he wakes up, we'll both know more about him."

Rose slipped outside to stand beside and a little behind her brother. She edged farther back, trying to put more distance between her and the stranger on the ground.

"Rose, honey, I left my rifle out by the well. Why don't you run and fetch it while Jack and I get our guest inside."

She didn't want to think of him in those terms, but figured the familiar expression would ease some of Rose's fears. She was often painfully shy around anyone she didn't know. Making it sound as if the stranger had come in on the stage might serve to reassure her that nothing was wrong. Lottie hoped.

Jack struggled to pick up the man's feet while she picked him up by the shoulders again. With the boy's help, she was able to maneuver him inside and down the short hall to the extra bedroom.

"On a count of three, help me heave him up on the bed." She adjusted her hold a bit and then counted quickly. "One . . . two . . . three."

It took them two tries, but finally she had the man on top of the bed. That taken care of, now she had to figure out what to do next. She took a few seconds to study his face. He certainly didn't have the look of someone who was seriously ill, even though his skin was clammy to the touch. Most likely it was heat stroke. Having settled on a possible diagnosis, she knew what to do.

"Bring me a pitcher full of fresh water and some rags."

Jack and Rose, who'd just come in with Lottie's rifle, hurried back out of the room. Lottie studied the stranger while she waited for them to return. If she had to guess, she'd say he wasn't much older than she was: twenty-four, maybe twenty-five. She touched the palm of his hand, noting that his hands showed signs of hard work. His chest and well-muscled shoulders did, too, for that matter.

She forced her eyes back up to his face. His lack of clothing didn't disturb her as much as the way her eyes kept drifting back to look at his smoothly muscled chest. The light dusting of dark hair that narrowed and spiraled down to disappear beneath his belt was nothing that she should be concerned with.

Unfortunately, his face was as compelling as the rest of him. His hair, a dark rusty brown, was longer than she normally liked, but she did admire the way it curled down around the nape of his neck. It had been a while since he'd last shaved, giving him a rakish look. Underneath that faint shadow of beard, his face was sharply defined with deep lines bracketing his mouth. Somehow, she doubted it was from smiling too much.

Jack came back in carrying the pitcher, dripping a steady stream of water on the floor each step of the way. Lottie didn't complain, knowing the small puddles wouldn't last long in the day's heat. Rose was right behind him, her hands full of rags torn from an old sheet.

She relieved Jack of his burden and filled the basin on the bedside table. After dipping a rag in the water, she wrung it out a bit and laid it over the stranger's forehead. That done, she repeated the process, this time using the cool cloth to sponge down his arms and chest.

Her efforts were rewarded with a faint stirring. His eyes fluttered and then opened. They were still unfocused, but his color was improving.

"Where?" he whispered.

"You're at the stage station at Marion Creek, mister," Jack answered before Lottie could get the words out.

She watched as he struggled to put the pieces of his memory into some semblance of order. When his gaze came back to meet hers, his eyes narrowed.

"You had a gun trained on me."

It wasn't an accusation so much as a statement of fact, so she nodded.

"We don't encourage strangers to hang around for long."

His hand drifted up to touch a bruise on the side of his face. He must have hit something when he fell. "What did you do? Knock me out cold?"

Lottie glared at the ungrateful fool. "I didn't have to. You managed to do that all on your own."

He looked as if he still didn't quite believe her, but that was too bad. She'd done more than she'd wanted to for him already. If he wanted to be ungrateful, that was his problem. For now, she had chores to do. He could see to his own needs and then be on his way. Without directing another word to her unwanted guest, she shooed the two children from the room.

"Rose, you have chickens to feed and weeding to do. Jack, you'll help me with the animals."

The two of them scurried out of the room ahead of her, but Jack, at least, cast one more curious look back at the man. Lottie fought the urge to do the same. She hadn't gone two steps out the door when he called after her.

"Look, I'm sorry."

She turned around to face him again. He'd managed to pull himself upright on the edge of the bed. It was obvious from the way his hands were shaking that the effort had cost him.

"I haven't had anything to eat and almost no water since some time yesterday or the day before. I wasn't feeling my best before that damned stage driver kicked me off in the middle of nowhere. The heat must have finished the job."

When he looked up at her this time, something in his eyes melted the last vestiges of her anger.

"If you can make it to the table, I can fix you something to eat before you go. There's some coffee left if you want a cup. It's been sitting since early this morning, so I won't promise how good it'll taste." Without waiting to see if he was able to stand or even walk, she hurried down the hall and left him to his own devices.

She spied his saddlebags sitting inside the door. Rose must have carried them in when she'd fetched Lottie's rifle. Being in no mood to face a half-naked man at her table, Lottie picked up the bags and returned to the back room. She carelessly tossed them through the door and stalked back to the kitchen.

The bacon was just starting to sizzle in the cast-iron skillet when her guest shuffled into the kitchen. He was moving slowly, as if not sure his legs would continue to support him. She watched him out of the corner of her eye as he pulled out a chair and eased himself down. It dawned on her that she still didn't know his name, nor had he asked for hers, which bothered her on some level. It seemed strange to have such intimate knowledge of his body without knowing a thing about the man himself.

Even so, neither of them seemed to be in a hurry to initiate introductions. She added a couple of fresh eggs to the skillet after the bacon was crisp. Without bothering to ask his preferences, she flipped the eggs over, let them cook long enough to set the yolk, and then eased them out onto a plate next to the bacon.

She slid the plate across the table to her silent guest. After pouring him a cup of coffee, she set it down and then walked outside to help the children with the chores. When he was ready to talk, he knew where to find her. There wasn't much worth stealing in the house, so she didn't worry about leaving him alone.

Out on the porch, she shaded her eyes and looked around for Jack and Rose. She found the two of them standing in the shade of a large syca-more tree, whispering together. When Jack caught sight of Lottie, he stepped back from his sister, look-ing guilty.

No doubt they'd been discussing their unex-pected visitor rather than doing their chores, not that she blamed them. Certainly, they were used to a large number of people passing through on a regular basis. Every time a stage arrived, the passengers would pile out, eager to stretch their legs and get a hot meal. Once in a while, the stage stopped overnight. Even then, Lottie and the children were too busy dishing up meals and making beds to spend any time visiting.

So although people came and went, they were all a faceless, nameless blur. This time was different. Since the man had yet to leave the confines of the house, she could only guess that he was in no hurry to leave. It would be safer for all of them, him included, if he were to start on the long journey to the next town. In good conscience, though, she couldn't throw him out in the middle of the worst hot spell they'd had in years, at least until he was feeling better.

At the best of times, mid-July was no time to be afoot in Missouri without the right supplies and water. Whatever he had in those saddlebags of his couldn't be enough to carry him through, especially on foot. She motioned toward the barn with a nod of her head. Jack immediately trotted off in that direction, leaving Rose standing by herself. For the first time in months, the little girl slipped her thumb into her mouth. Lottie knew then that she needed to do more to reassure the girl that everything was under control.

She knelt down to be at Rose's eye level. "You did that man a great kindness by bringing in his saddlebags without being asked. I know he appreciated it." Not that he'd said a word, the ill-mannered fool.

Rose's dark eyes slid toward the house. After a few seconds, she pulled her thumb back out of her mouth and carefully dried it on her dress. Lottie hoped that meant Rose was feeling better about the situation.

"Is he real sick?"

"No, I don't think so. With some rest and food under his belt, he should be fine by tonight."

"I'll pick extra lettuce and tomatoes so we have enough to feed him at dinner."

Lottie hadn't thought that far ahead, but leave it to Rose to think beyond the immediate. Despite her young age, she constantly amazed Lottie with her insight.

"I'm sure he'll appreciate that, too." Not wanting to discuss the matter any further for the moment, she turned Rose around and sent her moving toward the garden with a gentle pat on her backside. "Time to get that weeding done, young lady."

Rose skipped away, her fears clearly gone for the moment. That problem taken care of, Lottie joined Jack in the barn, bracing herself for another session of fending off questions she had no answers to. Jack was already at work, shoveling out the first stall. She picked up a pitchfork and started on the next one.

After a few minutes, she stopped and leaned over to look down at Jack. "Go ahead and ask me whatever has you all in a dither. I can't promise that I know the answers, but you'll probably choke if you don't spit it out soon." Jack giggled, just as she intended.

The boy motioned over his shoulder toward the house with his thumb. "Who is he?"

Before she could answer, a third voice entered the conversation.

"My name is Wade McCord, boy." The stranger stepped into the dim interior of the barn. He tipped his hat toward Lottie. "I want to thank you, ma'am, for the breakfast and the care. I sure didn't mean to collapse on you like that."

Her first impression had been right on the money. The man didn't smile easily. Even when he was being polite, his expression was guarded and somber. She set down her pitchfork and stepped out of the stall. It was time to get some answers to her questions.

She gave Jack a pointed look, which sent him back to work. Even so, she knew that he was concentrating more on what she had to say to Mr. McCord than on his chores. That was easily fixed.

"Come outside with me, Mr. McCord. We can talk more privately there." Without waiting for him to respond, she headed back out into the bright sunshine. The glare hurt her eyes, so she headed for the shade of a nearby tree. McCord was right behind her.

"Now, then, Mr. McCord—"

He immediately interrupted her. "I'm afraid you have the advantage, ma'am."

She frowned. As far as she was concerned, he wasn't going to be around long enough for her name to matter. Short of being downright rude, however, she had no choice but to answer.

"My name is Lottie. Lottie Hammond."

He swept his hat off his head with a flourish. "It is a pleasure to meet you, Mrs. Hammond."

"It's *Miss* Hammond, not *Mrs.*"

His eyes immediately flickered toward the barn, where Jack was hard at work. She waited for him to ask the obvious question about the children, but to her surprise, he didn't.

"*Miss* Hammond, it is. As I was about to say, I owe you for this morning, and I thank you."

She didn't want his gratitude. She wanted him

gone. Something in the set of his mouth made her think that he knew just what she was thinking.

"This is a stage station. The company allows no nonpaying guests."

"Now that is a problem, Miss Hammond." His eyes narrowed.

Others might find his glare intimidating, but not her. She stood her ground and stared right back at him. "I can't change company policy, Mr. McCord."

"No, but you could *ignore* company policy for a time, if you wanted to." His smile was anything but reassuring. Despite the heat of the day, a chill danced right up Lottie's spine.

"I don't want to."

Two

Wade knew that he'd seriously miscalculated Lottie Hammond. When his attempt at charming her hadn't worked, he thought intimidation might. But the lady had shown him quickly enough that she wasn't going to push easily. It was time to back up and try again.

"I'm sorry, Miss Hammond, if I've offended you." He took a small step backward, giving her a little more breathing room. "It's just that I have no way of going anywhere."

"You walked here. You can walk out. The road goes both ways."

Damned if he didn't admire her gumption. "That's true enough, I guess. However, I don't have any supplies and no money to buy any. Under the circumstances, I was hoping that you might see your way to letting me stay on until the next stage comes through."

She looked him up and down. "What happened to your money?"

"Lady Luck deserted me in the middle of a poker game. I hid out on the stage, hoping to catch up with her in another town."

"You're a gambler. I should have known." Lottie rolled her eyes to the heavens and shook her head.

"So tell me, Mr. Gambler, if you have no money for a ticket today, how will that change anytime soon?"

"I could help with chores until the station manager comes back. When he returns, I'll work something out with him."

He'd said the wrong thing again. Lottie had her hands on her hips, looking fit to be tied.

"I am the station manager, Mr. McCord. There is nothing to be worked out. The children and I do all the chores around here. I don't need anybody's help."

She glanced at the sky. The sun was almost directly overhead. Frowning, she gave him a look of pure disgust.

"However, I won't have it said that I sent a man out into this heat feeling sickly. You can rest today and leave in the morning. I will see that you have enough food to last you a few days."

With that announcement, she spun on her heel and marched back to the barn, leaving Wade staring after her. He felt like a total fool and annoyed at the same time. "Sickly" be damned.

Left with nothing to do, he sat down at the base of the tree and leaned back to do some serious thinking. He tilted his hat forward over his forehead, hiding his eyes from view. If Lottie decided to check on him, she wouldn't be able to tell if he was awake or asleep.

He'd never heard of a woman managing a stage station, but there wasn't any excuse for his not knowing the situation beforehand. The whole reason he was here was because of the rumors that this particular station was frequented by a gang of bank robbers and outlaws.

Lottie didn't strike him as a woman who would take up with men of that type, but considering she had two children without benefit of marriage, he didn't much trust his instincts in the matter. Somehow, he had to convince her to let him stay on, because he had a job to do. There'd be hell to pay if he reported back to his superior that he'd gotten himself thrown out for insulting the station manager.

The sound of approaching footsteps startled him out of his reverie. He waited to see what Lottie had to say this time. When the silence stretched into several seconds, he pushed his hat back and looked up.

Instead of Lottie, the little girl was standing a few feet away from him. She held out a cup toward him. Careful not to make any sudden moves, he slowly raised his hand to accept her gift.

The cup was full of fresh, cool well water. It had a faint metallic taste from the cup, but felt damn good going down his throat. His benefactress watched him, her dark eyes huge in her face. He wasn't much good at guessing age in children, but he figured her for under five years old.

He drank the last of the water and wiped his mouth on his sleeve. Smiling slightly, he held out the empty cup. "What's your name?"

"I'm not 'posed to talk to you." She grabbed the cup from his hand and took a couple of steps back.

"Well, I guess I understand, that since we haven't been properly introduced. My name is Wade McCord." He would have bowed if he'd been standing up, but as it was, he could only tip his hat.

She looked back toward the barn, probably to make sure that Lottie was nowhere in sight. "My name is Rose." The introduction was accompanied by a shy, dimpled smile.

He accepted the gift of her name with a smile of

his own. With her dark eyes and jet black hair, she was going to be capturing hearts by the bushel. He surrendered his gladly.

"Well, Miss Rose, thank you for the water. I appreciate your kindness."

Rose tilted her head to one side as she studied him. "Are you still sick?"

"I'm feeling much better now that I've had some water to drink and food to eat."

"I threw up once. Did you throw up today?"

Wade fought back the urge to laugh. Only the very young, like the very old, would ask such blunt questions.

"No, I didn't." When she looked disappointed, he added, "But I almost did."

She nodded, as if she'd suspected as much. "Do you want some more water?"

"Why, Miss Rose, I believe I would."

Rose headed back to the well. He watched as she stood on her tiptoes to reach the pump handle. Once she had her hands the way she wanted, she simply picked up her feet and let the weight of her body pull the handle down. After two such efforts, the cup was full to overflowing.

It was pure pleasure to watch her carrying the cup to him, trying not to spill most of its contents. With her forehead creased in concentration and her tongue sticking out slightly, she made the journey with at least half of the water still there. The rest had soaked the front of her dress and splashed down her legs and bare feet.

Her smile was triumphant when she started to surrender the cup to his hands. Unfortunately, she stumbled slightly, splashing a goodly portion of the remaining water onto his shirt. Wade ignored the sudden shower and sipped from the cup slowly, savoring the moment. Rose stood close by, probably to make sure that he didn't waste a drop.

"Rose, I told you to stay away from him!" Lottie came charging out of the barn at full speed.

Wade lurched to his feet, ready to protect the little girl from any retribution from the angry woman. He shoved Rose behind him and stood his ground. Despite his concern for her, he couldn't help admire the woman coming straight at him with fire in her eyes. Although he'd always preferred petite brunettes in the past, Lottie, with her silver-blond hair and furious blue eyes, was something to behold.

She came to a halt a few feet away. "Rose, you know better than to pester a guest." Her angry gaze flickered up to meet Wade's and back down to Rose's, who was peeking around him. "Even unwanted ones."

"She thought I needed water. I won't let you punish her for being kind."

"You have no say in the matter." Turning her attention to Rose, she gave her a stern look. "You go back to your chores, young lady. We'll talk about this later."

"Yes, ma'am," Rose answered respectfully. Then the little minx looked up at Wade and winked.

To Wade's relief, she skipped off toward the garden, apparently unconcerned about future consequences. Even so, Wade made his position clear.

"I meant what I said."

Lottie echoed his statement. "So did I." She watched Rose as she started in on the weeding. "It isn't safe for her to trust everyone who comes through here."

Wade mulled that idea over before nodding. "So it isn't only me that you've warned her away from."

That startled a laugh out of Lottie, and not a particularly nice one. "You have a high idea of your importance in the world, don't you?" Then, showing how dangerous she found him, she turned her back to him and walked away, still chuckling to herself.

About halfway to the barn, she looked back over her shoulder. "If you're looking for something to do to earn your dinner, you can help Jack finish shoveling out the barn."

Wade felt as though the woman had him spinning in circles. One minute she was warning him away from the children, and the next, she was putting him to work as Jack's assistant. He didn't know what to make of her change in attitudes, not that it mattered one way or the other. If shoveling shit all afternoon got him the job he needed, so be it.

With that decided, he rolled up his sleeves and headed for the barn.

Lottie had run out of excuses to go into the barn to check up on Wade McCord. So far, he'd been hard at work whenever she had slipped in. The stalls had fresh straw in them, and the animals had been fed. The last time she'd peeked in, he was sitting on a crate mending some tack she'd been meaning to get to for ages. She surely couldn't complain about his work.

And although she and Jack were perfectly capable of seeing to the needs of the mules and horses, it was nice to have a little extra help. Not that she'd let herself get used to that particular luxury. If she'd learned one thing running the station, it was that men were always just passing through.

Luckily for her and the children, she was perfectly

capable of taking care of herself. If some folks seemed shocked to see a woman doing a man's work, she didn't care. The work was hard, but it kept food on the table and a roof over their heads, which was more than either the children's father or hers had ever done.

It was time to turn her attention to putting dinner on the table. After adding some wood to the fire, she reached for her favorite skillet and put it on the stove to heat. While Jack and McCord had been hard at work, she and Rose had slipped down to the river and caught a mess of bluegill for dinner. With skill born of practice, she had the fish gutted, scaled, and ready for the pan. They were bony but tasted fine when dusted with cornmeal and flour and then fried up. A pan of hot cornbread and some fresh greens would complete the meal.

Once McCord had eaten and gotten a good night's sleep, she could send him on his way in good conscience. None of them would be safe if he stayed around too long.

The door opening brought a halt to that line of thinking. She looked over her shoulder to see who'd come in, although in truth she already knew. She forced her attention back to gathering the ingredients for the cornbread. For several seconds, he simply stood, watching as she worked. She could feel the weight of his eyes trained on her back.

It was a relief when he finally asked, "Is there anything else you'd like me to do?"

She wiped her hands on a towel as she turned to face him. "No. You've more than earned your dinner—and breakfast, too, for that matter. By the time you wash up, everything should be ready."

He went back outside to the pump. Her breathing became easier as soon as the door closed behind

him. What was there about him that caused an unfamiliar flutter in her chest whenever he walked into
the room? She'd known him for less than a day; he
should mean nothing to her.

Her curiosity aroused, she dropped the towel on
the table and gave into temptation. If she was careful, she could watch him from the window without
anyone's knowing. Why she would want to was a
mystery even to her, but that didn't keep her from
standing beside the window and lifting the edge of
the curtain to see better.

For the second time that day, Wade McCord had
taken his shirt off while he washed away the day's
dust and dirt. His shoulders were broad and surpris-
ingly muscular for a man who professed to making
his living with a deck of cards. Of course, if his luck
was always bad, perhaps he often ended up working
in someone's barn in order to eat.

Against her will, she admired the way the muscles
in his arm flexed as he worked the pump handle to
get the cool water flowing. Once it was coming in a
steady stream, he held his head under the flow and
then reared up, shaking the chilly drops from his
hair. It must have felt good, because he repeated
the performance.

The sound of laughter warned her that Jack and
Rose were also watching their guest. It didn't surprise her much that Jack had warmed to the man,
since McCord had done more than his fair share of
Jack's chores for him. Rose, on the other hand,
rarely took to anyone new. Yet there she was, talking
up a storm as McCord finished washing up.

He even manned the pump for the children so
they could wash their hands and faces. Without being told to. And if that weren't unusual enough on
its own, Rose was holding up her hand for McCord

to hold as they walked toward the house. Realizing she was about to be caught staring, Lottie went back to her dinner preparations.

The cornbread was browning nicely, and the fish was flaky and tender. The children took their places at the table. McCord hesitated before joining them.

"You sit there, Mr. McCord," Rose announced. "That other one is for Mama."

It was then that Lottie realized that she would be forced to spend dinner looking right into Wade McCord's eyes. A fresh batch of butterflies took up residence in her stomach. She would have rearranged the seating if doing so wouldn't have caused more problems than it solved. Both children were smart enough to suspect something was wrong if she suddenly started changing things around.

No matter what the man looked like, she could manage a single meal with a little effort. Besides, with some luck, she would finally manage to figure out exactly what color his eyes were. So far, they'd looked gray, green, and even light brown.

After setting the cornbread on the table, she took her seat. The children both held out their hands to hold hers while she said grace. Their guest didn't hesitate at all to join in the circle.

It was Jack's turn to say grace. "Thank you, God, for this food." He opened one eye and looked at McCord. "And thank you for bringing Mr. McCord to help me with my chores. Amen."

Lottie held her breath, waiting to see what McCord's reaction would be to be included in a small boy's prayers. His look of surprise was to be expected, but there was something else underneath it that she couldn't quite figure out. Just as quickly, the look was gone, leaving her wondering if she'd only imagined it.

"Take some bread and pass it on, Jack."

Once the food was being served, some of her tension eased. She could only be grateful that Rose and Jack kept the conversation flowing. They talked about the things that were important only to children, but to give McCord his due, he listened to what they had to say.

She didn't want to like him. Not at all. He simply had to go. In the morning, she would make sure he did.

Wade had been aware of Lottie's scrutiny during dinner, even though she'd done her best to act as if he weren't sitting right straight in front of her. For certain, she hadn't been happy that her two children were so accepting of him. On the other hand, he figured they might be his ticket to staying on longer than Lottie wanted him to.

For now, he'd given her some breathing room by going outside. The sun had almost disappeared behind the surrounding hills, but the day's heat lingered on, making him reluctant to go any farther than the porch. The katydids and cicadas droned out their music as the fireflies danced through the woods. He soaked in the peace of the moment, knowing it wouldn't last for long.

He reminded himself that he was here to do a job. If Rose and Jack liked having him around, Lottie might get past her immediate distrust of him. He hoped so, because his best shot at capturing Ambrose Bardell was to wait for the man to make an appearance here at the station. Others had tried to track the man but with no success, because the wily bank robber apparently knew every game trail, road, and path in the Ozarks. He'd led his pursuers in circles, making the deputy marshals look like fools.

Wade planned on changing all of that, and damn soon.

Old anger stirred in his mind. Some folks treated Bardell and others like him almost as folk heroes, but not Wade. He'd experienced firsthand the terror caused by a man so filled with greed that it left no room for morals. At that time, Wade had been too young and inexperienced to protect the woman he loved.

In the end, he'd lost her to another man, but his need to protect still burned hot inside him. He would end Bardell's reign of terror in the Ozarks or die trying.

The door behind him opened. He knew without looking that Lottie was checking up on him again.

"Dinner was real fine."

"It was nothing special." She took up a position on the other end of the porch.

"Don't underestimate the appeal of home cooking." Then, because she wouldn't appreciate it, he joined her at the other rail. Just as he expected, she frowned but held her ground. He liked that about her.

He let the evening sounds surround them both for the moment. Although he'd grown up farther west, he'd come to love the Ozark Mountains with their winding rivers and hot summer nights. A whippoorwill called out its sad sound as the last of the daylight faded away.

Despite the darkening shadows on the porch, his eyes were drawn to study his unwilling companion. He wondered what she was looking for in the gathering darkness. Or more likely, who.

"We get up early around here, Mr. McCord."

"Fine with me."

Lottie had been looking away from him, but something in his answer had her frowning in his direction. He wondered what . . . oh, hell. He was a gambler and therefore more likely to be going to bed at dawn, not getting up to do chores. He'd better reassure her pretty damn quick.

"I grew up on a ranch. I may be out of practice when it comes to getting up with the sun, but I think I can manage it for a day." He hesitated only briefly and added, "or two or three."

She clearly didn't quite believe him, but even more than that she didn't like the hint that he planned to be around longer than breakfast in the morning. Either way, he thought he'd successfully diverted her attention from his inadvertent slip.

"Where do you want me to bunk down?"

"You can have the room you were in earlier. It's not needed right now."

"When is the next stage due in?"

"Six days. We only get one a week most of the time because we're not on one of the major routes. They're talking about adding an extra run for the summer. No matter what time of the year it is, if the weather turns bad, we can get overnight guests."

That made sense. A normal stage station took far more people to run it than this one did. Still, he wondered how she'd come to manage the place. He couldn't imagine the stage line owners hiring a woman to do the job. That was a question better left for later, he decided. For now, that bed sounded pretty damn good to him.

"Well, I think I'll turn in, if that's all right."

Lottie evidently had the same idea, because they collided when they both reached to open the door.

Wade's hands shot out to steady her, and for a brief second, she was in his arms.

He had no way of knowing if she felt the same jolt of attraction that burned through him, but a bolt of lightning wouldn't have startled him more. He did know that it was a dead heat as to which one jumped back the quickest, ending the almost-embrace.

Lottie's breathing sounded ragged, but then so did his. Once again her hands were on her hips in a clear sign that she wasn't too pleased with him. Too damn bad. He'd done nothing wrong.

"Good night, Mr. McCord," she managed to choke out as she swept past him into the house.

Not to be outdone, he followed close on her heels. He waited until she was about to disappear into her room to call after her, "Good night, Lottie. Sweet dreams."

She didn't dignify his teasing with a response, but then, he didn't expect one. Despite her chilly departure, he went to bed feeling pretty pleased with himself and the world in general.

Lottie punched her pillow and rolled over onto her other side in an effort to find a comfortable position. It didn't work any more than any of the other attempts she'd made in the past hour. She didn't like cursing, but she might just make an exception tonight.

How could one man manage to upset her life so much in only one day? If there'd been any other way to handle the day's events, she couldn't think of it. Luckily, no one else had been expected to arrive. She shuddered to think what might have happened. Wade McCord struck her as a man who could handle himself under normal circumstances, but Ambrose and his men could hardly be considered normal by anyone's definition.

Finally, she gave up on sleep altogether and stared up at the ceiling. If she were going to be fair, she couldn't blame Wade McCord for her restlessness— not entirely, anyway. She loved living on the station with Jack and Rose, but that didn't mean that her life was complete.

And McCord had succeeded in reminding her of exactly what she was missing: someone to share that life with, a full partner. The touch of his hand on her arms, the feel of his gaze over the table, and a smile shared over something Rose said all made her ache for something she couldn't have.

And truthfully didn't want—not with a man who spent his time wandering from saloon to saloon, wasting both his money and his life on the turn of a card. He was handsome, she had to give him that; and he was good with the children, but so was their father. That didn't mean that he was good *for* them. Her thoughts were going in circles and getting her nowhere. She firmly closed her eyes, vowing that this time she'd let sleep overtake her as she banished the day's worries from her mind.

Instead, she told herself a variation on the bedtime story she'd told Rose earlier, all about a tall blond princess and a handsome knight who fought to protect her honor. The tale was a favorite, even though the hero's looks had changed slightly this time. Now, instead of the blue his eyes had always been, they were an ever-changing shade of hazel.

The sound of an ax biting deeply into wood dragged Lottie out of a fitful sleep. Her mind, dense with the fog of half-remembered dreams, took a few seconds to make sense of things.

When her eyes would finally stay open, she realized that she'd overslept. Bright sunshine streamed through the small window across the room at an angle that told her that she'd remained in bed hours longer than usual. She fought to untangle her legs from the sheets and sat up on the edge of the bed. Just as her feet hit the floor, Rose peeked in through the door. When she saw that Lottie was awake, her sweet face lit up.

"Are you surprised, Lottie? We decided to let you get some extra rest. Mr. Wade said it would be a nice thing to do."

Lottie reined in her temper, not wanting to frighten Rose. That didn't mean that "Mr. Wade" wasn't going to get an earful over his high-handed behavior. He was supposed to be on his way first thing that morning, not hanging around messing with her routine. She was reaching for her clothes when she realized that she hadn't answered Rose.

"I'm surprised, all right, Rose. Give me a few minutes to get dressed, and I'll get breakfast started."

"We already ate. Mr. Wade made breakfast for Jack and me."

"He did, did he?"

She gave the blankets a halfhearted pull to straighten them. Normally, she took some care to make her bed neatly, but not today. "And did he also feed the chickens and milk the cow?'

Why wasn't she surprised when Rose nodded?

"I assume that's him I hear chopping wood?"

Rose nodded firmly. "He said the wood box was almost empty. When he's done filling it up, he's going to rest a spell before he helps me with the garden." Her eyes sparkled with anticipation. "You can sit and watch if you want."

Lottie was going to do far more than just watch, but Rose wasn't the right target for her anger. "You go get started on the garden now before it gets much hotter out there. Make sure you water the tomatoes well." She kept her fingers crossed that Rose wouldn't argue.

Just as she'd hoped, the little girl hurried back outside. Somehow, even though Rose was doing just as she was told, it only made Lottie crabbier. No doubt McCord was better company at the moment than a sleep-rumpled Lottie. She pushed herself up off the bed and staggered over to the washbasin. Rather than refill it with hot water, she splashed the water left from the night over her face, hoping the cool water would clarify her thinking.

It helped some, as did brushing the night tangles out of her waist-length hair. She plaited it into a single braid that hung down the middle of her back. That done, she was ready to face the day.

And Wade McCord.

She marched straight through the kitchen, ignoring the call of the coffeepot sitting on the stove, and headed right on outside. A quick glance around reassured her that Rose was busy in the garden. Jack was nowhere in sight, which she hoped meant that he was at work in the barn.

She'd join him there shortly, as soon as she sent Wade McCord packing. With that goal in mind, she followed the sound of the ax around behind the house. He was right where she expected him to be. If he was aware of her approach, he gave no sign of it as he swung the ax high over his shoulder. In one smooth arc, he brought the blade down on an upturned log. The power behind his swing split the wood neatly down the middle. With the ease born of practice, he set the split log back on its end and used the ax to cut through it yet again. He tossed the two pieces aside and reached for another log.

He'd done an impressive amount of work in just one morning, judging by the pile of wood at his feet. She didn't want to be grateful, but neither could she disregard the favor he'd done her. The children weren't big enough to be much help cutting wood, so that particular chore always fell to her. He'd done enough to keep the stove supplied for close to a week.

Wade finally noticed her standing there. He set the ax down and wiped his face clean of dust and sweat with the bandanna he pulled out of his back pocket.

"Thank you." She said it grudgingly, but at least she'd said it.

"I figured I owed you." He rolled down his sleeves and picked up the ax. "Now that you're up, I'll put this back in the barn and then be on my way."

"You promised Rose that you'd help her with the garden." The words slipped out before Lottie could stop them. What was she thinking of? She wanted him gone. But a little voice in the back of her mind taunted her by whispering, *But not yet. There's no hurry. Tomorrow would be soon enough.*

As if he'd read her mind, Wade asked, "Are you sure? Yesterday you seemed pretty determined to see the last of me at first light."

"Yes, well, you didn't leave when you were supposed to, did you?" Now, what did she mean by that? What difference did it make when he left, as long as he was gone?

"No, I guess I didn't." He picked his hat up off

the ground. His saddlebags were lying nearby. "If I'm going to go any distance today, I'll help Rose for a few minutes and then be on my way."

She watched him walk away, feeling more confused than ever. If he'd argued or even hinted that he wanted to stay on, she'd have sent him hurrying on down the road before he had time to catch his breath, using her rifle to encourage him if necessary. But by earning his keep for the day and then offering to be gone, he'd neatly turned the tables on her. If she made him leave after all he'd done, well, it would be nothing short of rude.

Giving up on making any sense of the situation, she headed for the barn to check on Jack. She found him putting the finishing touches on the last stall. The barn hadn't been that clean—ever.

"Nice work, Jack."

He looked over the stall at her and grinned. "I bet we surprised you but good this morning, didn't we? The chores are about done, the wood is chopped, and we didn't need you at all!"

She knew he didn't mean that last comment the way it sounded, but it still hurt. Jack and Rose had depended on her their whole lives. One morning in bed wasn't going to change that, but still the idea rankled. Jack, however, didn't need to know that.

She closed the remaining distance between them. Reaching out to ruffle his hair, she assured him, "You and Rose did a fine job, that's for sure. I'm proud of you both."

"And how about Mr. Wade? It was his idea, you know."

Lottie knew hero worship when she saw it. "He did a lot, too." A lot she hadn't asked him to do. A lot she wished he hadn't.

"Why does he have to leave?"

For the second time, Wade walked into the middle of her conversation with Jack. "I don't live here, Jack."

"But you said you don't have a home, not anymore. Why can't you stay with us?"

Lottie put her arm around Jack's young shoulders, wanting to offer him some comfort. He accepted her touch for a few seconds, but then pulled away. Another reminder that he was growing up.

"It's all right with us if he stays on for a while, isn't it, Lottie?"

Two pairs of male eyes were trained on her, awaiting her decision. Jack's were hopeful, full of trust. Wade's were another matter. In the dim light of the barn, she could still feel the power behind his gaze. She met it head on and made up her own mind, even though knowing he clearly wanted to stay but wasn't going to beg or even ask.

"He can stay until the next stage comes through. I'll tell Buck that Mr. McCord has worked his passage back to Springfield."

Jack jumped up in the air and clapped his hands. "That's great! I'll go tell Rose." He gave Lottie a quick hug and then disappeared out the door, leaving her alone with McCord.

"I would have gone." He took a step closer to her.

She backed up before she could stop herself. "Yes, you would have, and you still will. The only difference is that you'll be riding when you leave instead of walking."

"What changed your mind?"

Lottie looked past him, out to where she could see Jack and Rose standing together. The truth was always the best answer to any question.

"I wish I knew."

Three

The lumpy bed made a poor substitute for a table, but Wade ignored the problem and dealt another hand of solitaire. He'd lost three straight games. This one didn't look much better, but he needed something to keep his hands busy.

Shuffle and deal. Shuffle and deal. Normally, the monotony was calming; instead, he was growing edgier as the evening wore on. Having a conscience was damned inconvenient.

He hadn't counted on liking Lottie Hammond, not to mention her children. Of course, no one had warned him in the first place that the stationmaster was a woman. Knowing ahead of time wouldn't have changed his plans, but he might have been better prepared to deal with the problems he'd encountered.

Shuffle and deal. Shuffle and deal. The cards were definitely against him tonight, just as they had been for the two days he'd been at the station. He glared at the queen of hearts peeking out from beneath the jack of spades. If he were willing to cheat, he'd pull the queen out from her hiding spot and use her to win the game. He both wanted her and needed her.

Just as he needed Lottie. Worse yet, he wanted

her in ways that had nothing to do with the job at hand. When he found himself reaching for the card against all sense of honor, he muttered a curse and swept the cards into a jumbled pile.

Thoroughly disgusted with both himself and the situation, he paced the length of the room and back. Five steps each way did little to help. After putting away the cards, he slipped out through the kitchen to the door. He paused long enough to listen. Lottie had put Jack and Rose to bed hours ago, not long after the sun set. Afterward, she'd kept herself busy doing household chores. He had to wonder if it was absolutely necessary to sweep the kitchen floor twice in one evening. Maybe she was feeling the same kind of edginess that he was.

The house was dark and silent, which meant that Lottie had retired for the night some time ago. Staring at the closed door to her room, he wondered if her bed was as narrow and lonely as his. His overactive imagination immediately supplied him with a picture of Lottie lying on her back, her glorious hair spread out on the pillow.

Damning both his wayward thoughts and the effect they were having on his body, he picked up his bags and slipped outside, hoping the night air and a little distance would help his mood. Walking carefully, he crossed the porch and headed for the woods and the stream that cut through the valley.

The moon was high in the sky. Although it was half gone in its monthly cycle, its silvery light was enough to guide his steps. The path wound through the woods to where the trees thinned out just before they gave way to the rocky riverbed. Caution kept him inside the tree line until he was sure he was alone. A mosquito buzzed near his ear. He managed to swat it on the second try. Before any of its friends could take its place, he quickly crossed the remaining distance to the edge of the water.

He was in luck. The stream pooled up deep enough for a man to bathe in. Stripping off his clothes, he waded in, letting the cold water do its best to soothe his night fevers. Once the water reached his waist, he stretched out and swam the length of the pool and back. Half a dozen trips later, he was feeling better about life in general.

Flipping over onto his back, he floated quietly and watched the stars overhead. He wondered how Lily was feeling. Her pregnancy had been uneventful as far as he knew, but he always worried. Despite the distance between them, he still cared very deeply for her. And worse yet, he honestly liked her husband; he just wished it had been himself.

He waited for the usual hurt to settle in. Instead, the memory of Lily only served to remind him of Lottie. She, too, was a fine mother. Physically, she was a far cry from dark-haired, dark-eyed Lily's slender build, but they shared some of the same strength.

Not liking where his mind was going, he decided it was time to wash up and get back to the house. He paddled over to the shallows and stood up. He rummaged through his saddlebags and found his soap and a threadbare towel. After working up a decent lather, he scrubbed himself clean and washed his hair. He dove back through the deeper water to rinse off. By then, he was feeling the effects of a long day filled with physical labor.

His shirt and pants stuck to his still-damp skin, making it hard to get them on. He gave up on socks altogether and slipped on his boots without them. If it had been lighter out, he might have risked going barefoot, but snakes were a very real threat. Cottonmouths were all too common in the area.

He was almost back to the house when he heard voices just ahead. Instinctively he reached for his gun only to realize that he'd left the house without it. Cursing himself for a fool, he continued along the path until he reached the edge of the trees. The house was still dark, but it was obvious that Lottie hadn't gone to bed.

She was standing out by the barn talking to a man. From his position, he couldn't tell much about her late-night caller except that he was tall. He had to be, because Lottie had to tilt her head back to look him in the face. That would put him several inches over six feet, about Wade's own height.

That little piece of information wouldn't go far toward identifying the man. For all Wade knew, he could be looking at his quarry, but Wade had no weapons with him, and short of knocking the man cold with a bar of soap, there was little he could do. He wondered if Lottie realized that her houseguest was not in his room. Not that it mattered. Wade would do nothing that would put her at risk. He judged the distance to the house, trying to decide whether he could get inside without being seen.

He considered his route carefully before setting out. Working his way along the edge of the trees, he waited until the house was between him and the other two before sprinting across the yard to the side of the porch. So far, neither of them showed any sign that they had noticed him.

Pausing long enough to catch his breath, he slipped down the side to the small window that marked his room. At least he'd done one thing right: it was open. He tossed his bags through the window, hoping they'd land on the bed. Then he pulled himself up through the narrow opening, turning his shoulder to ease the tight fit.

Once inside, he hurriedly stripped off again and laid his clothes out to dry in the night air. That done, he yanked back the covers on his bed and got in. About the time he pulled the sheet up to his chest, he heard the front door open.

Lottie didn't go straight to her own bed. Instead, he could hear her almost silent footsteps approach the door to his room. Since she didn't open it, he had to think that she also hadn't tried it before going out to meet her late-night guest.

Or should he say *lover?* He didn't like that thought one damn bit, but there wasn't much he could do about it. He fought to keep his breathing slow and even until he heard her move away. It was some time before his pulse slowed to where he could feel sleep creeping up on him.

For about the tenth time that morning, Wade caught himself watching Lottie. Try as he might, he couldn't keep his eyes from wandering in her direction. Several times she almost caught him staring, and the last thing he needed to do was make her suspicious.

Her late-night rendezvous still stuck in his craw. No matter who the man was, Wade wondered what they'd been up to, sneaking around late at night like that. Did they always meet out by the barn, or was this an exception because Lottie had an unexpected guest in Wade?

And had the two of them sought the privacy of the barn for anything other than to talk? He hoped like hell that hadn't been the case. He knew he had no claim on Lottie, but he'd hate to see any man using her that way. Telling himself to mind his own business, he turned his attention back to the weeds that needed cutting back from around the corral and barn. It had been some time since anyone had attacked the encroaching plants. Once again, he picked up the scythe and began swinging it back and forth. Despite the heat of the day, the familiar rhythm went a long way toward improving his mood.

As he approached the end of the barn, he noticed that Lottie had found a comfortable spot in the grass under the spreading limbs of the sycamore. Jack and Rose lay sprawled next to her as she read to them from a book. He wondered what story had the two youngsters so enthralled.

The scene brought back fond memories of his own childhood, only it was his father's voice he remembered patiently reading favorite stories over and over. But that was before both of his parents died, leaving him and his older brother on their own. Now Thad was dead, too, leaving Wade alone in the world. Once again, he turned his back to the others and started cutting the grass.

Lottie wondered what was wrong with her unwanted hired hand. He'd seemed remote and unapproachable since breakfast. She thought at first that she was imagining things, but even Rose was casting worried little looks in his direction every so often. Earlier, Jack had tried without success to engage Wade in conversation while they worked side by side. Finally, disappointed in the results of their efforts, the two children had turned to her for entertainment.

After she finished reading the story, she was going

to take the two of them down to the river to cool off. Maybe giving McCord some time to himself would improve his disposition. She hoped so, because she had enough to worry about without having to baby a man in a bad mood.

Come to think about it, he was now nowhere to be seen. Maybe he'd decided on his own to take some time for himself. Shrugging, she turned her attention back to the book. The faster she finished, the faster they could all head for the swimming hole.

Finally, she paused for dramatic effect, then uttered Rose's favorite part, where the prince saves the day.

Rose gave a happy sigh and smiled happily. Just as predictably, Jack rolled his eyes and shook his head. Of course, since he was the one to suggest the story in the first place, Lottie figured he didn't hate it all that much.

"What do you say we sneak down and go swimming?"

Rose and Jack squealed with excitement and took off for the house to gather some towels and the blanket they always took to sit on. Lottie didn't bother to wait for them, knowing they'd catch up with her at the river. Inside the woods, the air clung damply to her hair and skin, making her clothes cling uncomfortably. Although she wouldn't go swimming with the children, she looked forward to tucking up her skirt and wading in the shallows.

She was only a short distance from the edge of the woods when she realized that someone had reached the river ahead of her. Since she knew for a fact that it wasn't Jack or Rose, that left only one person it was likely to be. Sure enough, she spotted McCord on the far side of the deep pool as soon as she stepped clear of the trees. He was concentrating so hard on his swimming that he had yet to notice that he was no longer alone. It would be good manners on her part to call out some kind of greeting, but she gave in to the temptation to watch for a few seconds.

He moved through the water with the same grace with which he did everything else. For a man who professed to make his living staying up till all hours drinking and smoking, he seemed to be in good physical condition. He wasn't the type of man she was looking for in her life, but that didn't keep her eyes from hungrily watching each move he made.

She must have made some sound, because he stopped in midstroke to look around. When he spied her lurking in the shadows of the trees, some of the tension went out of his expression. He paddled toward shore. Until that moment, it hadn't occurred to her to wonder what he was wearing, if anything. When he found his feet and started to rise up out of the water, she gasped and turned away.

His laughter rang out, echoing off the bluffs across the stream. She knew she was being foolish; after all, she'd already seen him half naked—just not the half she was worried about. And, truth be told, more than a little curious about.

"You can turn around, Lottie. I'm decent." Laughter still colored his words.

She hated blushing, but there was no hiding it, not with her fair complexion. Squaring her shoulders, she turned back to face him. One look and she decided that decent wasn't the word she would have chosen to describe Wade McCord at that moment. And he knew it, too, damn him. His mouth curved up in a grin that dared her to call him a liar.

Her eyes skimmed over Wade's bare chest, his skin shimmering with droplets of river water. Despite her good intentions, her gaze continued downward to note that his trousers clung to his legs in a way that should be outlawed among decent folk. And then her wayward mind took note of the fact that he wasn't unaffected by her scrutiny.

This time, she wasn't sure whether her skin flushed from embarrassment or the effect Wade McCord was having on her. She could only be grateful that he kept his distance, especially because they wouldn't be alone for long.

Jack came flying past her, slowing only long enough to shuck off his shoes and drop the blanket he was carrying. That done, he went plowing right into the river at its deepest point. Rose wasn't quite as fast, but she was right behind her brother. Lottie was pleased to see that Rose had changed into a pair of trousers and a shirt that Jack had outgrown. It might not be ladylike, but they would afford her the freedom to swim in the river more safely than would a dress.

"Hey, Wade, come play." Jack was floating on his back, letting the slight current carry him along.

"Please, Mr. Wade."

Lottie watched in disgust as Rose batted her long eyelashes at McCord as she pleaded with him to join the two of them in the river. And there he went, wading right in up to his . . . his—well, to his chest, anyway. She'd known for a long time that Rose was going to be a beauty, but she wasn't ready to see her practicing her flirting skills at such a young age.

Especially on a man old enough to know better. Only minutes ago he had been looking at Lottie in a way that made her knees weak. She had half a mind to . . . The realization that she was getting angry over nothing brought Lottie up short. Why, she sounded jealous, and of a four-year-old, at that. The humor in the picture it made relieved the last of her tension.

Satisfied that the children were in good hands, she decided to wander upstream by herself. She still had a mind to do a bit of wading, but it didn't seem at all proper to lift her skirts in front of McCord, even if just to her knees. Once the river turned a corner, she sat down on a handy rock and pulled off her shoes, leaving them up where they'd be unlikely to attract any unwanted critters to hide inside them. That done, she grabbed the hem of her skirt at each side and pulled it up and knotted it so that her legs were bare. Walking carefully on the rocky shore, she waded in until the water lapped at her legs just above her ankles.

It felt like heaven. Just that little bit of coolness did much to ease the oppressive afternoon heat. Knowing the river bottom was unpredictable, she didn't go far. Once she found a level place to stand, she stopped, content to let the water rush past her. When a school of minnows played around her ankles, Lottie giggled and shooed them on downriver.

"Well, Lottie Hammond, if you aren't a picture!"

Lottie fought to keep her balance as she whirled to face the horseman coming out of the shadows just ahead. His horse splashed across the shallows to stop near her. She kept her voice to a harsh whisper. "Ambrose, what are you doing here? I told you last night to stay away until after the next stage leaves."

"You did at that, but I wanted to see this gambler friend of yours for myself." Ambrose tilted his hat back and gave her one of his most charming smiles.

It only served to make her angry. "He's not my friend," she snapped, sounding defensive to her own ears.

"Now, why don't I believe that?" He nudged his horse a few steps closer and leaned down to look her in the face. "You left Jack and Rose alone with him. You hardly trust me that much."

That was the truth, so she didn't bother to deny it. Even so, she glared up at Ambrose. "At least he doesn't rob banks for a living."

"Maybe not, but then you don't know that for sure. All you know is what he told you."

She watched as he dismounted. He wouldn't leave until he was good and ready, so there was no use in arguing with him. Ambrose had always come and gone as he wanted. She listened for a few seconds, making sure that Jack and Rose were keeping McCord busy down around the bend. From the sound of their laughter, they hadn't even missed her.

Thank goodness.

"You're right, Ambrose. I don't know much about Wade McCord, but I do know what is important. He'll leave on the next stage and won't come back. That's more than I can say for you." She wished she had her shoes on, so she could punctuate that statement by walking away.

"They're my children, too, Lottie. Despite what you think about me, I've done my best by them."

That was true, as far as it went. But trying to get her to take money he'd stolen from other innocent people wasn't her idea of providing for his children. She'd told him so frequently, but he wouldn't change his ways for her or them.

"I'm going to be gone for a couple of weeks on business."

Yes, and she could guess exactly what kind of business that was. She wondered what town would lose its money next, but she couldn't let that matter.

Those other people's misfortune meant that she and the children would be free of Ambrose for a while. That was as close to good news as Ambrose ever brought.

Then he ruined it. "When I get back, I'll be wanting to stay for a while."

"No." Fear gripped her insides and wouldn't let go. It was bad enough when he came for a day or two. But if he took up residence and the stage line found out, the owners wouldn't hesitate to throw her and the children out. "You can't stay, Ambrose. We've gone over this before."

"I want to spend time with the children without feeling like I'm saying good-bye before I get done saying hello." He whipped off his hat and dusted it against his leg in frustration. "They're getting so they treat me like one of your damn stage passengers instead of their father."

"That's not true. They both love you. Too much, if you ask me."

Besides, there was no mistaking their parentage. All one had to do was see Ambrose's dark good looks to see it reflected in his children. There was little doubt that Jack would one day be as handsome as Ambrose. And Rose, sweet Rose, had her mother's beauty and her father's dark eyes and entrancing smile. Lottie prayed every night that their looks were all they'd gotten from him.

"I mean to be with them. Remember our deal, Lottie. The children live with you, but only as long as I get to see them. Interfere with that and I'll take them so far away, you'll never find them."

"You wouldn't!" As much as she needed to believe that, she knew he meant every word he said. He'd been using the children as pawns to get what he wanted from her for years. Frantically she tried to come up with a solution that was satisfactory to both of them.

"The stage comes through on Fridays. Once it's out of sight, you're welcome to stay for five days. After that, you have to be gone."

"I get damn tired of hiding out in the hills and sleeping in caves. For once, I want to sleep in the same bed every night."

She'd feel sorry for him, except that he'd brought all his troubles on himself. Ambrose was a smart man and a natural-born leader. If he'd stayed on the right side of the law, his life would have been different.

"After Friday," she repeated firmly. "Five days. Now go before Wade sees you."

Ambrose lifted an eyebrow at her use of McCord's first name, but didn't say anything about it. She did her best to look resolute until he accepted her offer.

"You're a tough one to bargain with, Lottie." He swung back up into the saddle. "Like I said, a couple of weeks and then you can expect me."

He spurred his gelding forward into the river, splashing Lottie with water from head to toe. He knew full well what he'd done because he laughed as he disappeared into the woods upstream.

Her peaceful moment destroyed, Lottie waded back down to where she'd left her shoes. They felt hard and unyielding to her feet, not unlike the situation she found herself in. She took the time to pick up a handful of rocks and threw them as hard as she could against the nearest tree.

Acting childish might not change anything, but at least it let her express some of the frustration she was feeling. That done, she pasted a cheery smile on her face and walked back down to gather up Rose and Jack and head back for the house.

There were chores to be done and dinner to be cooked. Some things never changed.

Wade promised Jack that he'd be along directly to help with the early-evening chores. Lottie was clearly not happy that he was lingering at the river, which convinced him all the more that something had happened while she'd been upriver.

She wasn't likely to tell him anything of her own accord, which meant he'd have to do some scouting on his own. He waited until she and the children were out of both sight and hearing before leaving the river.

After pulling his shirt on without bothering to button it, he yanked on his socks and then his boots. That done, he checked the path that led back to the house to make sure that Lottie had indeed gone. Figuring he was safe for the moment, he worked his way upstream, looking for signs of where Lottie had been.

Just past the bend in the river, he found what he was looking for. The day was so hot that he would have walked right by the place if he hadn't been looking so carefully, because the rocks had almost completely dried off. Even so, he was able to make out where a horse had crossed the river.

If he'd had more time, he would have back-tracked across the water to see if he could tell for certain whether it was the same horse that had stood outside the barn the night before. But even without proof, he knew it had to be. Lottie's reaction convinced him of that.

If the man was an enemy, she would have either screamed for help or come running to warn them all. No, this was someone she knew and knew well. Someone she didn't want Wade to know about.

Ambrose Bardell.

Wade figured he should be feeling pretty good right now. He'd been almost in spitting distance of the one man the marshals were determined to bring to justice. Hell, no one else had even caught a glimpse of the bastard. But he wasn't feeling good, not in the least. The thought of a killer like Bardell talking to Lottie—or worse yet, bedding her—made him sick with a fury he hadn't felt in some time.

Memories of watching Lily fall prey to Cal Preston's charms washed over him. Granted, Cal had turned out to be a good husband to Lily, but at the time Wade's inability to stop it had been infuriating.

But he wasn't helpless now. Instead, he was a deputy U.S. marshal. Ambrose Bardell's time was over. Wade would see to it.

"Tomorrow is Friday." Lottie immediately shot to her feet and began clearing the table. Clearly, she'd hoped to issue her reminder and then get on with things.

Wade took one look at the children's faces and braced himself for the argument that he knew was coming. Earlier that morning, he'd heard Jack and Rose pleading with Lottie to change her mind. None of them knew he was outside the open window and could hear every word.

Her arguments had to do with the fact that they didn't need anyone's help. Theirs had more to do with how much they liked him. He'd waited for several heartbeats to see how she reacted to that idea. She hadn't—not in words, anyway. Rather than risk being discovered, he'd moved on, still not knowing what his fate was to be.

Now, hours later, it was clear that Jack and Rose still didn't want Wade to leave, which made it three votes against one. Too bad the one was Lottie, who outranked all of them when it came to matters concerning the stage station.

"I know. I'll be packed and ready."

Predictably, it was Jack who launched right into the fray. "We already told you that we don't want him to go. Not tomorrow. Not ever."

"Now, Jack, Mr. McCord has places he has to go. People who miss him."

Rose immediately looked to Wade to deny the truth of that statement. Once again, he was unable to resist those young-old eyes of hers. "That's not exactly true, Lottie. No one is expecting me anytime soon."

He bit the inside of his lip to keep from laughing at the nasty look she shot him for failing to back her play.

"You're right, though. I can't stay here forever. But," he added with as innocent a look as he could muster, "I was wondering if I could wait for the stage to come back through going the other way."

She was immediately suspicious. "Why? If you don't have anywhere to go, what difference does it make which way the stage is running?"

"Well, you see, I sort of left Springfield in a bit of a hurry, if you get my meaning."

She got it, all right. "In other words, you left owing money you still don't have."

He tried to look embarrassed. "That would pretty much sum things up."

She rolled her eyes to the ceiling, as if praying for patience. "I thought it would. All right, this is the way it will be: you can stay as long as you do as you're told and don't ask questions. I can pay you a little bit, but not enough to pay off any sizable debts you may have left behind. When you're ready to move on, you can pick the direction."

He hadn't expected her to give in so easily, which made him immediately suspicious. Even so, he'd take the deal and be glad of it. Jack and Rose took over the conversation at that point, a fact that Wade was grateful for—and suspected that Lottie was, too.

After the dishes were done, Lottie slipped outside by herself. She wasn't at all surprised to have Wade join her after a few minutes. He stood next to her, his hands in his hip pockets. By unspoken agreement, the two of them enjoyed the peaceful quiet of the evening for a time. Finally, Wade broke the silence.

"Thank you for letting me stay."

"Don't thank me. Thank Jack and Rose. They're the ones who want you here, not me."

"You have to admit that the work around here is too much for one woman and two young children."

That did it. The frustration of dealing with Ambrose and keeping secrets from Wade all came boiling out.

"How dare you! We've been doing fine on our own for a long time, Mr. McCord. It doesn't take a man to run a business or make a home. It takes someone who is willing to stick it out through good times and bad."

He held his hands up as if in surrender. "Now, I didn't mean to rile you up, Lottie."

"No, you meant to insult me and the way I provide for Jack and Rose."

"You've made a fine home for the three of you and you know it. But what would happen if you got sick or hurt? Who would harness the mules then?"

He was speaking to her worst fears, the kind she

had nightmares about. She clenched the porch rail until her knuckles ached. "I pray very hard that doesn't happen."

"You can tell me to go to hell, but what happened to the children's father? Why isn't he here with you?"

Oh, lord, did he suspect? No, he couldn't know about Ambrose. "That is none of your business."

The color of Wade's eyes turned stormy with swirls of green and gray. "And if I want it to be?"

Somehow he'd moved so close to her that she could feel the heat of his body. She tried to move away, but he stopped her. She could feel his breath on her neck, sending a shiver up her spine.

She whispered, "Don't."

He used the side of his finger to turn her face to his. "Don't what, Lottie? Don't ask questions? Don't do this?"

He brushed a kiss across her lips. Once, twice, and then his mouth settled over hers as if its whole purpose in life was to make her complete. His arms slid around her waist, pulling her so close that she could feel the racing pulse of his heart. She sighed and allowed him to deepen the kiss. An ache, sweet and heavy, spread throughout her body, leaving her shaken. Leaning against him for support, she gave in to the temptation to tangle her fingers in his hair where it curled down over his collar.

And his hands. What they did to her was too wicked . . . and so wonderful. She hadn't known a man's touch could make a grown woman beg for things she had no words to describe. He allowed her a brief respite from the onslaught of his kiss as his lips left her mouth to wander down the curve of her throat. At the same time he splayed his hand on her bottom and raised her up on her toes.

The feel of his body molded so perfectly against hers left her breathless and needy. She wasn't a weak woman, or a small one, but he made her feel feminine and protected within the shelter of his arms. When he lifted her up onto the railing and pushed his way between her knees, she lost all claim to sanity.

"Wade, please . . ."

"I'm trying to, honey, believe me I'm trying," he murmured from somewhere near her ear.

He drew a ragged breath as he pulled back. Even the slight distance made her feel as if she was losing something precious. Frustration made her cry out.

"Don't go."

He smiled, his eyes glittering in the darkness. "I won't, but we can't finish this here. Not with Jack and Rose sitting in the kitchen." He looked around. "Do you want to go out to the barn? I think I can wait that long before taking you." He brushed a kiss across her mouth and whispered, "Maybe."

She tried to make sense of his words, but her mind refused to cooperate. "Finish what?"

He drew close again, his voice a rough whisper on the night air. "I want to lay you down and make love to you, just not out here on the porch." He punctuated the statement with a heated exploration of the curve of her ear as he tugged her back down off the railing.

Somewhere in the fog of her mind, she heard Jack and Rose laughing over something inside the house.

Reality came crashing down over her. She pushed Wade away and almost lost her balance. She knew she'd already lost her mind. "Get away from me."

Fury had replaced passion in Wade's eyes, but at least he kept his voice low. "What the hell is wrong with you?"

"You and I were about to . . ." she fought for words. "I can't—I wouldn't . . ." In full panic, she tried to shove her way past Wade into the house.

His arms snaked around her waist and lifted her high in the air. Even as she fought to get free, she realized that he carried her as if she weighed nothing at all. All too quickly, they were into the trees beyond the house. Anger mixed with fear as she fought to be free.

"Damn it, Lottie, settle down." Wade sounded far more fed up than passionate. "I only dragged you out here because you'd have scared the children if you'd gone tearing into the house like some crazy woman." He plunked her down on her feet but kept his hands resting lightly on her arms. He clearly wasn't done with her.

"And quit looking at me like that. I don't know what you think of me, but I don't take a woman where she isn't willing to go." He gave her a look of pure disgust. "And you were willing, lady; don't think you weren't. Hell, I can't remember the last time I was that close to losing control because of a simple kiss."

Shame stained her cheeks. It seemed as if she was always blushing around this man for one reason or another. But this time, he was right. "Things got out of hand, and I got scared."

Wade stepped back, giving her room to breathe. "They sure did. I won't say I'm sorry for what we did—and almost did—but the timing was wrong. Next time we'll plan it better."

Next time? She ignored the ache of need that still pulsed within her. She drew herself up to her full height and looked Wade straight in the eye. If her hands were still shaking, at least it was too dark for him to see it.

"There should never have been a first time, much less a next time." She glanced back toward the house as she tried to straighten her clothes and her hair. "There can't be. I have the children to think of, not to mention a business to run. I offered you a job and a roof over your head, and that was all." She poked him in the chest to emphasize her final point. "*I* was not part of the bargain."

He shoved her hand aside and stepped closer. "I never thought you were. But what happened back there on the porch was just as much you as it was me. Don't tell me you didn't know what you were doing. I know better."

Now she was outraged. No one who knew her had ever accused her of being an easy woman. "And just how do you know that?"

He gestured in the direction of the house. "Hell, woman, you have two children. How could you not know?"

Lottie wanted to laugh and needed to cry. She wanted to throw the truth in his face: that Jack and Rose were her sister's children, not hers. But she had taken over the raising of them when Elsa died, agreeing to claim them as her own to protect them from Ambrose's enemies.

Until now that hadn't been a problem, but it was only logical that Wade would assume that she was far more experienced than she was. She couldn't tell him the truth and didn't want to lie.

So before the tears could fall, she walked away, hating herself almost as much as she hated Wade McCord.

Four

Wade had felt worse in his life, but at that moment he couldn't remember when. Cursing himself for a fool, he stomped off through the woods to the river. He needed some time alone to work off his frustration.

Stripping off naked, he dove into the water and prayed that its coolness would quench the twin fires of anger and need burning in his gut. Stroke after stroke, he wondered how he had let some simple lust blind him to the job at hand.

The devil in him argued that she was as much at fault as he was. For sure, the heat lightning that crackled between them had come from them both, not just him. No, the truth of the matter was that she'd enjoyed kissing him. That and more.

But he was a man of honor, and men of honor didn't treat decent women like whores. Whatever had happened in her past, Lottie had the right to be treated like a lady. He owed her an apology and his word that it wouldn't happen again.

Not unless she wanted it to, the devil added with a sneer.

Now thoroughly disgusted with himself and the whole situation, he waded out of the river and reached for his clothes. He didn't want to face Lottie, but putting it off would only make it harder.

He managed to dress himself in the dark as he trudged back along the path to the house. A soft glow showed through the kitchen window, which meant one of two things: either Lottie was still up or she'd been kind enough to leave the lamp burning for his sake.

That he almost knocked on the door, asking permission to come in, was a measure of how much the events of the evening had scrambled his thinking. He yanked his fist back and forced himself to reach for the doorknob. Stepping inside, he wasn't surprised to see Lottie sitting at the table, staring at a small picture in her hand. When she didn't immediately acknowledge his presence, he looked over her shoulder.

"My sister was the pretty one."

Lottie laid the picture aside, as if she couldn't bear to look at it for more than a few seconds. Wade wanted to protest the lie of her statement, but something held him back. Instead, he pulled out the chair next to Lottie's and sat down. He didn't have to wait long.

"Everyone loved her. It was as if the sun shone brighter just because Elsa smiled." She pushed the picture closer to him. "Even though I was older by a year and a half, she was the one that men wanted."

He heard the pain underlying her words as clearly as he did the pride in her sister. The men must have been fools to look past Lottie without seeing her beauty. Perhaps they were intimidated by the strength in her, but that only showed their own weakness.

"Then they were blind or stupid or both."

Her sad smile made him want to hit something. "You are being kind." She stood to leave.

His hand snaked out and pulled her back so quickly that she lost her balance. He controlled her fall so that she ended up sprawled across his lap, right where he wanted her. She fought to regain her footing, but he kept her pinned against him until he had his say.

"I may be many things, but *kind* isn't always one of them." She started to protest, but he put his hand over her mouth to stop her.

"Now, I have no doubt that Elsa was a beauty, and I'm sorry for your loss. But that wasn't Elsa out there on the porch with me, was it?"

When she didn't immediately respond, he repeated his question more firmly. "Was it, Lottie?"

Her blue eyes sparkled with tears—and maybe hope—when she whispered, "No, it wasn't."

He gentled his touch as he traced her luscious mouth with the tip of his finger. "If I weren't trying to be a gentleman, I'd tell you in exact detail the effect you had on me out there. Hell, I wanted you so badly after one kiss that I wasn't sure I could make it as far as the barn before finishing what we started. And if the children had been in bed, I would have taken you right there on the porch."

And she was having the same effect on him right now. Damn his good intentions, anyway. A kiss wouldn't hurt either of them, but after that he had to put some space between them.

She seemed to know what was going on in his mind, because she tilted her head to the right angle for his mouth to find hers. It took every scrap of his strength to limit his assault to the most innocent of kisses. She sighed and melted into him, her arms wrapped around his shoulders.

Finally, when he was at his limit of endurance, he managed to pull back. "Now, Lottie Hammond, let that be a lesson to you."

"Yes, sir." Her smile, while sweet, wasn't all that innocent.

"I came in here to apologize for the assumptions I had made about you. I should have known better."

"You're forgiven."

"I wouldn't be in such a hurry to do that, Lottie. Nothing's changed: I still want you." He caressed her sweet face. "But you deserve a man who'll put his ring on your finger before he climbs into bed with you. I'm not that man." Nor would she want him to be, once she found out the lies he'd been telling her.

Her pride took over again. She lurched to her feet and stepped away, this time making sure she was out of his reach. "Good night, McCord."

So she was back to calling him by his last name. Maybe that little bit of distance would help her. He hoped so. He watched her disappear into her room, wishing like hell that he could follow her there.

Instead, he deliberately turned Elsa's picture face-down on the table before he blew out the last lamp and found his way in the dark to his bed. Alone, as always.

Lottie bustled around the kitchen, slamming pots down on the stove and calling out orders like a general managing a campaign. Although well aware that the children were puzzled by her behavior, she was at a loss how to stop it. They gobbled down their breakfast and then practically ran out the door to get away from her.

Last night had left her rattled and out of sorts. Wade had yet to make his appearance this morning, and she was in no hurry for him to do so. What had she been thinking of, crying like a fool because no man had seen fit to tie himself to her? One look in a mirror, which she did her best to avoid, always served to remind her that she was too tall, too bossy, too everything.

The door to Wade's room had a telltale squeak when it opened. She'd been listening for it since she awakened at dawn. Even so, it managed to startle her. She almost gave in to the temptation to escape to the barn without facing him, but Wade needed breakfast even though her own stomach was jumping around too much to risk eating. Rather than look at him, she hurriedly put the eggs and bacon on the table and then kept herself busy at the stove.

The stage was due in along about dinner time, and the passengers would be needing something to eat before riding out again. For several minutes, she worked in silence while Wade ate his breakfast.

The scrape of his plate being pushed away warned her that the truce was at an end. "What do you need me to do?"

Now that question brought all kinds of suggestions to mind, most of which were totally inappropriate. Grateful that her back was still to the table, she latched on to the one thing that wasn't.

"Buck will bring the stage through late this afternoon. The mules need to be brushed and ready to harness. Coming this direction, the passengers will be expecting dinner, so we have more time to get the replacement animals harnessed up. I'd appreciate if you'd see to it that the stock is fed and then brushed and ready."

"Fine."

Wade stood up, but he didn't head out the door as she expected. Instead, he came around to her side of the table. She told herself it was only her imagination that the air around her had become heavy and hot.

"Lottie, about last night . . ."

She concentrated on cutting up the potatoes in exact cubes. "What about last night?"

"Turn around and look at me. I hate talking to the back of someone's head."

Lottie finished hacking up the last potato before doing as he ordered. "I'm busy. What do you want?"

"Aw, hell, never mind."

From across the room she could feel the force from the way he slammed the door closed behind him. For some reason, that cheered her as nothing else had in a long time. Even though his parting words, mumbled to himself, sounded suspiciously like "I'd rather deal with the mules."

It wasn't as if he'd never seen a woman wearing men's clothing to do hard work. Hell, on one cattle drive, Lily and her friend Thea had worn his castoffs more often than dresses. But damned if either of them had filled trousers in quite the same way that Lottie did. He was pretty sure he would have noticed. Somehow, the rough quality of her present outfit only served to emphasize her feminine curves. He'd never stripped pants and a shirt off a lover, but he was willing to give it a try. He hoped he wasn't drooling over the prospect, but he suspected he was.

To make matters worse, he felt like a fool holding the reins to a pair of mules while a woman harnessed their companions to the stage. His assigned job was to stay out of the way and let her work. In fact, those had been her exact orders when he'd tried to take over harnessing the team to the stage. When he'd tried to argue, she'd told him he could help or he could watch, but it was her job and she was going to do it.

Damn, it went against his nature to see any woman working that hard. Even though he knew she'd been harnessing mules long before he'd showed up, and would be after he was gone, it just didn't seem right.

"She's the best one on my whole damn route." Buck was leaning against the railing, watching Lottie as she pushed and shoved a mule into place.

"Have you known her long?" Wade kept his tone conversational, but the twinkle in Buck's eyes hinted that he wasn't completely successful.

"Why?"

"Just curious."

Lottie waved for him to bring the next pair to her. That done, he headed back into the corral for the last two. Buck picked up the conversation right where they'd left off.

"I guess I've known Lottie about eight years. Before that, her daddy ran the place. When he took off, she sort of slipped into the job."

Buck sent a stream of tobacco juice splashing to the ground. After he wiped the residue off his lips, he grinned at Wade. "The stage line owner about pitched a fit when he found out that he had a woman running one of his stations, but he couldn't argue that the job was getting done. Hell, he'd be damn lucky if his other places were as clean and well run."

"But I've got a question for you. How'd you come to be working for her?" The driver pushed away from the railing. "I remember kicking you off my stage, and I've never known her to take in strays."

"I was willing to work for next to nothing."

"Hmmph." Buck followed Wade over to the stage. The two men helped put the finishing touches on the tack.

Lottie straightened up from tightening a buckle. "Buck, did you get a chance to eat? I can bundle up some bread and meat for you to take with you."

"I had me a bowl of your stew, but some of your bread would sure taste good later tonight." He gave her a hopeful look. "And maybe a piece of that pie I saw cooling on the window."

"You old coot," Lottie laughed. "You know that's why I baked it."

Wade lagged behind, watching the two teasing back and forth. It was nice to know that she had some friends in this world, even if it was the crusty old stage driver. Buck had given Wade some things to think about.

What kind of father took off and left his daughter behind to raise two children and do a man's work? No wonder she didn't trust men.

A few minutes later, the passengers filed out and climbed back into the stage. Wade didn't envy them the long night ahead, trying to sleep while they jolted along the rocky road on their way back toward Springfield.

Buck was the last one out. He was carrying a sack, looking pretty proud of himself for wheedling yet another meal out of Lottie. He climbed far enough up the side of the coach to lay his precious package carefully on the driver's seat. That done, he jumped down and headed straight for Wade.

"It's only fair that I warn you that I'll be keeping an eye on things around here, boy." He motioned toward the house. "That there's a nice woman, and I won't much like it if she gets hurt by some damn drifter."

Another stream of tobacco hit the ground. "You understand what I'm telling you?"

"Yes, sir." Wade resisted the urge to salute, knowing the older man wouldn't appreciate the humor.

Buck suspected something wasn't quite right, but he didn't say any more. Instead, he climbed up to the driver's seat. Then, looking Wade straight in the eye, he picked up his rifle and checked it over. Content that his message had gotten across, he reached for the reins and snapped them over the mules' backs. With a lurch and a stream of curse words, the stage disappeared in a cloud of dust.

Somewhere along the line, Lottie and the children had come outside on the porch. The three of them stood side by side, waving as Buck and his passengers rode out of sight. As soon as they were gone, the children ran back straight for Wade. Lottie followed a few steps behind them.

"Did you check the team over before you turned them loose for the night?"

"Buck and I both did. He was worried that one of the lead pair was limping a bit. We didn't find anything wrong, but I'll check the whole bunch over again in the morning."

"Good, because we may be needing them again sooner than we thought. Buck says the owner wants to add that other run through here for the rest of the summer. He thinks he can get enough passengers to make it worthwhile. We'll have to bring in another team of mules and extra feed some time soon."

He knew that was good news for Lottie, even if it meant more work for her. For the time being, he could lighten her load as much as she would let him. In the long run, though, she was on her own. Despite her strength, the burden of responsibility would eventually wear her down, making her old before her time. She deserved better.

Rose caught his eye. "Mr. Wade, after dinner we get pie if we're good."

A smile tugged at his mouth. He winked at the little girl. "For a piece of pie, I think I can manage to behave." Then he looked over her head at Lottie, to make sure that she understood him. "At least for tonight."

She got the message. "See that you do." That settled, she dusted her hands against her pants. "Rose and I are going inside to wash up before we eat. You two should do the same."

Rose followed her inside, leaving the two males to take care themselves. Wade ruffled Jack's hair.

"You pump for me and I'll pump for you. Fair enough?"

"Sure."

Following Wade's example, Jack rolled up his sleeves once they reached the pump. The shock of the cool, clear water against his hot skin had Jack dancing and squealing with laughter. Wade knew just how he felt. The day had been a scorcher. Maybe he'd take Rose and Jack down to the river after supper and let Lottie have some time to herself.

Satisfied that they'd pass muster, Wade let Jack lead the way to the dinner table and that promised piece of pie.

The days fell into a familiar pattern. Wade had taken over care of the animals, but Lottie wasn't sure she was doing the right thing in letting him. It wouldn't do to become dependent on him.

On the other hand, his help had freed her up to do other things that she'd neglected for some time. The house was cleaner than it had been in years, and she'd managed to get to the mending that piled up all too fast with two growing children under foot.

To her surprise, Wade had assigned himself the task of washing the windows inside and out. With his help, Rose kept the garden weeded and watered. Even Buck had commented on how nice things were looking these days.

And by her count, Ambrose Bardell would be riding back any day now to ruin everything. She knew just what he'd been up to. Buck made a habit of bringing along a handful of newspapers for her when he came through. The last bunch had headlines detailing another daring bank robbery in a town less than a hundred miles due north of the station.

Although no names were mentioned, she knew from the stories that it had to be Ambrose and his men. Witnesses described a number of men all dressed in dusters and with bandannas over their faces riding into town with guns blazing. As the citizens ducked for cover, several of the gang marched into the bank, threatening customers and bank tellers with revolvers and shotguns. In a very few minutes, the bank vault was empty and the riders on their way out of town. By the time the sheriff organized a posse, the robbers had faded back into the hills. So far, no one had been able to trace their whereabouts. The only good news was that none of the townspeople had been seriously wounded. That wasn't always the case.

Filled with a familiar helpless fury, she wadded up the paper and tossed it into the wood bin, only to realize that Wade was standing across the room watching her. She waited for him to say something, since she normally shared the paper with him. To her relief, his question had nothing to do with her actions.

"Do you mind if I take Jack fishing for a while? The chores are all done for now."

"That sounds fine. Some fresh catfish for dinner sounds real good to me." Then she grinned at him. "But just in case they aren't biting, I'll be ready to heat up that leftover stew from last night."

Wade immediately protested. "I think Jack and I have just been insulted. We'll be back in a couple of hours with dinner in the bucket."

She watched him leave and worried. Despite his chosen profession, Wade had been a good influence on both the children. It wasn't often that they got to see a grown man pulling his weight around the station. Even when their father was around, he rarely did more than care for his own horse. He said it was because he was lying low, but she figured him for plain lazy.

Although Ambrose complained about not seeing enough of his children, he wasn't willing to change his ways. Lord knows, he'd promised Elsa often enough that he'd settle down some time, but so far he hadn't made much of an effort to do so. Maybe things would have been different if Elsa had lived. In truth, Lottie had no doubt that he loved the children—just not enough to be a real father to them.

On the other hand, she knew he wouldn't much appreciate Wade's spending so much time with Rose and Jack, either. She supposed she should discourage it, too, for the sake of the children. Who knew how long Wade would stick around? Once he left, he'd leave a big hole in their lives, not to mention hers. She hadn't forgotten that night on the porch, even if Wade had. In fact, sometimes she found herself drawn to the window to watch Wade working around the place, wishing he were there to stay. Once or twice, he'd stopped what he was doing to look back around, as if he felt the weight of her gaze on him.

Heaven forbid that he'd catch her mooning after him like some lovesick young girl. She was definitely old enough to know better. But no matter how many times she forced herself away from the window, nothing seemed to keep him out of her dreams at night. Some of those had the power to make her blush for hours afterward.

The sound of a horse approaching had her reaching for the rifle next to the door. Glad that Rose was still napping, she eased the curtain to the side to see who would be approaching in broad daylight. Ambrose usually knew better than to do such a foolish thing, but after their discussion the other day, she didn't know what to expect from him.

Even at this distance, she knew the rider wasn't Ambrose. It was likely one of his men passing through on his way home. One of the reasons lawmen hadn't been able to catch up with the gang was that they almost always dispersed as soon as a job was over instead of staying together.

Ambrose gave them a specific date to meet back up with him, but there was no contact between jobs. That way, they were able to live relatively normal lives most of the time.

She kept the rifle cocked until she knew for sure who the rider was. When he got within hailing distance, he took off his hat and waved it over his head. Then he whistled: two long notes followed by three short ones.

The signal was the right one, so Lottie stepped out onto the porch and waited for her unwanted guest to come the rest of the way in. She recognized him by the time he pulled up at the water trough and dismounted. She joined him there.

"Hello, Miss Hammond. Sorry if I startled you."

"You didn't really, Jeb. I just try to be careful." She handed him the cup that she kept hanging on the pump. "On your way home?"

The young blond man smiled and nodded. "Yes, ma'am. I just stopped by to tell you that Ambrose will be coming in some time tomorrow night. He thought you might like to know ahead of time."

She struggled to hide the anger his words stirred up. It wasn't Jeb's fault that she didn't want Ambrose anywhere near the place. She also knew that he would expect her to offer his young accomplice some hospitality.

"Are you hungry?"

"I appreciate the offer, but I'd better get back on the trail. My ma will have my hide if I don't get there in time to help bring in the corn."

Lottie stayed with him while he filled his canteen and finished watering his horse. She'd always had a soft spot for this particular boy. Most of his money went to helping his widowed mother raise his seven younger brothers and sisters. He was a farmer at heart and would likely return to that way of life if given half a chance. Most of Ambrose's men, however, liked killing too much to give it up anytime soon.

Jeb swung back up in the saddle. "I'll be going now, Miss Hammond."

"Tell your mother hello for me." She put her hand on his horse's neck. "You be careful, Jeb. Ambrose's luck can't go on forever. The lawmen are getting closer to him all the time."

The boy looked around, as if he was afraid that Ambrose might hear him before saying, "I'll try, but the money never seems to go as far as it should. The young'uns are always wearing out their shoes, or Ma needs a new milk cow. You know how it is."

Yes, she did. The resignation in his eyes almost broke her heart, but she summoned up a smile and sent him on his way, insisting that he take a sack-full of fresh cookies with him. His mother had to know what he was up to, but with all those mouths to feed, maybe she had no choice.

Just like Lottie. She went back inside, desperately trying to figure out how to keep Wade from meeting up with her brother-in-law.

Wade stayed right where he was for fear that any movement would alert Lottie and her unknown guest that they weren't as alone as they thought. He wasn't close enough to hear what they were talking about, but even from a distance it was clear that Lottie was not happy about something.

She didn't seem particularly alarmed by the man himself. If she'd shown any indication of fear, he would have shot the other man without hesitation. But several times she had smiled in response to something that was said, so she wasn't threatened by him. Something he'd said had her upset.

Wade was willing to bet that it had something to do with Ambrose Bardell. In fact, he was probably looking at one of Bardell's men right now. He wasn't fooled by the youth of the lone rider. Being a killer had little to do with age.

For now, there was nothing he could do but head deeper into the woods without letting Lottie know that he'd been anywhere near the house. He'd wait a few minutes and then approach from a different direction. It was doubtful that she'd tell him about her visitor at all, much less the truth about him.

The minutes dragged by as he waited to put time

and distance between his arrival and the other man's departure. He didn't want to leave Jack alone too long, so he gave up and left the woods. He found Lottie in the kitchen.

"You can put that stew back."

Lottie screamed and whirled toward him with a large butcher knife in her hand. Wade backed away, holding his hands up in mock surrender. When Lottie recognized him, her fear turned to fury.

"Don't you ever sneak up on me like that again!"

"Sorry, I didn't mean to startle you like that, but I figured you would have heard the door open." He didn't point out that he'd done precisely the same thing on numerous occasions without her reacting in such a fashion.

It was then that she noticed that she was still holding the knife as if to ward off an attack. With a nervous laugh, she let it drop to the table. Wiping her hands on her apron, she stepped away from the table.

"What did you need?"

"I came up to get a couple of apples for Jack and me to eat. The fish are biting, so we'll be there a while longer. I thought you'd want to know that we'll be having fish for dinner instead of stew."

"Well, that sounds good to me." She picked a couple of apples out of the bowl on the table and tossed them to him. When he didn't immediately leave, she asked, "Was there something else?"

So much for her telling him about her guest. He considered asking her but didn't want to put her in a position where she felt it necessary to lie to him.

"No, we'll be back in another hour or so." He was almost out the door when she called him back.

"Wait a minute."

When Wade looked back to see what she wanted, it was obvious that she wished she'd kept her mouth shut. Looking around for an excuse to have stopped him, her eyes lit on the plate of cookies. Her relief was all too evident as she quickly wrapped several in a napkin and brought them to him. "I thought you might want some cookies to go with the apples."

Seeing how worried she looked, he tried to lighten her mood. "Do I have to share them with Jack? If I eat them on the way, he'll never know."

Her smile was weak at best, but at least she tried. "Just be careful."

He walked out wishing he didn't have to go.

Later that evening, Lottie was still jumpy and out of sorts. She didn't seem inclined to talk about what was bothering her, but she asked Wade to go for a walk with her. They'd gone some distance toward the river when she finally decided to talk.

"I need you to ride into Springfield tomorrow to take a message to the stage office there."

"Can I ask what it's about?" He wished they'd stop and sit down so he could watch her facial expressions. The sun was well on its way behind the surrounding hills, so it was like hearing a voice coming out of nowhere.

"Well, we're supposed to be getting those additional mules and supplies. In fact, I expected them before now. I need to know when they're coming."

Wade did some quick thinking. If he were a true gambling man, he would bet that she was more worried about getting rid of him for a few days than she was about any missing mules or feed. Even knowing that, he had no choice but to go along with her plan. The only real question was whether he should argue a bit before giving in. After all, she didn't know that he knew anything was going on.

They reached the river's edge. Rather than respond right away, Wade pretended an interest in skipping rocks across the stream. In between throws he commented. "Seems like Buck could have taken a message for you today."

Lottie had an answer ready. "He's not going to be in Springfield long enough to talk to anyone about it. Even if I had given him the message to take, he wouldn't have been there to get an answer, much less bring it back to me anytime soon."

She tossed a few rocks of her own. Her first one skipped four times before landing on the opposite shore. Wade applauded her little dance of victory.

"If they start that second run through here, I won't have enough mules to handle the stages coming and going. I'll rest easier knowing you're there in Springfield."

He bet she would. As soon as he was out of sight, Ambrose could come calling with no one being the wiser. Well, he'd have to see about that. And if it was just Ambrose, Wade would need to trail him back to the rest of his men. Once Wade found out all he could, he'd wire for the other marshals in the area to back his play.

For now, though, he'd play along with Lottie's feeble attempt to keep him out of the way.

"Well, if I'm going to leave in the morning, I'd like to get a good night's sleep. Will you and the children be all right while I'm gone?"

"We always have been. No reason for that to have changed." She picked up the front hem of her skirt slightly, making it easier for her to walk across the rocky terrain without tripping. She lost no time in heading back to the house, leaving Wade to follow as he would.

Five

"When will you be back, Mr. Wade?"

Rose had already asked him that question twice before. She'd shown her displeasure with the answer by sucking her thumb and staring up at him with a frown. This time, he knelt down in front of her, placing his hand on her shoulder.

"I will be back, Miss Rose. And if I can find one pretty enough, I plan on bringing my best girl a new ribbon for her hair."

She considered the matter. "I like yellow."

He tugged on her braid with a smile. "Now, that's exactly the color I was thinking." Wade turned to Jack. "And I figured you for some of that candy they have lined up in jars at the mercantile."

"Can I have one of each color?"

At least one of them was easy to please. Lottie, on the other hand, kept looking at the sun and back at Wade. Evidently, he wasn't riding out as early as she liked.

"You shouldn't spend what little money you have on the children."

"Well, I'd spend it on you, but you won't tell me what you want."

"What I want from you," she reminded him, "is the date my mules are being delivered."

With that, she tugged Rose and Jack back away from the horse she was lending him. Wade swung up in the saddle.

"I'll be back as soon as I can."

That put some worry into her expression. "Now, don't risk hurting the horse or yourself by rushing too much. And remember to stay in town until you get a definite answer, even if it takes a week or more. The stage company will put you up at the hotel if you show that letter I gave you."

He patted his pocket to show her that he had the letter tucked away safe.

"Say good-bye, children."

"Bye, Mr. Wade."

"Bye, Mr. Wade. And remember: yellow would be best, but I'd be happy with blue."

"Rose! Where are your manners?" Lottie scolded.

Wade winked at the little girl to let her know he understood that such things as hair ribbons were important enough to make sure he got it right. With that, he urged his horse forward and started down the long road to town. He was careful not to look back, although it seemed as if he could feel Lottie's eyes following him until he was well out of sight.

In some ways, it felt good to be on the road again. He'd spent most of the past seven years on the move, a habit that Lily and Cal deplored. They both insisted that the ranch was still his home. He just never felt that way. Strangely enough, he'd felt more at home at the stage station after only a few days than he could remember feeling in a long time. Sometimes, he forgot for hours at a time that he was only playing a role and that he had his real job to do—one that could destroy the life that Lottie had so carefully built for the children and herself.

He knew he was doing the right thing by the letter

of the law. But he was also paid to protect the innocent, which meant Rose and Jack. And even Lottie. Damn, he couldn't wait for this job to be over. He'd never felt so torn between duty and desire. For certain, once Ambrose was in jail or dead, he would take some time off, maybe even to pay one of his rare visits to Lily and Cal.

That decided, he pulled up and guided his horse off the road and stopped just out of sight. He waited a full thirty minutes or more to make sure that he wasn't being followed before circling back toward the station. Going cross-country would take him longer to get back, but it was safer than following the road.

If his guess was right, Ambrose wouldn't show up until late in the afternoon or even after dark. Wade needed to find a good spot from which he could watch the station without being seen. He had a place or two in mind, but hadn't really had a chance to scout them out.

When the trail turned uphill, Wade dismounted and led his horse up the rocky incline. Together, they worked their way back and forth across the steep slope as Wade made sure to keep the hill between him and the stage station. The last thing he needed was for someone to spot him.

Finally, when he was in easy reach of the crest, he hobbled his horse and let it graze. Then, taking his rifle with him, he made himself comfortable against the base of a tree and sat back to wait.

Bardell managed to surprise him. It wasn't much past high noon when a group of horsemen cantered out of the woods that led to the river. They rode straight for the house as if they owned the place.

When they stopped right at the front step of the porch in a cloud of dust, Lottie was there to greet them with her rifle resting in her arms.

From this distance it was easy to see the tension in the set of her shoulders, even if he couldn't quite make out facial expressions. He leaned forward, trying to understand better what he was seeing.

When several of the riders started to dismount, Lottie brought her rifle up in warning. All but one of the men stayed in their saddles, but did she really think one rifle would stop a gang like Bardell's if they were of a mind to come inside?

The one individual joined Lottie on the porch, slipping his arm around her waist. Wade gritted his teeth, foolishly wishing he were down there to knock the no-good bastard flat for daring to touch her. It didn't help his mood any that she accepted the man's embrace without protest.

He'd give anything to hear what Lottie was telling the others. Presumably, she won the argument, because all those still mounted moved away from the house. Several stopped near the barn long enough to water their animals and fill their canteens, but the rest kept going. Wade made note of the direction but otherwise held his position.

He wanted Bardell, and there wasn't a doubt in his mind he was looking right at him. Lottie stayed right where she was, rifle at the ready, until the last of the riders had ridden out of sight. When they were gone, some of his own tension eased, but not all of it. Bardell, if indeed that's who it was, still had his hand on Lottie as if he owned her.

And maybe he did. Lottie had yet to tell Wade the name of Jack and Rose's father. The thought that they could be the offspring of a cold-blooded son of a bitch like Bardell made him sick.

And then there was Lottie. Could her unknown lover be Bardell? The scene in front of him argued that such was the case, but Wade wasn't ready to believe it. What he wanted was to shake her until her teeth rattled.

By all reports, Bardell was a handsome man, but hard and violent. Not at all the kind of man Wade would have expected Lottie to be involved with. He'd thought more of her than that, but it wouldn't be the first time that a woman he cared about had fallen for a man of dubious character.

Lily had been drawn to Cal, a gambler, from the first day they met. Wade had done everything he could to convince her that it was a mistake, that her future lay with him instead. The fact that she and Cal had been married for seven years now didn't lessen his pain at all.

Of course, it was obvious that Lottie had been involved with Bardell long before Wade had entered her life, but he still felt betrayed on some level. If she belonged to another man, she should have slapped him senseless for daring to kiss her as he had. Since she hadn't, then he had to assume that she was freer with her favors than she'd led him to believe.

There was movement on the porch. Jack and Rose came running outside. Bardell bent down and held out his arms. Both children flew into his embrace. Wade watched as Bardell threw back his head and laughed, spinning in circles as the children giggled and hollered.

Wade couldn't hear a word they were saying, but it was clear that they, too, were happy to see the man. He'd seen enough for the moment. He slipped back over the edge to where he'd left his horse. Grabbing his canteen, he took a swig of water and immediately spit it out, trying to wash away the bitter taste in his mouth from the scene he'd just witnessed.

It didn't work worth a damn.

From his vantage point, there was little more that Wade could learn. A few minutes after Bardell had arrived, Jack came back out to see to his father's horse. Wade wondered what other secrets Rose and Jack had been taught to keep.

Not that it mattered. His job hadn't changed because for a few days he'd enjoyed being a part of the scene below. And he was as mad at himself as he was at anyone else. He'd violated the one rule that he held on to with both hands: never let anyone get close enough to hurt him.

How could he have been so damned stupid?

He turned his back on the stage station below and walked away. It was obvious that Bardell was settling in for a visit. While he was staying put, Wade had time to follow the rest of the gang. He couldn't take them on by himself, but if he could find their hiding place, it would be easy enough to wire for help.

For now, he was too tired to do more than ride far enough to set up camp out of sight of the station. Luck was with him. He found a quiet little meadow that boasted both plenty of grass for his horse and a spring bubbling up out of a cluster of boulders. He wouldn't risk a fire, fearing the smoke would alert others of his presence. His dinner would be cold, but the vestiges of the day's heat would keep him warm enough through the night.

His meager supplies wouldn't last him another day, but that didn't matter much. In the past, he'd made do with less. Besides, after he trailed the gang long enough to find where they were headed, he would turn back and ride like hell for Springfield. Despite everything that had happened, he still needed a job at the station for a while longer.

Lottie had sent him on a mission; she'd get her answers, and he'd get his man. Seemed like a fair trade to him.

Talk about arrogance. Bardell's men rode as if half the lawmen in the region weren't looking for them. Wade had to wonder why they felt so safe. Their day-old trail led straight down the valley.

It was either a miracle or blind luck that had kept previous posses from stumbling across their route before now. Wade could follow it from the trees higher up the hillside with no trouble at all. When the valley narrowed down, he dismounted and worked his way on foot for some distance.

Finally, the trees thinned out, leaving him little cover. Rather than risk discovery, he turned back, satisfied with what he'd found so far. Certainly, he knew more about the movements of Bardell and his men than anyone else had previously.

It was time to head for town to report in. First, he'd take Lottie's message to the stage office. Afterward, he'd send a letter off to report his findings. A wire would be faster, but he didn't trust the telegrapher to keep his mouth shut about the contents of the message. All that mattered was that if something happened to him, another marshal would have a place to start.

He tried telling himself that he'd done a fine job so far. But if that was so, why the hell did he feel so damn bad?

* * *

Lottie needed to get away, only there was no place to go. Tomorrow the stage was due in, and Ambrose showed no sign of wanting to leave. If it was a sin to hate, then she was the worst sinner of all. She looked around for something to do that would allow her some relief from the tension that was threatening to tear her apart from the inside out.

It wasn't the stage she was worried about. No, Wade was at the heart of her fretting. Her trumped-up errand couldn't have kept him waiting in Springfield for more than two days at the most. Certainly, she hoped that he would stay gone for the duration of Ambrose's stay, but surely he was on his way back by now.

That is, if he was coming back. Just as quickly as that idea formed in her mind, she shoved it back down in the dark recesses of her mind. Of course Wade would return, if only to bring Rose her ribbon and Jack some candy.

Ambrose chose that moment to wander in from outside. It wasn't the first time that he'd caught her staring down the short stretch of road that was visible from the front window. He joined her, slipping his hand around her waist. She stiffened and moved away.

"Still watching for your lover to come back?" He might as well have been asking about the weather for all the emotion in his question.

"He's not my lover." She turned to face her tormentor. "He's my employee."

Ambrose's mouth quirked up in a half smile. "Lottie Hammond, I never knew you to tell a lie before."

She glared up at him. "I am not lying."

The sudden sympathy in his eyes hurt. When Ambrose was like this, she could almost remember why Elsa had been so drawn to him. He reached out to touch her shoulder briefly.

"You're not only lying to me; you're lying to yourself." Knowing from past arguments that she didn't like being crowded, he stepped back. "Don't trust him, Lottie."

"Who are you to judge anyone? At least he doesn't make his living stealing from other people."

She wanted to bite her wayward tongue as she quickly looked around to make sure Jack and Rose weren't within hearing. She and Ambrose never spoke about what he did for a living, at least not around the children. They liked to maintain the illusion that it was his job that forced him to travel— they just never talked about what that job was.

"I'm sorry, Ambrose." She felt compelled to add, "Not for what I said; just that I wasn't careful."

He glared back at her. "I meant what I said, too. Don't trust this McCord."

"And why not?"

"Something about his story doesn't seem right to me." Ambrose frowned as he gave the matter some thought. "He claims to be a gambler who sometimes drinks too much. You told me yourself that was his excuse for being on the stage with no ticket." He looked at her as if asking if he had his facts straight.

Since she'd already told Ambrose that much, she shrugged and nodded.

"Buck told me the same story when he came back through."

"I guess that's what bothers me. For a man with the need for liquor riding him hard, he seems to do without it mighty easily." Ambrose pulled out a chair and sat down at the table. "Most men can leave the stuff alone if they need to, but for others it's not that easy."

Lottie didn't want to hear any more, even if what Ambrose had said made some sense. She herself had wondered a bit about how easily Wade had fit in with their life on the station. He had a way with animals that spoke of years of experience. That wouldn't have left much time for card-playing.

Not wanting to discuss it any longer, she walked out of the kitchen, leaving Ambrose to entertain himself. Before she was out the door, she looked back. "The stage is due tomorrow. You need to be gone."

He was on his feet and following her outside. "I've already told the children that I'll be gone when they wake up in the morning. But I won't stay gone long. I like it here."

Her laugh sounded bitter to her own ears. "You've only been here a few days and already you've about worn a hole in the floor with your pacing. Another week and you'd be going crazy."

"And McCord wouldn't be? Maybe I should ask what you're doing to keep him entertained and satisfied."

Her hand connected with his face before he could stop her. He grabbed her wrist and twisted her arm up behind her back. She cried out in pain but refused to beg for mercy. Abruptly he released her and shoved her out of his way.

"Don't push me, Lottie. I won't stand for it."

She rubbed her wrist and ignored the tears trickling down her face. "It's bad enough what people think of me for having children without a wedding ring, Ambrose. I don't need you thinking worse of me, not when you of all people should know better."

Ambrose stood glaring at her. She'd seen him angry before, but she hardly recognized him at that moment. He was all hard edges and chilling eyes. For the first time, she had a clear look at the man who would rather kill than make an honest living.

Then, just as quickly, that man was gone and the smiling charmer her sister had married was back. "I'm sorry, Lottie. I feel like a fool for being jealous of a man I've never met." His smile didn't reach his eyes. "There's been times I hoped that you'd finally take me up on my offer of marriage."

She did her best to disguise the wave of revulsion that washed over her at the thought. It was true that he'd offered to marry her, but he hadn't liked her conditions. She'd told him the only way that she'd take up with the likes of him was if he gave up robbing folks and took up farming. He'd given that idea all of about two seconds of consideration and then laughed off the whole conversation. Maybe he hadn't been joking after all. If so, she wasn't about to encourage him in that line of thinking.

"You know we'd drive each other crazy, Ambrose. I'm not like Elsa." That was nothing but the truth. Elsa had thought Ambrose was the ideal man: tall, handsome, exciting. Lottie, on the other hand, saw beneath the obvious to the cold streak that ran through him. She'd been a little afraid of him from the first day they'd met.

There was nothing else she wanted to say to him, except to hurry him on his way. She held her tongue, though, because if she pushed too hard, he'd dig in his heels and stay.

"Jack could use some help in the barn."

Her brother-in-law reached out and caressed her face before walking away. She stood her ground long enough to make sure he'd really gone. On her way back into the kitchen, she used the corner of her apron to scrub her face clean. Once inside, she desperately looked for something to keep her hands busy. Finally, she decided to spoil Buck again with another apple pie. At that moment, he was the only adult male for whom she was willing to do anything at all.

Just after dawn, the sound of the door closing woke Lottie from a sound sleep. Her heart pounded in her throat as she grabbed her wrapper and made her way through the kitchen. With shaking hands, she picked up her rifle and then cautiously moved the curtain aside.

Several horses and their riders were milling around out by the barn. They parted right down the middle as one last man led his horse out of the corral and mounted it. Ambrose was leaving. *Please, God, don't let him come back anytime soon.*

As he kicked his horse into motion, the others fell into formation behind him. As they disappeared into the early morning mists, they looked ghostlike and faintly evil. She waited until the last one disappeared before hurrying to the back room to make sure that Ambrose had taken all his things with him. She sagged against the doorway, feeling weak with relief. Her first chore would be to change the bed linens, erasing the last sign that Ambrose had ever been there. When Wade returned—if he returned—his room would be just as he had left it.

Feeling much happier than she had in days, she decided that she might as well be about the day's work. There was laundry to do and a stage to prepare for.

* * *

The view from the ridge hadn't changed in the days he'd been gone. Lottie was outside hanging up laundry while Rose sat on the porch talking to one of her dolls. Jack was not in sight, but he wouldn't be far. Both of the children were good to stay close by so as not to worry Lottie.

Damn, he didn't want to go down the last slope to the station. There had to be another way to lay a trap to capture Ambrose Bardell and his bunch. One without having to live with his woman and care about his children.

And if things went down the way he expected them to, Wade would ride away, leaving Bardell's widow and orphans behind. The man would either be dead or on his way to a hanging. Son of a bitch, what a mess.

But he had no choice in the matter—not and still live with himself. Cursing again, he kicked his horse into starting down the hillside. The sooner he got there, the sooner he'd get this mess over with.

To give himself something to look forward to, he promised himself a bath in the river as soon as the children were down for the night. Normally, he'd take them along, but somewhere along the trail, he'd realized that Lottie was right. It wasn't fair to Jack and Rose to make a spot for himself in their lives if he was going to ride away without looking back.

It wasn't a surprise that Jack caught sight of him first. His welcoming shout carried the distance to where Wade was, still only halfway down the hill. The boy came flying along the road, his bare feet kicking up dust to hang in the heavy summer air. Rose was doing her best to keep up, but her dress slowed her down some.

The simple joy in their faces felt like a kick directly to his gut. He was a damned fool for thinking there was still time to build some distance between Bardell's children and the lawman sworn to bring him down. Granted, their father had hurt his share of people, making widows and orphans out of strangers. How was what Wade was doing any better?

Especially when his victims had names and faces he knew personally. He pulled back on the reins and waited for Jack to reach him. The boy was huffing and puffing by time he made it up the steep hillside. Wade leaned down and offered him a hand up behind him on the horse. Together they rode down to where Rose waited. Wade tried to ignore the feel of Jack's trusting arms wrapped tightly around his waist.

When they reached Rose, Wade held his hand out to her. She giggled as he pulled her up to sit sideways across the saddle in front of him. The horse probably didn't appreciate the extra weight after the long ride, but that didn't seem to matter once it caught the familiar scent of the barn.

Both children laughed with glee when the horse broke into a bone-jarring trot, causing both of them to bounce with each step it took. Wade kept Rose snugged up tight against his chest, trusting Jack to be able to hold on long enough to reach the house.

Lottie was waiting on the porch. Strands of her hair had worked their way out of the knot at the base of her neck, and her apron was soaked with water from the wash. She'd never looked better to him. She wiped her hands on her apron and then reached up to catch Rose as Wade handed her down. Jack managed to dismount on his own. Wade followed suit.

"You made it back finally."

"Sorry that it took so long. The man with the

answers you wanted was out of town; I had to wait for him to return."

"And?"

"The mules are on their way." Wade pulled his saddlebags down off the horse and tossed them up on the porch. "Should be here within the week. He said the extra feed has been ordered, and they'll send it along directly."

He didn't mention that the man had been puzzled to find Wade waiting for him. Seemed he'd already sent a letter to Lottie with the same information two weeks before.

He felt a tug on his sleeve. Rose was waiting not so patiently for him to take notice of her. He resisted the urge to pick her up, much as he'd seen her father do.

"Did you need something, Miss Rose?" It wouldn't hurt to tug on her braid.

"Mr. Wade, did they have yellow?" She chewed her lip as she waited for his all-important answer.

Lottie rolled her eyes. "Rose, where are your manners? If Mr. McCord was kind enough to bring you something, he'll let you know soon enough."

"Tell you what, Miss Rose. While I take care of this tired horse, I'd appreciate you fixing me one of your special cups of cool water. After that, I might just have something in my bags for someone around here."

Three pairs of eyes immediately looked to the bags he'd tossed on the porch. Wade didn't say a word but walked off leading the horse to the barn. Jack ran past him to open the corral gate. The clank of the pump handle told him that Rose was willing to do her part to hurry things along.

With Jack's help, it didn't take long at all to give the horse a quick brush down. They turned him loose in the corral with a fresh supply of hay and water. That done, they could get on with the serious matter of presents.

Rather than bring the water to Wade, Rose had carried it over to the porch, no doubt to be closer to the wonders that waited for her tucked somewhere in his bags. She handed the cup to him willingly enough, but didn't take it at all kindly that he took the time to savor the water.

Jack's shuffling feet and Rose's frown warned him that he'd dragged the suspense out long enough. He opened the bag, making sure that no one could see what was in there.

"Well, Miss Rose, they did have yellow ribbon, but you didn't tell me that ribbons came in sizes. They had thin ones and wide ones. Not only that, ribbons come in nice blues and even a red or two." He frowned. "I couldn't make my mind up which one you would have picked out. I surely didn't want to disappoint my best girl."

He took the time to wink at her and laughed when she winked back. "So, I stood there for the longest time trying to choose just the right one." He paused, trying to sound sorrowful. "I'm sorry to say that I couldn't do it."

Rose tried to look brave, but the slight quiver in her chin gave her true feelings away. "That's all right, Mr. Wade."

"So I bought you some of each one."

With a dramatic flourish, he pulled out a wad of ribbons and sprinkled a rainbow of colors down on Rose's head. She danced for the joy of it, spinning in circles, letting the bright-colored strands dangle from her head and arms until she got dizzy and sank to the ground. Then she gathered up her treasure with greedy hands. But before she ran off to count her new ribbons in the privacy of her room, she took the time to throw her arms around Wade and plant a big kiss right on his cheek.

"Thank you, Mr. Wade."

Jack had watched all this, still keeping one eye on the saddlebag. Wade figured the boy had already waited long enough, so without further delay, he pulled an enormous bag of candy out and tossed it to Jack.

"Now, don't go eating all that at once. You get sick on that and Miss Lottie here will have both our hides nailed to the barn."

"No, sir, I won't. I'll make these last maybe a year."

Both adults chuckled, knowing full well the temptation of candy and the nature of little boys. Jack was about to follow his sister into the house, but stopped before he reached the door.

"Thank you, Mr. Wade." Then he was gone, already counting the different flavors in the bag.

"You shouldn't have spent so much on them, Mr. McCord, but I thank you for doing it. They don't complain about much, but I know they miss out on some things living out here."

"It was my pleasure. Besides, who else do I have to spend money on?" He pretended to give the matter some thought. "Oh, yes, there's you."

This time he wasn't so sure about the choice he'd made. It was hard to guess what Lottie needed or would even accept from him. The storekeeper had wrapped this one in brown paper tied up with string. Wade held it out to Lottie. He made note that her hands were almost as shaky as his when she took the full weight of the gift in her hands.

"You shouldn't have."

"I wanted to."

"But the money . . ."

"Lottie, will you just open the damn thing instead of arguing with me?"

He would have yelled at her for being so slow, but then he realized that she was savoring the moment. It made him wonder how long it had been since someone had given this woman anything at all.

"It's a book!" Her hands caressed the cover as she traced each letter of the title with her fingertips.

She looked up at him, her eyes full of wonder. He'd made the right selection after all. He'd thought long and hard over the possible choices and kept coming back to the few books the store had available. Somehow, he thought the gift would appeal to her imagination, but the deciding factor was picturing her still taking pleasure in the story long after he was a dim memory. If that was all of her future that he'd be able to share, so be it.

His eyes followed each move her hands made as she learned the feel of the book's cover and gently turned the pages. For a few precious seconds, he allowed himself to wonder if she would take the same pleasure in exchanging touches with a lover. The idea alone was enough to have an immediate effect on him, sending an ache pulsing through him. He turned away, not wanting Lottie to take note of his body's almost painful response to being near her.

"Well, uh, I'd better take my things on in and start working to get the team ready for Buck." He stepped up on the porch, intending to do exactly that, when Lottie put her hand out to stop him. Her touch did little to ease his need.

"Thank you, from all of us. You didn't have to do this." She held her hand up when he started to protest. "Let me finish. You didn't have to, but it was sure nice that you did."

She ended her breathless little speech by daring to brush a quick kiss on his cheek. He froze, fighting the urge to do far more than kiss her back. Something of his thoughts must have shown in his expression, because her eyes widened in surprise. For an instant, he thought she leaned slightly forward, as if drawn to the heat she saw reflected in his eyes.

But one of them had to resist the momentary lapse. Bitterly, he reminded himself that she belonged to Ambrose Bardell in some way. As long as the other man had a prior claim, Wade's honor wouldn't allow him to take her, even if she was offering.

Frustration blunted his manners. "Like I said, I'll go see to the mules." Dropping his bags on the porch, he turned on his heel and stalked off, cursing the day that he'd first laid eyes on Lottie Hammond.

Buck bit into his plug of tobacco as he glared at Wade. He'd been his usual teasing self with Lottie, but it was clear that her favorite driver was not happy with the hired hand. That made two of them.

Wade was successfully ignoring both of them, which only served to make her madder. Maybe she'd been a little too forward in showing her gratitude for the gift he'd brought her, but that shouldn't have turned him into a bear nursing a sore paw. And even if it had, she wasn't about to apologize.

Buck muttered something as Wade led the next pair of mules out of the corral. The only sign that Wade had heard from him was the slight falter in his step. She hoped that Buck would keep any further comments to himself, because he shouldn't bear the brunt of Wade's foul mood when he wasn't the cause.

She let Wade position the two mules and didn't protest when he started working on their harnesses. Normally, she preferred to do it all herself, but she was willing to compromise if it kept him from exploding in front of the passengers. But there was no denying that the storm was coming; she could feel it every time he looked in her direction. Well, let lightning flash and thunder roll. She wasn't one to duck trouble. She yanked on a strap, making the wheel mule shift in protest.

"Sorry," she crooned, patting the animal on the neck.

Wade was checking the far mule's blinders. He stopped long enough to frown in her direction. "Were you talking to me?"

She glared right back at him. "I have nothing to apologize to you for. I'm not the one with a burr under my saddle."

"And I am?"

Deciding that didn't even deserve a response, she patted her mule again and said, "I'll bring the last two out."

"Like hell you will. That's my job."

He dropped the handful of harness he was working with and walked off before she could protest. She looked to the heavens for patience. What could possibly have him this riled up? Her own temper flared in response. Only her determination to keep their problems from interfering with the smooth handling of Buck's passengers, not to mention the mules, had kept her from tearing into Wade before now.

She watched as he sweet-talked one of the more temperamental mules. As far as she was concerned, Wade fit right in with all the critters in the corral. Words like stubborn, bullheaded, and cantankerous described him just as well as the two animals that were following after him.

That idea made her feel like smiling for the first time since she'd made the mistake of kissing his cheek. Words had failed her, so she'd acted on impulse, something she regretted as soon as it was over.

"That pie was damned good, Lottie." Buck joined her at the stage. He'd evidently given up on trying to puzzle out Wade's behavior. Since she wasn't having any better luck, she didn't blame him a bit.

"I'm glad you appreciated it." She straightened up. "We'll have the team all hitched up in a few minutes. You'd better go wrap up your extra vittles if you're going to take them."

"I wouldn't miss a chance to eat more of your good cookin', gal." Buck looked over to see where Wade was. "If he gives you any trouble, let me know. I keep my rifle handy for just such emergencies."

She could always count on Buck to make her feel appreciated. "That's mighty sweet of you." Pitching her voice loudly enough to carry to her hired hand, she said, "I figure I can handle any mule that I come across, but it's nice to know that you'd be willing to help out."

Her tart comment had Buck laughing and slapping his knee. Wade, of course, failed to see the humor in the situation. Somehow, that made Lottie feel better. "Of course, if a mule quits being useful, I might be tempted into using my own rifle."

That set Buck off again. He wandered toward the house, still chuckling and shaking his head.

A few minutes later, he led out the six passengers

and got them settled in the stage. He had his usual bundle safely tucked under his arm as he climbed up to his seat.

Rose and Jack waved at him from the porch. "See you soon, Mr. Buck."

He waved back at them and reached for the reins. Lottie joined the children while Wade disappeared back into the barn. She'd deal with him later, after the stage pulled out and the children went to bed. Then she'd knock some sense into him if necessary.

Six

It had been a while since she'd heard any stirring from the children's rooms, but she went in to check on them for certain. As usual, in only a short time, Jack had completely unmade his bed. The blanket and sheets were wadded up around him. She tugged them a little straighter and picked his pillow up off the floor. He cuddled into it as soon as he felt it, and sighed in his sleep.

Rose was his complete opposite. She looked more like one of those fancy porcelain dolls Lottie had seen in a store once. She gently brushed a lock of Rose's hair back from her face and then pressed a kiss on her forehead. She never tired of watching the two children sleep, enjoying their innocence and dreading the day that they grew up and started their own lives.

The minute she'd been dreading ever since the stage pulled out was upon her. Earlier, when her own anger was hot, she would have relished taking Wade McCord down a peg or two. Now, she only wanted to say good night and seek out her own bed.

Alone. And maybe that was the problem.

Wade, with his dark eyes and rare smiles, had only to look at her to make her hunger for his touch, to recreate the moment of heat they'd shared on her porch. Curiosity was no reason to allow a man to bed her, but the tension was becoming unbearable. If it were only her, she'd do her best to ignore the whole mess.

But sometimes when she was looking, she caught him looking back. Although she might not have her sister's experience with admirers, that didn't mean that Lottie didn't know when a man was interested. The only real question was whether he really wanted her, or she was just handy.

She hesitated only briefly before walking past her bedroom door and straight outside. Sleep wouldn't come anytime soon, not with the restlessness riding her so hard. She pulled the door closed behind her, stepping out into the night air.

When she didn't immediately spy Wade, she didn't know whether to be relieved or annoyed. He couldn't have turned in for the night, not without her knowing. She looked around the station. The barn door was closed and the animals in the corral were quiet.

That left the river.

She closed her eyes and let the image of him gliding through the water fill her mind. It was doubtful that he'd have kept even the minimum amount of clothing on when he knew the children wouldn't disturb his solitude. She already knew what he looked like without his shirt on, and that day at the river he'd waded out of the water with his trousers clinging to him like a second skin, leaving very little else to her imagination.

Her feet moved of their own accord, taking her directly toward the path through the woods. She didn't know what she expected to happen once she found Wade. She only knew that she had to find out.

A few feet shy of the trail, a faint sound brought her to an abrupt halt. Tilting her head to the side, she held her breath, hoping that she had been mistaken. A few seconds passed before she knew she'd heard the whistled signal used by Ambrose and his men.

"Told you I wouldn't stay gone." Her brother-in-law stepped out of the shadows at her side.

She managed to bite back a scream at his sudden appearance. With considerable effort, she kept her voice to a harsh whisper. "What are you doing here? Are you insane?"

"Maybe, but I told you I was going to spend more time here. The stage is gone again."

She took a desperate look around. "Keep your voice down. Wade might hear you."

Ambrose shook his head. "He's still down at the river."

Her pulse sped up. "What were you doing watching him?"

"Checking out my competition." Ambrose took her arm and led her back toward the house.

She pulled free of his grasp but fell into step beside him. "What do you mean, your competition?"

"Don't act coy. You were sneaking down to meet him at the river. What am I supposed to think?"

Presented with a perfect target for her temper, she let it fly. The man made his living stealing and killing but dared to sit in judgment over her. "Ambrose Bardell, don't you go insinuating anything. You have no claim on me to begin with, and I'm a grown woman who can make her own decisions."

"And you've decided to take up with some gambler you know nothing about."

"We've been all through this, Ambrose. It's time for you to leave."

"And if I don't want to?"

He reached for the doorknob, but Lottie shoved her way between him and the door. "I mean it, Ambrose. Leave now, before Wade finds you."

"Are you worried about him or about me?"

"I'm worried about the children. Go." She didn't want to beg, but she would if it became necessary.

"I do have some business to see to, but you better get your loyalty straightened out. We have a deal, but you act like you've forgotten about it."

She drew herself up to her full height. "I never for one moment forget who those children belong to." Let him make of that what he wanted to.

From the narrow-eyed look he gave her, he suspected that she wasn't referring to him. Even so, he stepped back. "I'm going, but when I get back, he'd better be gone. I won't share."

He didn't say whether he was talking about the children or her. It didn't matter. She'd fight him on both fronts.

His footsteps echoed through the night, making her cringe with the fear that Wade would hear and coming running. Since it was unlikely that he'd taken his gun with him, he'd be facing a known killer unarmed. She closed her eyes and prayed, for what exactly, she didn't know.

In no mood to face anyone else, she slipped inside the house and threw herself down on her bed. Sometime later she heard Wade come in. His footsteps seemed to hesitate outside her door, but maybe she only wanted them to. It wasn't long before the house was completely silent. With grim determination, she closed her eyes and willed sleep to come.

* * *

Wade tried without success to gauge Lottie's mood. For the past several days, she'd been unpredictable and jumpy. It was as if she was constantly looking over her shoulder, watching for something or someone.

He knew for a fact that Ambrose Bardell had paid her another visit the other night while he'd been down at the river. Wade had caught sight of him as he was leaving. If the other man was aware of Wade's scrutiny, he'd given no sign of it.

He wondered how long it would be before she came up with another excuse to send him away again so that Bardell could come calling. Buck had already given her an update on the mules, and the feed had been delivered the day before.

She appeared at the kitchen window, looking in his direction. He turned his attention back to the rail he was repairing in the corral fence. It had worked loose and needed to be reinforced before the additional animals arrived.

When that was done, he'd start on the loose shingles on the roof of the house. He wouldn't be here when winter hit, but he wanted to look back and know he'd done his best to make the place snug for Lottie and the children. Not that they were his responsibility.

Even if he wanted them to be.

Sure enough, Lottie was on her way out to see him. This time, he had no excuse for not tracking down Bardell's men. He looked around the station, taking note of the chores he'd outlined for himself, and knew he'd never get them all done now.

He set the hammer down and waited for Lottie to reach him. A trickle of sweat ran down the side of his face. He swiped at it with his handkerchief, but it was a losing battle. Short of staying in the river or hiding in the shade, it was impossible to avoid the effects of the day's heat.

"I've been looking for you." Lottie looked around, acting surprised to find him there.

He wondered if she knew what a lousy liar she was. "I've been here the whole time."

"Yes, well, I need to ask a favor from you."

"Anything." He leaned back against the fence. "What do you need?"

Several strands of her hair had slipped free of her braid. He reached over and tucked them behind her ear. He wondered what she'd do if he told her how much he dreamed of those silken strands spread out on his pillow. That every night when she walked into her bedroom, he kept hoping she'd invite him to go with her. He kept those thoughts to himself, knowing there wasn't much chance of that being the favor she had in mind. Luckily, she was too busy trying to collect her own thoughts to wonder about his.

"I hate to ask you, but I need some things in Springfield. I could go myself, but I know you're used to more excitement than we have around here. I was thinking you might not mind shopping for me. You could even stay a few days." She paused as if the idea had just occurred to her before adding, "In fact, I insist on it. You've been working too hard in this Ozark heat. You must miss the card games; besides, the rest would do you good."

He had worried that he wouldn't be able to fake surprise when he was already expecting her to send him away. Her suggestion that he actually needed to be playing cards was the only real surprise. Hell, she'd been railing at him since the first day about his choice of careers, and now she was encouraging it. He had no choice but to take her up on it. He wiped the back of his hand across his mouth, as if imagining the burning taste of whiskey.

"Well, I have to say that sounds real good to me. When do you need me to be ready to leave?"

She glanced at the sky as she pretended to give the matter some thought. "This afternoon would be best. No use putting it off. I'll have the list ready for you." Almost as an afterthought, she added, "It's past time that I paid you again, so I put your money on the table in your room."

Mighty generous of her. Not only did she want him to go back to gambling, but she was willing to give him a stake to get started with. "I'll just finish reinforcing the fence and then get ready."

For a second, he thought she was going to argue, but then she walked away. He watched her go, wishing that she trusted him enough to tell him the truth. He gave some thought to how he was feeling at the moment. He was definitely mad, but wasn't sure why. Finally, it hit him. It had been a long time since anyone had felt the need to protect him. Thinking back to the last occasion, it had been when Lily had insisted on treating him like a boy instead of a man.

He hadn't liked having a woman try to hide him behind her skirts then, and he damned well didn't like it now. Frustration bubbled up inside him because both times he'd been powerless to stop it. Picking up the hammer, he pounded it against the railing, taking his mood out on the innocent fence.

He wasn't normally much of a drinking man, but he might make an exception for the night. It had been late when he reached Springfield, but that only meant that his fellow card players were a few drinks ahead of him. One of the rules that Cal had taught him was that poker and liquor were both better enjoyed long after the sun had set.

After checking in at the hotel, Wade had picked a saloon at random and gone looking for a card game. His requirements weren't hard to meet: clean glasses and a few pretty women to make the scenery interesting as the night wore on. Of course, the fancy women got better-looking as the liquor took effect, but that was all right. He probably got more handsome in their eyes for the same reason.

Hell, now that he thought about it, maybe a trip upstairs with one of the ladies would improve his mood and his luck. As the cowboy across from him shuffled and dealt, Wade looked around the room, studying the possible choices. It didn't take long for him to decide that none of them would do.

Time was, he hadn't been all that damn picky, but he wasn't in the mood for a brunette or even a redhead. No, he'd developed a definite penchant for silvery-blond hair and big blue eyes. And tall— definitely tall, with the kind of legs that wrapped around a man's waist and wouldn't let go. Damn, he was back to thinking about Lottie Hammond and what she might be doing at that moment. The idea of her spending the night with Ambrose Bardell had Wade reaching for the bottle to pour himself yet another drink.

He reached for his cards and fanned them out, hoping that at least Lady Luck hadn't deserted him. It was some comfort to see that she'd presented him with three nines. Depending on how she was feeling about the other men at the table, his hand might just net him a tidy profit.

"I'll raise you two dollars."

He tossed the chips on top of the pile and waited

to see what the others would do. The man on his left studied his cards and then threw them down on the table with a look of disgust. The cowboy counted his chips before meeting Wade's bet. The only serious gambler of the lot was seated on Wade's right. He didn't hesitate to meet the bet and then added a couple more chips above that. Interesting. Once again, the lady seemed to be flirting with more than one of them. Well, she had no patience with a man who was unwilling to pay her price. Wade met the bet.

"I call."

The cowboy had a pair of tens. The gambler gave him a pitying look and laid down his two queens. Wade smiled at them both and showed his nines. The lady might be flirting, but it appeared that she was his date for the evening. He raked in the chips as the gambler picked up the cards and started the dance again.

Wade squinted and cursed the bright sun. It was his choice to be out riding at such a god-awful early hour, but he didn't have to like it. His head hurt like a son of a bitch, but there was no one to blame but himself. He knew what he was doing last night, at least until he started on the second bottle. After that, everything was pretty hazy.

The only good thing that had come out of the evening was that he'd made it back to the hotel with his winnings. A fool who got that drunk risked being robbed or even worse. The lady had been watching over him; that was certain. But now the warm, mellow feeling the whiskey had given him last night had been replaced by a sick stomach and a headache that threatened to split his skull right down the middle. He took some comfort from the fact that he was hurting too badly to spend much time thinking about Lottie and her outlaw lover.

It had taken him all of ten minutes to pick up the urgently needed things that Lottie had managed to come up with for him to buy. He surely understood why she couldn't live another week without an extra bar of soap to do laundry with, and a spool of white thread. There were a few other things on the list, but none of them were as important as getting him out from underfoot for a few days.

His errand accomplished, he was now free to go after Bardell's men. This time he would trail them all the way to their hideout. Once he got the lay of the place, he could figure out the best way to go after them. Despite his behavior the night before, he wasn't stupid enough to take them on by himself. Help would be quick in coming now that he'd sent the letter telling his superior what he'd found out so far.

His conscience bothered him some about leaving Lottie's name out of the report. At the worst, she was really only guilty of having poor judgment when it came to men. Once everything broke loose, she'd probably take some satisfaction in telling him that he was another of her mistakes.

His horse slipped sideways a little coming down the steep hillside, jarring his head again. He muttered a curse as he guided the animal onto a more gradual line of descent. Not for the first time that morning, he wished he'd slept in and tackled the job of tracking the gang later in the day or even the next day. But it was too late to turn back now. He'd reached the entrance to the valley he'd discovered the last time.

Once again he kept to the trees, going slow and

watching for fresh sign of the gang's passing. When he reached a small stream, he dismounted and let his weary horse take a long, cool drink. He did the same and then dipped his bandanna in the water. Without bothering to wring it out, he wiped his face and neck, hoping to ease his headache somewhat.

Now that the sun was almost directly overhead, the day would only get hotter and more miserable. If he had a lick of sense, he'd find the biggest tree in the woods and lie down in its shade until the heat eased up some. Maybe after a nap he'd feel like a human being again.

To that end, he looked around for a place to stretch out that couldn't be easily seen. But before he could pick out a likely spot, his horse jerked its head up and turned to sniff the slight breeze.

The two of them were no longer alone in the valley. He stroked the horse's nose, soothing its sudden restlessness. Even as he calmed the animal, he put his other hand on the butt of his gun, ready to draw it if necessary. It was another minute or two before he heard for himself what had the gelding shifting restlessly.

A group of mounted horsemen had just come into sight. The bastards must feel immune to bullets, because they were riding right down the center of the valley, not even bothering to keep their voices down. There was no doubt in his mind that he was looking at the core of Bardell's gang. Based on all reports, the number of men who rode with him varied anywhere from eight to twelve men. He studied the group, trying to pick out the leader. Although he'd only gotten a couple of brief glimpses of the man, he was pretty sure he'd be able to pick him out. If he was correct, then Bardell wasn't with them this time.

He kept to the shadows, doing his best to keep his horse quiet. There was no way he could take on this many of them by himself. Once they were out of sight, he'd go back to trailing them until they holed up somewhere. Afterward, he'd ride like hell for Springfield and the telegraph office. He'd risk the telegrapher's sharing the contents of Wade's message with the wrong people to get some help in rounding up this many of Bardell's killers.

He waited until they'd been out of sight for several minutes before mounting up, intending to follow them at a safe distance. Finally, he led his long suffering mount down the hillside, figuring that both of them would fare better on the rocky slope. Once they reached the bottom, Wade took time to tighten the cinch before swinging up onto the gelding's back.

Wade debated whether to continue along the hillside or risk the more easily traveled but less protected valley floor. Caution won out over comfort. Besides, the plan wasn't to catch up with the riders, only to see where their trail led.

When the trees thinned out to the point that they offered little cover, he gave up all pretense of hiding and took to the main trail that Bardell's men had used. He'd gone only a short distance farther when he realized that the valley came to an abrupt end. Only a narrow passage offered an escape from the high rocky bluffs that had taken the place of the stands of oaks and maples.

Overhead, a pair of turkey vultures dipped and turned, their ugliness at odds with the grace with which they soared in the hot afternoon sky. As omens went, the sudden appearance of the scavengers was a dandy. His plan to follow the trail until he knew where the gang went to ground no longer seemed wise.

Once he had a reassuring number of fellow marshals at his back, he'd be more willing to risk finding out where the next leg of the trail would take him. With a final look at the blind turn ahead, he tugged on the reins, turning the gelding aside. He was more relieved than he cared to admit to put some distance between himself and the ruthless men he'd been following.

Maybe it was only the vestiges of last night's excesses that had him feeling jumpy, but he'd learned to listen to his gut feelings. More than once he'd avoided potentially deadly situations by the fraction of a second that some sixth sense had given him.

This time, it didn't do him a damn bit of good.

Riding straight for him were two more of Bardell's men. Either they'd doubled back to ensure that they weren't followed, or they'd posted lookouts. How they had come to be chasing him didn't matter at the moment, because both of them had their rifles aimed right at him, spitting smoke and fire.

Wade felt the impact as pain blossomed in his chest, followed by another blow to his lower right leg. As he reeled in the saddle, he wondered if the roar he was hearing was the sound of the shots or his heart pumping his life's blood down the front of his shirt.

He managed to keep his senses about him enough to realize that he was almost a dead man. But if he let the bastards catch up with him, he'd be one for certain. Leaning forward, he grabbed on to the front of the saddle with both hands and gave the gelding its head. Using another burst of strength, he kicked the animal in the ribs as hard as he could.

The horse lurched forward, breaking into a run almost from a standstill. Wade was thrown back in the saddle by the sudden change in speed and direction. With concentrated effort, he managed to pull himself forward, leaning down over the horse's neck. The position offered the dual benefits of making it easier to stay in the saddle while presenting a smaller target to the other two riders.

Now that he'd been seen, there was no reason for stealth. His only chance was to put as much distance as possible between himself and his pursuers. His luck held for a few minutes; he actually thought he was going to make it as the space between them increased slightly. His attackers chased after him, but not with any great urgency. No doubt, they were experienced enough to know when their shots had been well placed. They had to figure that weakness would eventually bring their quarry to bay.

The cover of the trees was getting closer by the second. As if sensing the urgency of the matter, the gelding jumped a fallen log, landing on the far side with more agility than it had shown to that point.

Wade wished he could reward the horse for its efforts, but that would have to wait. At the moment, Wade had all that he could do to hold on. He gave up trying to guide the horse as it picked its way among the trees and undergrowth. Branches tore at both horse and rider, making it that much harder for Wade to keep his seat.

Finally, his luck ran out along with his strength. When the gelding lurched to the left to avoid a cluster of boulders, Wade fell off to the right. He wasn't sure if he screamed or only wished he could as he hit the ground, bounced, and then rolled down the hillside. A tree stump broke his fall and damn near did the same for his back.

For a hellish few seconds, he remained conscious, facedown in the dust and dirt. The vile smell of his own blood mixed with the pungent odor of rotting leaves, filling his senses. He'd never realized that pain had a flavor all its own. Praying for a mercifully quick death, or at least oblivion, he gratefully gave himself over to the darkness that washed over him, leaving him at peace.

"Damn it, Lottie, open the door! Get your backside out of bed and let me in."

Startled out of a sound sleep, Lottie lurched toward the kitchen, trying to reach the door before Ambrose kicked it in. Since he'd ridden out only hours before to rejoin his men, his immediate return could only mean something was horribly wrong.

She didn't bother with a lamp, finding her way through the darkened room with the ease born of familiarity. Throwing the lock, she yanked the door open and stood back.

Her brother-in-law stood outlined in the doorway, but he wasn't alone. He had the body of another man thrown over his shoulder. Ambrose, staggering under the weight of his burden, bolted straight through the kitchen, heading for the room that he used and unwillingly shared with Wade. She slammed the door and followed after him.

Jack was peeking out of his room, his eyes wide with worry. "What's wrong?"

There was no time to offer much in the way of comfort. "Nothing your father and I can't handle," Lottie replied. "Go on back to sleep. I'll tell you more in the morning." She took the time to tuck him back into bed, knowing that if she acted calmly, he would accept her words as the truth.

That done, she pulled his door closed again and charged down the hall after Jack's father. In all the years that she'd known him, he'd never brought any of his wounded to her house. It was part of their agreement that he would keep his other life as separate from her and the children as possible. If he'd dared to do so now, it could only mean that trouble wasn't far behind them.

With some effort, she kept her voice down to avoid waking Rose or further upsetting Jack. "How dare you bring one of your men here! You'll bring the law down on all of us."

Ambrose deposited the wounded man on the bed and stood back. "This isn't one of my men." He struck a match and lit the lamp on the bedside table. "I suspect he's yours."

"What? Who?" She pushed past Ambrose to see, but she knew before she pulled back the blanket that Ambrose had wrapped the injured man in. "It's Wade. What happened? How badly is he hurt?"

Without waiting for an answer, she pulled the blanket completely away. The sight of Wade's blood-stained shirt made her dizzy with panic. She swayed and then caught herself. There'd be time for hysterics later, but right now she needed her medical supplies if Wade was to stand any chance of surviving the night.

She ran for the kitchen. After filling a kettle with hot water from the reservoir, she grabbed her sewing basket, the sharpest knives she owned, and a pile of clean rags. On the second trip, she added soap, some towels, and a bottle of whiskey. Frantically she looked around for what else might be of help, but decided she had enough to get started. If she was missing anything, she'd send Ambrose for it.

To her surprise, Ambrose had already started peeling off Wade's shirt. It wasn't the first time that she'd seen his bare chest, but last time there hadn't been a bullet hole with blood still seeping out. Her stomach lurched miserably.

"Is the bullet still in him?"

"Didn't get a chance to look."

Using a surprising amount of care, Ambrose turned Wade onto his side far enough to see if there was a matching hole in his back.

"No, we'll have to dig it out." Easing Wade down onto his back, Ambrose asked, "Do you want me to do it?" He didn't look too happy about the prospect.

"Have you done anything like that before?" Not that she had, but she suspected she'd done a fair amount more nursing over the years than Ambrose had.

"No, not alone. I've held a few men down, though, while someone else went digging around for the bullet."

"That's something, at least. Let's get the rest of his clothes off and then we'll get started."

It took both of them a great deal of energy to pull Wade's trousers and boots off. That was when she saw that he had another bullet hole in the lower part of his right leg. Luckily, this one appeared to have passed through the muscle without hitting the bone or a major blood vessel. Once they got his chest wound taken care of, she'd worry about this one.

"Go wash your hands good with hot water and plenty of soap. I'll sharpen the knife and get myself cleaned up."

There wasn't time to think about what she had to do. Murmuring a prayer as she put a fine edge on the knives, she laid out thread and a needle, then quickly tore the rags into narrow strips for bandages.

She pulled a chair close to the bed and arranged her supplies on the nearby table. Finally, she washed her own hands thoroughly and then reached for the smaller of the two knives. She drew a deep breath and then reached out to touch Wade's chest near the wound. He flinched slightly. She wasn't sure what to think about that except that it had to be a good sign that he was strong enough to still feel pain.

Ambrose filled the doorway. Without looking at him, she gave him his orders. "Get on the other side and do your best to hold him down. He may be unconscious, but there's no telling what he'll do when I go poking around with this knife."

Ambrose situated himself on the opposite side of the bed, half sitting, half kneeling. Using both hands, he pushed Wade down onto the bed.

"I think I can hold him, but don't be squeamish. The faster you get that bullet out, the better off we'll all be."

With all the courage she could muster, Lottie probed the open wound with her fingertip. It was too much to ask that the bullet would be easy to find. Blood pooled up around her finger and then poured down his side.

"You'll never find it that way. Use the knife, Lottie."

"I'm trying, damn it." Tears blurred her vision. She blinked rapidly to clear her eyes. Grasping the knife firmly, she sponged away the worst of the blood and then went in after the bullet.

Time stood still for the time it took her to probe the wound until she felt something solid that moved when she touched it. It could only be the spent bullet. Wade stirred restlessly, feebly kicking with his legs. Ambrose managed to keep him still enough for Lottie to work.

Finally, she worked the bullet close enough to the opening that she could grasp it with her fingers. It was doubtful that Wade would want it for a souvenir, but it didn't seem right to throw it away. For the moment, she dropped it on the edge of the table to be dealt with later.

Figuring it wise to let the wound bleed clean, she waited a minute or two before washing away the last of the blood that was caked on his skin. Once everything was as clean as she could make it, Lottie reached for her needle and thread. It wasn't the first time that she'd stitched a wound closed, but the feel of the thread sliding through flesh made her stomach churn.

That done, she turned her attention to the less serious injury on his leg. By comparison, that one was hardly more than a scratch.

"You can let go now." She met her brother-in-law's gaze. "Thank you for your help. He would have died without you."

"He might still. He'd lost a lot of blood before I got to him." Ambrose stood up and stretched. "I guess I'll bunk down in the barn."

Lottie pulled a clean cover over Wade and tucked it close around him. "You can sleep in my bed if you'd like."

When he didn't immediately leave, she looked up from the pile of dirty bandages and bloody rags. "Is something wrong?"

Ambrose shook his head. "I've been trying to get

in your bed for years. If I'd known all I had to do was bring a half-dead body with me, I'd have tried that a long time ago." With that, he walked out, shaking his head and chuckling. At least he took the kettle of rust-colored water with him.

She didn't bother to respond, knowing he was trying to get a rise out of her. Normally, she would have made a point to laugh it off, but referring to Wade as a body was far too grim a jest. Once again, she found herself laying her hand on his forehead. His skin felt feverish. It was worrisome, but considering the severity of his injuries, not unexpected.

She needed some fresh water to bathe his face, but that would have to wait for a while. Her hands were shaking, and her legs felt in danger of collapsing. If she didn't get some nourishment herself, she wouldn't be much good to anyone. Gathering up what she could carry, she made her way to the kitchen, using the wall to support her.

To her surprise, the sun had already made its way above the hills to the east. She hadn't noticed what time Ambrose had jarred her out of a sound sleep, but several hours must have passed for the day to be this far gone. She'd been planning on only fixing herself something to eat, but the children would soon be up and about.

She put water on to boil for coffee and set out a griddle for some flapjacks. They were a favorite of both children and Ambrose as well. With all that had gone on, Lottie didn't much care what she ate as long as it was quick and easy. Just as she expected, by the time she had a stack of pancakes piled up, Jack and Rose were both sitting at the table with big smiles on their faces.

It felt good to sit down. From the way both kids dug into their breakfasts, she figured she could count on a few minutes before she had to tell them about Wade.

"What was going on last night? I thought I heard you talking to my father."

She reached over and ruffled Jack's hair. "You've got good hearing. It was your father." The truth was better than any lie she could think up. "He brought Mr. McCord back. He'd been shot."

"Is he all right?" Rose pushed herself back from the table, ready to run to Wade's room.

"Your father helped me get the bullet out. Now Wade is in God's hands."

Breakfast gave her back some of her strength. "You two have chores to do. I need to clean up the kitchen, and then I'll check on my patient. If he's up to visitors, I'll call for you."

As usual, Rose relaxed once she knew what to expect. Jack wasn't fooled so easily. "Where did he get shot?"

Lottie deliberately misunderstood him. "I don't know where your father found him. I suppose somewhere between here and Springfield."

"That's not what I—"

Lottie rolled her eyes toward Rose, who was putting her dishes on the counter. "Like I said, somewhere near Springfield. Now, don't you have some chores to be doing?"

Jack got the hint, but the stubborn set to his mouth made it clear that he wasn't happy about it. Shooting his sister a dirty look, he walked out of the house without another word. Rose finished clearing the table before joining Jack outside.

Lottie did a slapdash job of cleaning up the kitchen. That done, she slipped into her bedroom to get her clothes. She had almost made it back out when Ambrose stirred and looked up.

"How's your lover? Is he still breathing?"

"Go back to sleep, Ambrose. I'm in no mood for your sense of humor."

He rolled over onto his back and rubbed his eyes. "Sorry, Lottie. I'm a bear when I haven't had enough sleep. Give me a couple of minutes, and I'll give you a hand."

"No, don't." Lottie softened her words with a smile. "I got more sleep than you did last night. Rest for as long as you need to. You can relieve me later when I cook dinner."

"If you're sure . . ." He was already snuggling back into the covers as he spoke.

"Good night, Ambrose."

He raised his eyebrows as he looked toward the sunlight streaming through the window, and back to her. "Good night?"

Lottie laughed as she pulled the door closed. "Somehow, good morning didn't seem right. Either way, sleep well."

Seven

Ambrose leaned back in the chair, balancing it on two legs. He'd done nothing for the past hour except stare at the unconscious man in his bed. He couldn't think of anything more boring, because McCord hadn't moved more than an inch all day. Even so, Lottie had insisted that someone needed to be right there in case he did, and right now that someone was Ambrose.

He'd thought about telling her no, but that would only serve to force her to do it all herself. He might be a bastard most of the time, but he figured he owed Lottie. She'd given up her own hopes for marriage and children to raise Jack and Rose. She'd never hesitated to let him know how little she thought of him and his ways, but she'd never once shown any regret when it came to the children.

Hell, he even admired her hardheaded honesty, not that he'd ever say so. It did rankle him good and proper when she refused to accept any money from him. A man needed to see to the raising of his children, but Lottie didn't care. The most she would allow was an occasional visit. Even then, she couldn't wait for him to be out the door and on his way.

He rocked forward in the chair and stood up. It

had grown too dark for him to see much out the window, but he'd go crazy if he sat still much longer. If he'd known bringing the wounded gambler back to the house was going to be so damned inconvenient, he would have thought twice about saving the bastard's worthless hide.

He leaned down to take a closer look at McCord. His color was better now than it had been earlier. Just his luck. The son of bitch was going to insist on getting better. It was jealousy, pure and simple, making him feel that way. Not only did the man spend more time in his bed than Ambrose did, but Lottie was fighting some pretty strong feelings for the man.

She didn't know any more about McCord other than that he gambled for a living and drank too much. Somehow, Ambrose doubted the first fact and thought the second was a lie. He ought to know. Half his gang were hard-drinking men. This man had given up the bottle far too easily for it to be a real problem for him.

But those weren't the only reasons that Ambrose didn't trust McCord. Although he'd let Lottie think that McCord had been shot on his way back from Springfield, Ambrose had found his horse west of the station. He'd backtracked the horse's trail until he found McCord.

The only people who rode through that particular valley on a regular basis were his own men. Strangers were actively discouraged or killed outright. One of his prime rules was that someone had to guard the entrance to the gang's hideout at all times. He had little doubt that it had been one of his men who'd shot McCord. The only question was what he'd been doing there in the first place.

Especially when he was supposed to be on a supply run for Lottie in the opposite direction. He

looked around for McCord's saddlebags. Jack had
carried them in after he'd unsaddled the gelding
Lottie had loaned him. The bags were on the floor
under the bed. Lottie had probably shoved them
there out of the way.

His hands itched to search them. He had too
many questions about the so-called gambler to ignore such an opportunity. Before he dragged them
out, though, he peeked down the hall to check on
Lottie's whereabouts. She'd never tolerate such an
invasion of a guest's personal belongings.

That was too damn bad, to his way of thinking.
If he was going to prove that McCord was lying, then
he'd use whatever means he could. Satisfied that
Lottie was busy putting Jack and Rose to bed, he
should have enough time to go through the bags
quickly.

If he found anything interesting, he'd do a more
thorough search later after Lottie was asleep. He
untied the flap on the first bag and dumped everything out on the table. It wasn't much: a clean shirt,
a dirty one, a worn copy of a dime novel—nothing
to tell him much about the man. He scooped the
few items back in and tied the bag shut.

That left the other side. He figured he didn't have
much time to waste. Lottie was planning on reliev-
ing him after she tucked the children in, because it
was Ambrose's turn to read a story to them—another mark against McCord. It rankled that he'd
been the one to buy a book for Lottie to share with
them. Hell, if she'd told him they needed new stories, he'd have bought them a whole trunk-full.

And damn her, she would have refused them, saying that they were bought with money he'd stolen.
How could one woman be that damn hardheaded?

Looking back, he'd loved her sister, but Elsa had

lacked the strength that Lottie had in abundance. Elsa had liked pretty things enough to turn a blind eye to how he'd paid for them. She had been almost childlike with her delight in bright colors and pretty trinkets. Her first pregnancy had weakened her; the second had killed her. He suspected Lottie would have birthed a baby and been able to hitch up a team of mules two hours later. He smiled at the thought but knew he'd keep it to himself. Lottie wouldn't appreciate knowing what he thought of her, or that he thought of her so often.

Should he risk discovery and open the second bag? He hesitated only briefly before untying the leather thong that held it closed. A worn deck of cards fell out first, followed by a bundle that contained McCord's shaving gear. Below that were two pairs of socks. He tossed them aside to get to the few remaining items in the bottom of the bag.

Still nothing to convict McCord of anything other than having socks with holes in the toes. Hardly a crime. Thoroughly disgusted, he shoved everything back. When he picked up the second pair of socks, something pricked his finger.

He muttered a string of curses as he wiped a small drop of blood off on his jeans. He started to put the socks away but thought better of it. As far as he knew, socks didn't normally have sharp points. Before he could unravel the mystery, he heard Lottie coming down the hall. He crammed everything but the socks into the bag, retied the knot, and tossed the bags back under the bed.

When she walked in, he was across the room, staring out into the night.

"How is he?"

"Less dead than he was a few hours ago."

She clearly didn't like that remark. "That isn't funny."

"You asked. I answered."

Turning her back to him, she immediately started fussing over McCord. His blankets weren't straight enough; his pillow obviously needed fluffing; his forehead needed touching. All the while, the man lay there, both unresponsive and unappreciative. The sight made Ambrose want to punch the bastard, wounded or not.

Ambrose didn't bother to look back as he stalked out, the socks tucked inside his shirt. There would be time later to solve the mystery. That idea had him smiling.

One way or the other, McCord's mask was going to come off.

Pain. Lots of it. Waves of it intermixed with deep pools of feverish torment.

Why did breathing hurt?

He should know the answer, but he damn well didn't. More to the point, his eyes weren't working, either. Despite repeated efforts to open them, they remained pasted shut, blinding him to the world around him.

What the hell had happened?

He managed to move his legs, but his right one screamed in protest. Coupled with the full weight of an Ozark mountain sitting right on his chest, it all added up to more than he could handle. He called back the darkness, embracing its welcoming touch as it slid over him, easing him back down into the world beneath the pain. . . .

* * *

It was time. The blackness no longer served any purpose. The pain, while still severe, was at least manageable. Drawing a deep breath, he concentrated on opening just his right eye. To his amazement, both popped open. Even the dim light of the lamp startled him with its brightness. Reluctantly he let his eyelids drop down to give himself time to adjust to seeing again. This time, he was able to keep them open for several seconds before he needed to blink them clear. Definitely a step in the right direction. Having conquered that particular milestone, he debated what to try next.

His most pressing need was to figure out where he was. The last thing he remembered clearly was riding Lottie's gelding back from somewhere. Springfield? Yeah, that sounded right.

A voice other than the one in his head spoke up from somewhere off to his right.

"Damn well about time you showed some sign of living. I don't know why she bothered, but Lottie has damn near killed herself trying to keep you alive. Personally, I was tempted to hurry you along."

Wade had never heard that voice before, but something told him he should recognize it anyway. As quickly as he could manage it, he turned his head in the direction of the speaker.

"Who?" was all that he could manage.

"You'll figure that out on your own presently. For now, let's just say that I'm the idiot that dragged you back to the station to let Lottie work her wonders."

"Bardell." It wasn't a question.

"You are quick."

Wade's sight was still blurred, but he could make out enough details to recognize the man he'd seen on Lottie's porch. He seemed to be tossing something in the air and catching it. Something shiny. Something silver.

"Lottie know that you've been going through my things?"

Bardell laughed. It wasn't a pleasant sound at all. "No, not yet, anyway. I figured she'd get mad at me for daring to search your bags, but then she expects such things from me."

He flipped the star up again. "On the other hand, she's going to really hate knowing that you've been lying to her and the children all along, Marshal McCord."

There was no use denying it, but Wade tried anyway. "That belonged to a friend who was killed."

Ambrose quirked an eyebrow. "Really? Considering the condition you were in at the time I found you, I'd say this badge was bad luck." He tossed the badge onto the bed. "Personally, I'd get rid of the damn thing."

Wade knew he wasn't thinking clearly, because he found himself actually liking Ambrose Bardell. Maybe he'd hit his head somewhere along the line. He hoped so. He'd hate like hell to drag a man back to face a hanging whom he genuinely liked. But then, maybe Ambrose had other plans for his future.

"Why haven't you told her?" For some reason, he knew the answer to that question was important.

Bardell gave the matter some thought. "Damned if I know. If you had died like you should have, then there wasn't any reason to say anything. I would have buried your secret with you." He grinned at Wade.

The man's smile was so infectious Wade found himself smiling back.

"Sorry to disappoint you."

"It isn't too late."

A threat was a threat, no matter how it was delivered. He looked around the room for his guns, but even knowing where they were wouldn't help. Right then, he was too weak to move much more than a finger. Ambrose would have a good laugh watching him crawl for his revolver.

"Well, I've done my duty watching to make sure you were breathing." Ambrose got to his feet. "Lottie will be happy to know you're awake." His eyes turned cold as he added, "I don't want her hurt. I'm not sure what's brewing between the two of you, but if she cries, you're a dead man."

Then he reached over and picked up the badge again. "On second thought, I'll hold on to this for you."

Wade watched him leave and then let his eyes drift shut. If he'd been puzzled by the relationship between Lottie and Bardell, that last remark made him even more so. For sure, if Lottie was his woman, he'd shoot another man for looking at her wrong. Bardell wasn't warning Wade to stay away, just to tread carefully. It made no sense.

Sleep tugged at the edges of his mind. It wasn't the blackness that had blocked out the rest of the world, but the normal kind—the kind that healed. Figuring things would be clearer when he woke up again, he gave himself up to it. At least for now, Bardell didn't seem in any hurry either to tell Lottie who Wade really was or to finish off what his men had started.

Someone was staring at her. Lottie glanced over to the bed to see Wade's eyes open and focused.

"Have you been sitting there long?" His whisper was rough and harsh.

At the first word out of his mouth, her hands stilled as she shifted her attention from her needlework to him. Her sewing forgotten, it fell to the floor as she stood. Her first need was to touch his forehead; the cool feel of his skin beneath her fingers relieved a tight knot of worry that had ached in her chest for three days.

"Welcome back." Blinking back the burn of tears, she tried to smile. "Your fever seems to have broken."

She pulled her hand back to her side, unsure what to do next. Her eyes lit upon the pitcher sitting on the table.

"You must be thirsty."

He nodded. She immediately reached to pour him a glass of water. Gently she lifted his head to support him as he sipped the water. When he'd had all that he could handle, she eased his head back down on the pillow. He managed to capture one of her hands with his before she moved back again.

"Please sit by me for a minute or two."

"I don't want to jostle you."

"Please."

Slowly she perched on the edge of the bed. Even that small movement made him wince, but he turned his head away trying to hide it from her.

"I seem to have lost track of the days. How long have I been here?"

How could she explain Ambrose? She settled on being vague. "A friend found you three days ago. You'd been shot twice, once in the chest and again in your right leg." Her eyes darted away from his, hoping he wouldn't ask questions she wasn't willing to answer.

"Thank him for me."

"I will."

A voice from the door startled them both. "You can thank me yourself, McCord."

Lottie jumped to her feet, feeling flustered at having been caught sitting on the bed with Wade. "I didn't know you two had met."

Ambrose stepped farther into the room. "I was here when he came to last night. Remember?"

"Oh, of course." She stepped farther from the bed, distancing herself from Wade. "I guess I didn't realize that the two of you had that much of a conversation."

Ambrose flashed her a smile as he slipped his arm around her waist. "Actually, we didn't have much to say to each other. I just reassured him that he hadn't woken up in hell."

Wade was frowning at both of them. "To tell the truth, until I saw Lottie sitting there, I still wasn't sure about that."

Their conversation had Lottie hovering between the two of them. They were saying more than what was on the surface of the words, but she didn't quite know what to make of their cryptic remarks.

"Either way, we didn't get around to formal introductions, Lottie. Why don't you do the honors?"

She looked at the two men, not happy with either of them at the moment. "Very well: Wade McCord, this is Ambrose."

That said, she grabbed her brother-in-law by the arm and dragged him from the room.

"Wade, you need to rest. Ambrose, I'm sure you have better things to do than aggravate both him and me." She gave him another shove in the direction of the kitchen.

He tried to slip past her. "I had promised to relieve you as soon as the children were asleep. Just because he's out of the woods doesn't change the fact that you need some rest yourself." His hand cupped her chin. "Besides, you look like hell."

"How nice of you to say so." Leave it to him to be brutally honest. "I don't want you pestering him."

"Now, Lottie, you keep telling me that I should spend time with a better class of people. Since you seem to think so much of McCord, I'd think you'd want me to be around him."

How could a known bank robber manage to look so innocent? She didn't trust the gleam in his eyes one bit.

"Now is not the time, Ambrose. He doesn't know who or what you are. Let's keep it that way for as long as we can."

"He knows I'm the one who dragged his worthless carcass back here. That alone should make him think well of me, don't you think?"

He leaned against the wall, ready to wait her out. There was no arguing with Ambrose when he made up his mind to be obstinate. She stood toe to toe with him and gave him his orders.

"Fine. Go sit with him. Don't let him do too much. If he falls asleep, leave him alone."

Ambrose held up his hands in surrender. "Yes, ma'am."

She suspected he was laughing all the way back down the hall to Wade's room, but she let him get away with it. Granted, she had some misgivings— make that a lot of misgivings—about letting Ambrose be around Wade, for obvious reasons. The trouble was that she didn't trust herself either. She'd known for some time that she'd allowed herself to become infatuated with the gambler.

But when he'd gone missing, she'd been almost frantic. Her hands still shook every time she remembered the feel of her fingers chasing the bullet as it slid through the torn, bleeding muscles in his chest. There was little doubt left in her mind that she'd gone way beyond infatuation.

It would have been all right to flirt a bit. And as long as her heart hadn't been involved, she might have enjoyed letting Wade teach her all about what went on between men and women.

After all, it had been weeks since that night he'd kissed her, but she could still remember the smoky green of his eyes when he'd lifted her up onto the porch rail. The thrill of having a man between her legs for the first time had colored her dreams ever since.

The sudden rush of remembered heat drove her from the kitchen and out onto the porch. For a few seconds, she stood with her eyes closed, breathing deeply of the night air. From out in the woods, a whippoorwill sang out its mournful call. Lottie turned her head, listening as the elusive bird told the world of its problems.

The sad song fitted her mood perfectly because there was no denying that she was a fool. She of all women should know better than to want a man with no roots and no qualms about taking other people's money.

Her own father had done his best to teach her that lesson early on. From everything she'd ever heard about him, he'd been shiftless from the day he was born. Unfortunately, her mother hadn't seen past his handsome face until it was too late. He'd worn her out, dragging her and their daughters from one town to the next.

Oh, it was true that sometimes he'd sober up and swear to do better by them.

She was grateful that his good intentions had lasted long enough to convince the stage line owner to set him up with the station and a job. Her mother had lived long enough to see her family finally have a solid roof over their heads. From the beginning, Lottie had loved helping her father with the animals and seeing to the needs of the stage passengers.

But once her mother died, the need to drink was stronger than her father's need to take care of the family. Lottie had been the real station manager long before her father had taken to the road, running away from the demons that haunted him.

Then there was Ambrose, another example of what she didn't want in a man. Charm didn't count for much as far as she was concerned.

Shaking her head, she looked up at the stars. Come to think about it, the only man she'd ever known who held a steady job was Buck. Of course, he chewed tobacco, cussed with every breath, and wasn't too fond of bathing. Maybe she was looking for a perfection that simply didn't exist.

Wade had definitely shown promise. Despite his chosen career, he'd certainly worked hard enough around the station. She'd found watching him with Jack and Rose to be pure pleasure. Perhaps that was how he'd slipped under her guard, lodging himself in her heart despite her lifelong resolve that no man at all was better than someone like her father or Ambrose.

She whispered another prayer, grateful that his life had been spared. So far, he hadn't been able to tell her anything about who had shot him. Likely, it had been some of his gambling acquaintances, fed up with his not paying his debts. If she had to worry about that happening every time he went to town, she'd lose her mind.

She'd do her duty by nursing Wade back to health. But once he could sit a horse, she'd send him on his way while she had the strength to do so. Once he disappeared over the hill back to where he came from, she would set about piecing her heart back together.

The whippoorwill had stopped singing. No doubt, he'd decided to take his troubles to a more sympathetic ear. She wished him the best, but she had enough problems of her own.

Ambrose had been right about one thing, though. She needed her rest, and it was long past time to turn in. Morning chores would need doing, no matter if she got any sleep or not.

Wade spread his cards out on the quilt. "Full house, queens over tens."

Ambrose didn't bother to show his cards. Glaring at Wade, he tossed them down. "Cheating bastard. If I could figure out how you were dealing off the bottom of the deck, I'd take a horse whip to you."

There was no use in taking offense. Ambrose had been cursing Wade and his own bad luck since they'd taken to playing cards. Under other circumstances, Wade would have felt obligated to shoot his opponent for such talk. But to his dismay, he found himself liking Ambrose.

He studied him as he dealt the next hand. It was hard to reconcile his easygoing companion with the cold-blooded killer he'd been told to bring to justice. Jack and Rose were obviously crazy about their father, and he was good with them. Wade had yet to figure out exactly what sort of relationship Ambrose had going with Lottie.

Since Wade was still pretty much confined to bed, he didn't know for certain where Ambrose was bedding down. He assumed that the outlaw was sharing Lottie's bed, but then, maybe not. Even though Ambrose would occasionally slip his arm around Lottie's shoulders, there was no real warmth in the gesture.

They acted more like old friends than lovers. But, perhaps he was seeing what he wanted to see. He'd hate like hell to find out that she preferred the company of a murdering son of a bitch like Bardell. He'd already lost one woman to a gambler; a bank robber would be even more of an insult.

The man in question brought Wade's attention back to the game. "You going to deal or did you fall asleep on me again."

"If Lady Luck was as cold to me as she is to you, I'd give up cards for good."

He finished dealing each of them five cards and set the deck down. Before he could pick up his cards, Ambrose grabbed them. He looked damned proud of himself as he organized the cards and spread them out.

"That was my hand," Wade protested, but with no real heat. If Ambrose hadn't been willing to play cards with him, he'd have died of boredom days ago.

"I just wanted to see if my luck would turn if I got what your lady meant you to have."

"Did it help?"

"No, she hates you, too." Ambrose picked up one of their improvised chips and tossed to the middle of the bed. "Ante up if you want to see your cards."

Wade, unable to hold back a chuckle, grabbed

his side. Everything made him hurt, especially laughing. He threw a couple of his own chips down. "I hate to tell you, but I think you missed your chance. The lady was definitely on your side in this one."

"Damn it all, anyway." Ambrose gave his hand a disgusted look before making another move. Finally, he gave up and threw down his cards and his few remaining chips. "Take them, McCord. You're going to get it all eventually. This will make it easier on both of us."

Wade gathered up the cards and then dumped the buttons back into the small sack Lottie kept them in. She wasn't too happy about their gambling with them, but even she had to admit that Wade needed something to do to keep from going crazy.

That done, he eased himself back down on the bed. He was getting stronger every day, but he still needed a fair amount of extra sleep. Usually, Ambrose would leave the room when their card game ended. This time, he sat staring at Wade.

"Something on your mind?"

The outlaw didn't answer right away. He seemed content to sit quietly as he leaned his chair back on two legs. Wade gave up on getting any answer and let his eyes drift shut. Sleep felt a long way off, but staying completely alert took far too much energy.

"Lawman, you puzzle me."

Once again, Ambrose kept his voice low enough to keep their conversation private. Evidently, he still wasn't ready to tell Lottie the truth about Wade. What kind of game was the man playing?

"How so?" he prodded when Ambrose didn't say anything else.

"Lottie's a beautiful woman."

Wade wasn't sure whether Ambrose was stating a

fact as he saw it or asking for Wade's opinion. He did know that the woman in question wouldn't appreciate being the subject of their conversation.

"Your point?"

"Near as I can tell, you've been living under the same roof with her for weeks without once doing anything about the itch you have for her."

That had Wade sitting right up. "What itch?"

"Hell, a blind man could see that the two of you are interested in doing a bit of nuzzling." Ambrose brought the chair back down solidly on all four legs with a loud thump. "I just kind of wonder why you haven't made your move, especially when she obviously feels the same way about you."

Wade was almost sputtering. "What kind of bastard are you? Offering her to me like that?" If he wouldn't have fallen over trying to stand, he would have done his damnedest to knock Ambrose through the wall.

"Well, since her pa is gone and probably dead, I'm her closest male relative. Someone has to find out what you're up to."

"Nearest relative? Is that what you call yourself? Hell, she has your children!"

Suddenly all the humor vanished from Ambrose's eyes. "That's true. When my wife died, Lottie thought it best to pretend they were hers. That's why they use her last name. I don't fit her idea of a proper father for her niece and nephew."

It was the first time Wade had seen Ambrose turn serious for any length of time. "I may not always like her methods, but Lottie has been a good mother to my children. I can't fault her for that."

Wade mumbled some response, but he wasn't listening anymore. He was too busy trying to get his mind around the fact that Lottie was the outlaw's sister-in-law, not necessarily his lover. He let his eyes drift shut, the need to sleep too strong to resist.

He was only dimly aware that Ambrose had slipped out of the room, his question about Wade's intentions left unanswered.

Eight

Lottie sometimes wondered if there was a man alive who could stand to stay in one place without getting the urge to see what was on the other side of the next hill. Or mountain. Or river. She knew for certain that if such a man existed, she'd never met up with him.

Ambrose was bad enough. Despite his claim to want to stay at the station, he'd taken to leaving for a day, maybe two, and then coming right back. He knew very well that she didn't like his being around that much, but he ignored her protests. When he was at the station, he divided his time between playing with his children and playing cards with Wade.

She prided herself on being self-sufficient, but she wouldn't have minded getting a little help out of him.

As far as her other houseguest, he was only a few days out of a sickbed, and already he was wearing a trench on the porch. Pacing back and forth, he'd walk until his strength gave out. Then he'd sit on the bench and fidget until he worked up the energy to walk again. Every so often he'd look in her direction, letting his eyes slide by and then back again, not really making contact but watching her nonetheless.

Of course, if she didn't spend so much time looking back, she wouldn't be so acutely aware of what he was doing. After nursing him, she'd seen about all of him there was to see, but she still hadn't looked her fill. Even now, with his hair grown too long, her hands itched to brush back the lock that insisted on falling down over his forehead.

Then there were his eyes. As changeable as the weather, they varied in color from dark green to almost brown, depending on his mood. At that moment, something had him frowning, so they'd gone all smoky. If she remembered correctly, they looked about the same as on the night he kissed her. In a moment of weakness, she wished she had the courage to entice him into kissing her again in order to know for sure. She was so intent on Wade, she didn't hear Ambrose walk up behind her. When his hand touched her shoulder, she was startled into yelping.

Feeling guilty, and not a little embarrassed, at having been caught staring, she lit into him. "Ambrose Bardell, I've warned you about sneaking up on me like that."

Jack and Rose were right behind their father. All three of them were trying not to laugh, which didn't help her temper one bit.

"Now, Lottie, we didn't mean to scare you. We only wanted to ask you something."

One look at their faces, and she knew she wasn't going to like it, whatever it was.

"All right, what are you three up to now?"

Jack and Rose looked at their father, waiting for him to plead their case.

"I'm asking you to hear me out before you make any decision." He waited for her to nod before going on.

"I need to go up to St. Louis on business." Then,

knowing how she felt about his business, he added, "Legitimate business."

Dread took up residence in her stomach even before he could finish speaking his piece.

"Jack and Rose have never been there, and I want to take them along. We'll take the train out of Columbia."

Her first urge was to throw herself between Ambrose and the children, but she managed not to. After all, they were his children. If she protested too much, he might just decide to take them anyway. Maybe for good.

"How long would you be gone?"

"A week, maybe. No more than two for sure."

It was her worst nightmare, but he'd never lied to her about things like this. Although it would be the longest trip he'd taken them on, in the past he'd always been prompt in bringing his children back to her. She supposed she should be grateful that he went through the motions of asking her permission at all.

"When will you leave?"

His answer was lost in the uproar from Jack and Rose as they realized that her question meant that she was saying yes.

"I'll go pack!" Jack yelled. "I'll need my extra shirts."

Rose was hopping up and down, tugging on Lottie's skirt to get her attention.

"Can I take all my ribbons that Mr. Wade bought me? I want to be pretty in St. Louis."

Ambrose knelt down to his daughter's level. "You'd be the prettiest girl no matter where you were. And I'll buy you all the new ribbons in St. Louis, if that's what you want."

He kissed her on the forehead and watched her

disappear into her room, presumably to start her own packing. He stayed down as he watched her with a strange longing in his face.

"You don't need to be jealous of a few ribbons, Ambrose." Lottie patted him on the shoulder. "They couldn't possibly love you any more than they do."

He got back up to his feet. "I know, and I owe you for that. You've done everything you can to make them look up to me. That's not easy, considering." His moods changed with the wind. "Is there anything I can bring you back from St. Louis?" Pure deviltry chased the sadness from his eyes. "Maybe some fabric for a pretty new dress?"

She definitely didn't trust his sudden interest in her wardrobe. "I'd get more use out of new pair of dungarees. Dresses only get in the way when I'm hitching up mules."

He tipped his head to one side, as if considering the matter. "Yes, I'm thinking a few yards of blue gingham—something that would bring out the color of your eyes. I've always thought they were one of your best features. The right dress might just make a man take notice."

He'd definitely caught her staring at Wade again. Her face flushed hot.

"I don't know any man that I'd want to take notice."

"Liar." Ambrose wasn't laughing when he looked past her to where Wade was back to pacing on the porch.

"Don't be any stupider than you have to be, Ambrose. I'm not looking in that direction."

He repeated his previous comment. "Liar. And don't fool yourself, Lottie Hammond. He's looking back."

She stepped around Ambrose and took a position at the stove. Picking up a knife, she began to peel potatoes for the venison stew she had planned for their dinner. With luck, her brother-in-law would take the hint and leave. But no, he'd evidently decided to dig in his heels on the matter.

"Lottie, you know I'm damn grateful for all you've done for me and mine. But it doesn't set easy with me to know that you've given up all hope for a man and family of your own."

His words hurt more than they should have, but maybe that was because she'd been having some of the same thoughts herself.

"I don't know what you're talking about. I have a good life. And I have a family—yours." She used the back of her hand to wipe a stray tear from her cheek. "My, these onions are awfully strong."

Ambrose ran his hand through his hair, clearly frustrated with her. "Damn it, Lottie, raising my children isn't the same as having some of your own. Besides, even though you love Jack and Rose, they don't warm your sheets at night. Don't miss your chance."

With that, he disappeared outside, leaving her stunned. Was he actually encouraging her to invite Wade into her bed? He knew how she felt about shiftless men. As much as she wanted to believe that Wade was different, she prided herself on looking at things dead on, not twisting the facts to fit her needs. Warm her sheets, indeed. She slammed the pan down on the stove to start cooking. Despite what some folks thought, she was a decent woman and planned to stay that way. No matter how lonely it got.

* * *

Wade was feeling better than he'd been letting on, figuring that it never paid to let an opponent know your full strength. And despite how friendly Ambrose had acted ever since he'd brought Wade back for Lottie to patch up, he was still Wade's enemy. The man was a killer and a felon.

If Wade was having time reconciling the Ambrose he'd always heard about with the real one, that was his problem. He had a job to do, and when the time came, he'd do it. Ambrose would be tried and convicted based on the facts of his crimes. If he was lucky, he'd go to prison; if not, he'd hang. Wade's eyes strayed toward the house, thinking about the three people who would be most hurt by that. He tried to tell himself that Lottie and the children were three more of Ambrose's victims, hurt by his total disregard of the law. But he knew they wouldn't see it that way. Without a doubt, they'd lay the blame squarely on Wade's shoulders when the time came.

After all, he'd lied to them about who he was, and lived with them under false pretenses, all to trap their father and brother-in-law. Although Lottie had never even hinted at Ambrose's means of making a living, she knew. So if he was guilty of deceit, so was she. She'd also let him think that Jack and Rose were hers.

To give credit where it was due, she'd done her best to keep him out of the house when Ambrose was around. But who was she really protecting? Certainly not Wade, or else she would have warned him that armed and dangerous men were frequent guests at the station.

He hit his fist against the porch rail. He wasn't making any damn sense, not even to himself. These were dangerous times, and killers were everywhere. There was no reason for Lottie to think he couldn't take care of himself. But by blaming her, he'd have an easier time living with his own conscience.

It was time to put some space between himself and those folks in the house. He eased down off the porch, taking his weight on his left leg. The right one was almost healed, but any sudden jolt still reminded him that it had a ways to go. If he took his time, though, he might just make it to the river before he had to sit down and rest.

A short distance into the woods, he heard footsteps behind him. Despite Lottie's frowns, he'd taken to wearing his gun all the time, even to the breakfast table. For now, Ambrose seemed unlikely to make any threatening moves, but his men would not have any such qualms. They'd already done their best to kill him once, and that was before anyone knew he was a marshal.

A twig snapped a few feet away. His gun was in his hand before he drew another breath. Hurrying his steps, he took refuge behind the trunk of an oak tree and waited. A heartbeat later, Ambrose came out of the shadows, holding his hands up.

"Didn't mean to scare you, McCord."

His smile was meant to be reassuring, but Wade didn't trust it. He waited until he stepped out from behind the tree before holstering his gun.

"A man can get shot when he least expects it, Bardell."

The outlaw dropped his hands slowly, his grin widening even more. There was nothing friendly or warm about it. "I'd guess you'd know better than most."

Wade prided himself on respecting his own limits. But at that moment he wanted nothing more than to knock Bardell back on his ass. He'd be satisfied if he got in one good punch before the man got in a few licks of his own.

Instead, he let the murmuring of the river soothe his anger. Turning his back on Ambrose, he limped his way out onto the gravel bar along the river. He sank down onto a driftwood log and gingerly stretched his sore leg out in front of him. The sunshine reflecting back up from the light-colored limestone rocks made him squint. He closed his eyes and let the warmth of the day seep into his skin.

It felt damn good to be alive, even if every step he took still hurt.

"We're leaving in the morning."

He'd hoped Ambrose would find someone else to pester. Maybe he could offend him into leaving.

"You and your men going on another killing spree?"

"Not this time." The bastard didn't even sound ashamed. "I was talking about Jack, Rose, and me."

"They're not leaving for good, I hope. That would kill Lottie."

"Despite what you think about me, I do have feelings for her." Ambrose stood facing the river, his back to Wade. "I have some business to attend to and thought they'd enjoy a trip to St. Louis. Besides it would give Lottie a break."

The man had no clue. "Some break. She can do all the chores instead of just the ones the children are too little to help with."

Ambrose picked up a handful of rocks and tossed them into the river. "Hell, we both know she works too damned hard, but half the time she won't let me in the house, much less accept my help."

He wandered closer, finally stopping right in front of Wade. "For some reason, though, she seems to trust you."

For a minute, Wade thought Ambrose was going to grill him about his intentions toward Lottie again. When he did speak again, it was a whole different topic.

"You never said who shot you."

Wade shrugged. "You never asked."

Disgust marred the handsome outlaw's face. "Don't play games with me, McCord. Did you get a good look at him?"

Why was Bardell asking him to describe his own men? It didn't make sense. He had nothing to lose by telling him. "The first time Lottie sent me on a wild-goose chase, I hung back and watched the station. You rode in with your men, and then they rode out again. I followed their trail far enough to find your little valley."

"And the second time?"

"I headed right for the valley, trying to figure out where you and the others were hiding that made it so hard to find you. I got a bad feeling when I reached the far end of the valley, but before I could get out of sight, two men came riding like hell straight for me. I didn't get a clear look at either of them, but one was riding a blood bay and the other was on a paint. If I had to guess, I'd say the second man was older, maybe even gray-haired."

If he'd been hoping for any great revelation from Ambrose, he was sorely disappointed. Instead, the outlaw merely nodded, as if Wade had merely confirmed his suspicions.

"I don't suppose you're so grateful that I saved your life that you'll walk away and forget where you saw me."

"I'm a deputy U.S. marshal." That said it all.

"We'll be back in a week to ten days. If you've got a lick of sense, you'll stay the hell out of that valley

for a while." He tilted his head to the side and stared
down at Wade. "Be good to Lottie while I'm gone."

Wade wasn't sure what Ambrose meant by good,
but all kinds of images flashed through his mind.
Somehow he doubted Ambrose would approve. But
then again, who knew? Knowing Ambrose, maybe
he would.

Lottie wandered over to the window. Sighing, she
turned around, searching the room for something
that needed doing. The children had only been
gone for one day, and already she was miserable.

Yesterday, the tears had held off only long enough
for Ambrose and the children to reach the top of
the first hill. When they'd turned back to wave at
her one last time, she'd smiled and waved back. At
least they were far enough away that they couldn't
see the wet streaks down her face.

They'd done their best to make their leaving easy
on her. With their father's help, Jack and Rose had
gone into a flurry of activity at first light. They'd
done their daily chores before breakfast and were
ready to leave by midmorning. While she'd appreciated their efforts, she would have just as soon done
the work herself. Anything to keep herself busy.

Now, to make matters worse, Wade had taken to
hiding from her. He might not see it that way, but
what else could she call it? He'd disappeared into
the barn yesterday just before the others left. She
hadn't seen him the rest of the day except to shovel
his dinner down before walking out again. She
didn't know quite what to think of his behavior.
Either he was mad about something or else he was
afraid of her. Since she'd done nothing to offend
him that she knew of, that left the second reason.

And what possible reason could he have for being nervous around her?

Did he think that she'd attack him somehow now that their chaperons were long gone?

True, the idea had occurred to her, but she'd quickly suppressed it. Ambrose's lecture had made her think of things better left alone. She figured a woman couldn't very well miss something she'd never experienced. Even if Wade was willing, how could she let him go once he'd been in her bed? In *her*?

Too restless to stay inside, she marched outside, determined to find something useful to do. She paused on the porch steps and looked around. The garden was flourishing. The two apple trees were heavily laden with fruit, but it wasn't quite time to start picking them.

Her eyes came to the barn. Maybe Jack had left something undone—some tack that needed mending, maybe. With that thought in mind, she headed across the yard. Along the way, she tried to locate Wade, but he was nowhere in sight.

She found him as soon as she walked in the barn door. He was sitting on an upturned crate, playing solitaire on a piece of lumber.

He must have been desperate to avoid her to take up card-playing in the stifling interior of the barn. The shame of driving a man to such extremes caused her to spin around and head right back out into the sunshine. For an instant, she thought he'd failed to notice her, but no such luck.

He was right behind her.

"Lottie, did you need me for something?"

She had to get away before he saw the tears. "No, I didn't mean to disturb you."

He cursed under his breath as he limped after

her. "You didn't disturb me. Now, what did you want?"

"Nothing. Just go back to what you were doing." She almost made it to the house before he lunged forward and grabbed her by the arm. The sudden jolt spun her around and right up against his chest.

The air around her became heavy and difficult to breathe. She tried to convince herself that it was the shock of being so roughly handled. Then her eyes met Wade's; as she watched, they darkened to the deep, smoky green they'd been the night he'd kissed her.

Could that mean . . . ?

Before she could finish the thought, he shook her gently. "Why did you run from me?"

Embarrassed by all that had gone on, she tried to look away. Gently but firmly, he used his fingertips to tilt her chin, raising her gaze back up to his.

"What did I do to frighten you?"

"I wasn't frightened." She tried to pull free, but his hand tightened on her arm, not enough to hurt but enough to keep her pinned against him. "Please let me go."

"Why did you run?"

There was no getting out of answering. "I know you've been avoiding me. I didn't want you to think that I wasn't respecting your privacy."

He closed his eyes and drew a deep breath. "And here I thought I was the one trying not to be underfoot."

His thumb traced the edge of her jawline as he spoke, sending shivers of heat coursing through her. She gave in to the need for his touch and pressed her cheek firmly against his hand. As she did, he loosened his hold on her, allowing her to slip her arms around his waist.

For an eternity, she feared he'd back away, leaving her more alone than she'd ever been. Instead, he used his own arms to anchor her firmly against him and lowered his mouth ever so slowly to claim hers. Her heart did a stutter step as she gave herself up to the joy of his kiss.

At first he teased and tempted her, brushing his lips along the width of hers before staging a serious assault on her senses. When she moaned out her pleasure, he deepened the kiss. His answering groan emboldened her into shyly touching his tongue with hers.

Her fingers, restless and curious, traveled up his body to the back of his neck, finally giving in to the temptation to tangle in his hair. She loved learning all the textures that made up Wade McCord: his hair, soft as silk; the powerful strength and gentle touch of his hands; the slight roughness of his beard against her skin.

Kissing made her ache in places that she had no name for. With mindless abandon, she pressed herself against the hard length of him, silently cursing the thicknesses of fabric that separated them. Wade pulled away, his eyes wild and dark with need. She hated the small space he'd created between them.

"Lottie, we need to think about where this is headed. One more kiss like that, and I swear I'll lay you down and take you right out here on the porch." She didn't want to think—only to feel, to learn what this man made her hunger for. On some level, she was aware of the effort it took for him to give her the choice to go on or to stop. Though she appreciated the gesture, she was in no mood for gentlemanly behavior.

"Then take me. Now." She tugged his face back

down to hers, offering herself up, trusting him to lead the dance.

A man could only withstand so much, and Lottie Hammond was an armful of temptation.

Take her he would, but damned if he was going to roll around on a rough-hewn porch with her. Under other circumstances, he would have swept her up in his arms to carry her inside. But with his leg as it was, the best he could do was give her another hot, wet kiss before tugging her up the steps and into the house. She followed willingly, clearly as anxious as he was to be about their loving.

Once inside her room, he did his best to slow things down a tad. He gentled his kiss while at the same time letting his hands learn the lines and valleys of her sweet body. Her breasts curved into the palm of his hand as if they'd been made for each other.

He cupped her bottom with both hands, lifting her against him. To his pleased surprise, she responded by wrapping one of her legs around his, pushing the core of her body against his. In just that amount of time, the entire universe narrowed down to the need to be on her, in her.

He went for her buttons, working them loose with hands that were clumsy from desperation. Finally, she brushed them aside and finished the job herself. He pushed the dress off her shoulders, letting it pool on the floor around her feet. That done, he backed her against the bed and pushed her gently down onto the quilt.

She pouted. "You still have all your clothes on." She pushed herself up on her elbows and waited impatiently for him to shed his shirt and pants. The minx even giggled when he cursed his boots for being stubborn.

He hesitated before lowering his drawers, not sure how she'd react to sight of his male member. Deciding that last barrier could stay in place a while longer, he crawled onto the bed alongside her warm woman's body. This time when he kissed her, he thrust his tongue into her mouth, a forewarning of what was to come. She moaned and lay back, pulling him over her. He shifted so that he was cradled within the haven of her arms. It felt like coming home.

So much for his resolve to take things slow and easy. Trying to regain some control, he moved to the side and turned his attention to her breasts. He nuzzled the valley between them and then used his tongue to tease her nipples into firm little buds through the thin cotton of her chemise.

Her hands pushed him away. At first he thought he'd been too rough, but instead she tugged at the ribbon that held her chemise closed. When the bow was undone, she slipped the straps down off her shoulders, offering him free access to the beauty underneath.

While he suckled first one sweet-tasting breast and then the other, he worked her undergarments the rest of the way off. That done, he ran his hand up the insides of her thighs. At first she rebelled against the unfamiliar invasion, but then sighed with pleasure as he taught her to trust his touch. When he tested her readiness with one finger, then two, she dug her heels into the bed and arched up.

"Please, Wade, I feel . . ." Words seemed to fail her. She tossed her head back and forth. "I need you to . . . please."

He knew what she was asking for even if she

didn't. He skimmed his drawers down his legs and then moved up and over her. Her eyes widened at the blunt pressure of him paused at her body's entry. He supported his weight with his arms as he positioned himself to enter her damp heat.

"Lottie, this is a hell of a time to ask this, but have you ever . . ."

She shook her head before he could even finish the question. He'd known the answer anyway. There was no getting around the pain he would cause her.

"This will hurt you some, honey, but I promise I'll make it up to you." Then, before she could tense up, he thrust straight and deep. Once he'd broken through the thin barrier, he used what restraint he could muster to hold still. With slight nudges and withdrawals, he teased her body into accepting him, into wanting him again.

Finally, of her own accord, Lottie locked her legs around his waist and dug her fingertips into the muscles of his back. He needed no second invitation. With gathering strength and speed, he taught her how to meet each movement of his body with one of her own.

He drove them both hard toward an explosion of pleasure that sent first her and then him flying. Her panting need ended with a keening cry of release, echoing in the silence of the house. He shouted with her as his body poured out its passion deep inside her.

When the tremors finally passed, he leaned down long enough to kiss her forehead and then her mouth. Feeling their bodies still joined, the reality of what they'd done hit him full force. Finally, he rolled away, taking her with him.

Her smile was a bit shaky as she tried to deal with all that happened. "That was . . ."

SPECIAL
INTRODUCTORY
OFFER!
4 FREE
Ballad
Historical
Romance
Novels!
A $23.96 value
absolutely
FREE!
Passion...Adventure...Excitement...Romance...
Ballad Historical Romances

Introducing Ballad,
A LINE OF HISTORICAL ROMANCES

*A*s a lover of historical romance, you'll adore Ballad Romances. Written by today's most popular romance authors, every book in the Ballad line is not only an individual story, but part of a two to six book series as well. You can look forward to 4 new titles each month – each taking place at a different time and place in history.

But don't take our word for how wonderful these stories are! Accept our introductory shipment of 4 Ballad Romance novels – a $23.96 value – and see for yourself! You only pay for shipping and handling.

*O*nce you've experienced your first 4 Ballad Romances, we're sure you'll want to continue receiving these wonderful historical romance novels each month – without ever having to leave your home – using our convenient and inexpensive home subscription service. Here's what you get for joining:

- *4 BRAND NEW Ballad Romances delivered to your door each month*
- *30% off the cover price with your home subscription.*
- *A FREE monthly newsletter filled with author interviews, book previews, special offers, and more!*
- *No risk or obligation…you're free to cancel whenever you wish… no questions asked.*

Passion-
Adventure-
Excitement-
Romance-
Ballad!

*T*o start your membership, simply complete and return the card provided. You'll receive your Introductory Shipment of 4 FREE Ballad Romances. Then, each month, as long as your account is in good standing, you will receive the 4 newest Ballad Romances. Each shipment will be yours to examine for 10 days. If you decide to keep the books, you'll pay the preferred home subscriber's price – a savings of 30% off the cover price! (plus shipping & handling) If you want us to stop sending books, just say the word…it's that simple.

A $23.96 value – **FREE** No obligation to buy anything – ever.
4 FREE BOOKS are waiting for you! Just mail in the certificate below!

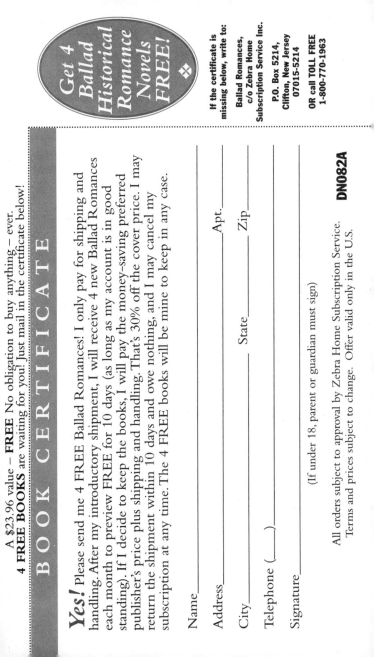

BOOK CERTIFICATE

Get 4 Ballad Historical Romance Novels FREE!

Yes! Please send me 4 FREE Ballad Romances! I only pay for shipping and handling. After my introductory shipment, I will receive 4 new Ballad Romances each month to preview FREE for 10 days (as long as my account is in good standing). If I decide to keep the books, I will pay the money-saving preferred publisher's price plus shipping and handling. That's 30% off the cover price. I may return the shipment within 10 days and owe nothing, and I may cancel my subscription at any time. The 4 FREE books will be mine to keep in any case.

Name _____

Address _____ Apt. ____

City _____ State _____ Zip _____

Telephone (____) _____

Signature _____

(If under 18, parent or guardian must sign)

All orders subject to approval by Zebra Home Subscription Service.
Terms and prices subject to change. Offer valid only in the U.S.

DN082A

If the certificate is missing below, write to:

Ballad Romances,
c/o Zebra Home
Subscription Service Inc.

P.O. Box 5214,
Clifton, New Jersey
07015-5214

OR call TOLL FREE
1-800-770-1963

Passion...

Adventure...

Excitement...

Romance...

Get 4
Ballad
Historical
Romance
Novels
FREE!

PLACE
STAMP
HERE

BALLAD ROMANCES
Zebra Home Subscription Service, Inc.
P.O. Box 5214
Clifton NJ 07015-5214

"Incredible." He finished the thought for her, adding the best smile he could muster.

Tucking her head against his shoulder and cradling her body close, he cursed himself for a fool. He'd wanted her, maybe even needed her. And God knows, he'd taken her.

But he'd also lied to her.

Would she ever forgive him when she found out? And if he'd planted his seed in her belly, what would become of their child if its mother hated its father? The image of Lottie carrying his baby made him want to smile and weep at the same time.

Unable to answer even the simplest of his own questions, he closed his eyes and prayed for sleep's temporary oblivion.

Nine

At first, she'd been thrilled to lie cuddled next to Wade, finding unexpected pleasure in the feel of her lover's body stretched out beside her. Although she'd known the basic facts of what went on between a man and a woman, the actual experience had been like seeing a black-and-white sketch suddenly filled in with all the colors of the rainbow.

Everything had been fine until she happened to glance up at his face. One look and she knew something had gone horribly wrong.

Wade lay staring up at the ceiling, his expression bleak. Under other circumstances, she would have tried to comfort him. But since it was likely that she was the source of his pain, what could she possibly do or say? Especially when she didn't know what she'd done wrong.

After time had passed without his saying a word, she rolled away from his side. That he let her go without protest hurt. Her eyes burned, but she wasn't about to give in to the tears. She was stronger than that. She had to be, because she wasn't going to give him the satisfaction of knowing he'd managed to ruin her one and only bedding.

She waited an eternity for his breathing to get deep and even. Inching to the side of her bed, she slipped out from between the sheets and sat up. When he showed no response, she gathered up her scattered clothes, blushing at the memory of how anxious she'd been to shed them.

After one last glance back to make sure he was still asleep, she paused to study his face. Even in slumber, he looked angry. She was sorrier than she could say that they'd given in to the impulse to do more than kiss. How could she face him across the dinner table knowing she'd left him unsatisfied or disappointed?

When he stirred restlessly, she practically ran from her own room to find sanctuary in the kitchen. She used water from the reservoir to wash off Wade's scent from her skin. That done, she dressed. Once again she found herself at the window wishing she had something to do.

Like start the day over, and this time keep her distance from the temptation of Wade McCord.

He had let her think he was asleep, but he'd been achingly aware of each breath she took. Hell, one look at her elegant back as she sat up had him hard and wanting her again. He'd almost reached out to pull her back into his arms, but his conscience had reared its ugly head.

Even knowing she'd been a virgin hadn't kept him from selfishly taking what he wanted. He'd had his share of women in the past, but they'd always known he was theirs only long enough to scratch a mutual itch.

Lottie wasn't like that. If she had been, she wouldn't have waited for a down-on-his-luck gambler for her first taste of passion. He turned on his stomach and buried his face in the pillow, to cuss himself only to realize that the pillow smelled like Lottie's hair, a cross between sunshine and lavender. He breathed deeply, making a memory of the short time that he and Lottie had found something special in each other's arms.

If she'd known the truth of him beforehand, he would have proposed as soon as his mouth could have formed the words. Instead, he'd tarnished something special with the lies his life had become. And once she did know who and what he was, she'd hate him with all the strength she could muster. Hellfire and damnation, what a mess.

Giving up on sleep, he climbed out of Lottie's bed, knowing it was his first and only time to be there. At least his clothes went back on easier than they'd come off. Picking up his boots, he headed for the kitchen, hoping for a few more minutes to hate himself before he had to face Lottie.

Lady Luck wasn't with him, for sure. Lottie stood at the window, looking lost. He was halfway across the room before he stopped himself. The last thing she needed right now was him grabbing at her again.

The look she gave him chilled him to the bone.

"There's chores to be done. Are you up to throwing out hay to the mules while I pump fresh water into the trough?" She crossed the room and walked out the door without waiting for him to answer.

There was no emotion at all in her words. For some reason, that made him mad. It didn't help that the way she phrased her question implied that he was weak. Hell, even if he'd been wrong to bed her, he'd made damn sure he'd satisfied her and then some. And if she was referring to his two bullet wounds, her concern was still not appreciated. Not one bit.

He hopped on one foot and then the other while he pulled on his boots. That done, he charged out the door. Ignoring the twinge in his leg, he practically ran to catch up with her. He put on a final burst of speed to step in front of her. When she tried to step around him, he blocked her way.

"I can toss hay all damn day long."

"Fine." She tried to go around him again.

"And I'll pump the water." He stood his ground, hands on his hips, waiting for her to do something besides look through him. "Well?"

"Fine. Throw all the hay you want, and then pump the well dry if you want."

Having got what he'd demanded but not really what he wanted, he turned on his heel and limped toward the corral. Lottie waited until he'd thrown the first pile of hay over the fence before walking away. She disappeared into the house, slamming the door loudly enough to rattle the windows.

He wasn't sure which one of them had won the battle, but at least he could work off some of his frustration with the pitchfork. Working with the mules might even give him some insight into how to handle Lottie. For certain, when it came to hard-headed stubbornness, she had them beat hands down.

"You two sit right there and don't move."

Ambrose tugged on his daughter's braid and ruffled Jack's hair before walking away. They'd spent most of the morning watching the boats move up and down the Mississippi. Both children were amazed at the sheer size of the river. Rose had been especially tickled when some well-dressed folks had waved at her from one of the paddle wheelers heading upstream.

But now it was time to get down to business. Most of his men spent every dime they stole by the time he'd picked their next target. He'd done his share of hell-raising, too, but he'd always put aside a certain amount from each take for his children's future. Lottie might be too proud to take a penny of his money, but he hoped that someday Jack and Rose would accept the inheritance he'd been saving up for them.

He'd planned on having many more years to watch them grow up, but lately a sense that time was running out had been riding him hard. Maybe McCord was right about luck's being a woman, and a fickle one at that. Hell, the fact that McCord had followed Ambrose's trail right to Lottie's door was enough to convince him.

But McCord wasn't the real threat, not by a long shot. Someone among Ambrose's own men had been stirring up trouble; he didn't know who it was yet, but that didn't really matter. He'd suspected something was wrong for some time, but McCord's story about how he'd come to be shot confirmed it. The one rule that had protected Ambrose and his men from the law for so long was that they never stayed together any longer than it took to pull off the robbery and divide the money. Once they rode away from their hideout with money in their pockets, they scattered until he called them back together. Between times, they all returned to their normal life, whatever that might be.

But if McCord was right, his men were gathering without him. During the past year, once or twice a robbery had been wrongly attributed to his gang. At first he'd figured someone was copying their methods, but now it appeared that maybe some of his men were cutting him out of the deal.

Once he figured out who was behind the problem, he'd have to face the treacherous son of a bitch in a fight for control. He wasn't a bad shot, but as McCord said, a man never knew who the lady was going to choose on any given day.

"Mr. Bardell, Mr. Benchly will see you now."

Ambrose followed the secretary into his lawyer's inner office. Benchly always looked at Ambrose as if he had brought a nasty smell into the room, but the greedy bastard was more than willing to take his money. Ambrose didn't give a damn what the man thought of him as long as he did his job.

The well-dressed lawyer didn't bother to stand when Ambrose came in. It was one of several ways that Benchly let Ambrose know that he wasn't a favored client.

"Mr. Bardell, I'm surprised to see you again so soon. Do you have more, uh, funds for me to invest?"

The slight hesitation was Benchly's way of telling Ambrose that he knew full well that the money wasn't really Ambrose's at all. He charged an exorbitant amount to keep that bit of knowledge to himself.

"No more money right now, Lawrence." Ambrose could play games, too. The man hated it when Ambrose used his first name. "I want to make a change in the directions I've given you." He pulled a sealed envelope out of his pocket and tossed it on the desk.

Benchly left it lying where it landed. "Anything I should know about the changes?"

"Just that it involves a U.S. marshal. If I were you, when the time comes, I'd follow the directions in that letter very carefully. Wade McCord wouldn't take it kindly if you try to cheat him out of a single penny."

He helped himself to one of the lawyer's expensive cigars. After biting off the tip, he struck a match and puffed until the end of the cigar glowed red and a cloud of smoke floated across the desk. "Any questions?"

"No." There was a decidedly pinched look to Benchly's mouth.

"Take your fee from my account, but make sure you don't overcharge me. I'd really hate that." He gave the older man a smile designed to be threatening rather than friendly. When he stood, he made sure that Benchly got a good look at the revolver he wore riding low on his hip.

His business done, he walked out whistling a cheery tune.

Wade had no idea where Lottie was. Dinner had been interesting. Neither of them had spoken a single word, relying on gestures to convey their needs. He wondered how much longer they could go without talking. Maybe they could make a game of it, the winner take . . . nothing.

As soon as she'd finished eating, Lottie had disappeared into her room. He washed the dishes and put them away, figuring he owed her something for cooking enough for both of them. He wouldn't have been surprised if she'd thrown him out, saddlebags and all.

Just in case, he went into his own room and checked his few belongings. Ten minutes would be more than enough time to shove it all in his bags. It would be a long walk back to Springfield, but he'd

try it if she ordered him to go. Or perhaps she'd
loan him the gelding to get that far. Buck could
return the horse when the stage came through
again.

Hell, here he was calmly making plans to leave
when that was the last thing he wanted to do. Never
mind that his job wasn't done.

He cursed himself for the worst kind of coward.
No woman deserved to be treated the way he'd been
acting toward Lottie. He owed her an apology and
an explanation as close to the truth as he could
make it.

Having made his decision, he headed straight for
her room, wishing he had the right to charge right
in and repeat that afternoon's performance. Instead, he stopped just shy of the door and knocked.

No answer. He knocked again and called her
name. Deafening silence. Finally, he opened the
door and peeked in. The room was empty, the bed
rumpled with the blankets trailing off onto the
floor. He knew how it had come to be that way, but
now wasn't the time to think about that.

Where was she? Not on the porch or in the barn.
He checked behind the house before deciding that
she must have gone down to the river. He headed
down the path, almost glad to be facing her away
from the house, away from her bedroom. The river
promised to be neutral territory for both of them.

He almost charged out of the trees in his hurry
to find her, but at the last minute, he slowed down
to take a look around. The woods were quiet, too
quiet. Maybe the silence was what warned him that
not all was as it should be. Moving forward slowly,
he slipped off the trail and behind a stand of dog-
wood saplings. He listened with his eyes closed, hoping to pick up some sign that Lottie was nearby and

safe. The slight breeze carried the murmur of voices from upstream. He worked his way in that direction, doing his best to hurry without revealing his presence.

Just around the bend, he spotted her. She was facing the far side of the river, where a trio of riders stood. He dropped back farther into the woods for fear one of the men would spot him slipping through the trees. Once he judged he was directly behind Lottie, he started forward again, this time with his gun drawn and ready to fire.

Strangers could always spell trouble, but two of these particular men weren't exactly unknown to him. After all, they'd damn near killed him. He couldn't say for sure that he recognized the men, but the horses were definitely the same.

He crouched down behind some deadfall trees and strained to hear what Bardell's men were saying to Lottie. From the sound of her voice, she was angry and making no attempt to hide it from her unwanted guests. He wondered if her hands were clenched because of temper or to hide the fear she was fighting. The others might not pick up on it, but then, he knew her better than they did.

"Tell Bardell to be ready or we'll ride without him."

Lottie's chin came up in defiance. "Tell him yourself. It's none of my business. I've told you before to stay away from the station."

The rider on the paint spit and laughed. "You talk pretty big for a woman out here all alone."

"Who says I'm alone?"

Wade shook his head. She needed more practice lying if she was going to convince hard cases like these three.

The rider's companions laughed at something

their friend said. The sound made Wade's stomach churn. He didn't give a damn what happened to himself, but Lottie would be caught in the crossfire if he had to take action to protect her.

To that end, he shifted back and to her left. If she had to take off running, she'd have a better chance of reaching cover if she ran toward the trail back to the house. Once he was in position, he picked up a good size rock and tossed it into a pile of brush upstream from where he stood.

Just as he expected, all three men reached for their guns as they stared across the river. When all they heard was the river, they relaxed slightly but kept their hands on their guns.

"Now, Miss Hammond," the graybeard drawled, "why don't you invite us on up to the house for refreshments?"

Her back went ramrod straight. "No. I was there when Ambrose gave you all orders that the house is off limits to the likes of you three."

She shouldn't have said that, but Wade figured fear had overruled her good sense. It didn't matter, anyway. None of them was going to live to cross the river, not if he could help it. At this range, he should be able to fire fast enough to hit all three of them before they had time to scatter.

"I figure you welcome Bardell into more than just your house. I want some of that same hospitality."

Lottie had the good sense to back up, putting as much distance between her and the riders as possible. She wouldn't get far if they came after her on horseback, but they didn't know Wade was backing her up.

The first one urged his horse forward. Wade didn't hesitate. He pulled the trigger at the same time he shouted. "Run, Lottie, run."

For once, she didn't argue. Hiking her skirt, she took off toward the woods as fast as she could go. Wade charged through the woods still firing, hoping to confuse them enough so they wouldn't realize that he was alone. He hit the old man in the shoulder, sending him reeling in the saddle. His partners grabbed at his reins and led his horse back into the woods.

Wade waited until he got a clear shot and used his last bullet to send the last rider's hat flying. With luck, their horses would run far enough to give Wade and Lottie time to get back to the house. He needed to reload and get his rifle. The bastards might give up for the time being, but he wouldn't bet on it. Lottie was waiting for him about halfway back to the house. She was breathing hard but otherwise seemed unharmed.

"Damn it, I told you to run. What if it had been one of them instead of me?"

"I could tell you were on foot. They had horses."

There was no time for arguments. He'd yell at her later for endangering herself unnecessarily. For now, they needed cover and they needed ammunition.

When they reached the station yard, he paused long enough to listen for riders. So far, Bardell's men weren't anywhere close. Wade took Lottie by the arm and pulled her toward the house.

"Let go of me. I'm not helpless."

He ignored her complaint as he dragged her up onto the porch.

"Get the rifle and bring it to me. Then take cover. Don't move unless I tell you to."

She drew herself up to her full height and glared at him. "I said I'm not helpless and I meant it. I do not need a man"—she gave him a pointed look—

"at all. This is my home, and if there's defending to do, I'll be the one holding the rifle."

Damn, he wanted to kiss her right then and there. Three killers could be down on them at any second, and all he could think of was how much he wanted this woman. Her fire and strength made him ache with need, but now wasn't the time.

"Damn it, woman, you'd argue with God himself."

She knew she'd won. "I'll bring your rifle and the extra box of bullets. Where do you want me?"

The answer to that was obvious, and he let her know it by giving her a long, lingering look from her toes to her face, lingering over certain favorite spots. When she blushed, he grinned.

"We'll talk about the real answer to that question later. For now, take your rifle and watch out the back window. Keep your head down and don't take any foolish chances."

Then he surprised them both by using his free hand to pull her face up for a kiss. She backed away, looking stunned. Before he could feel too pleased with himself, she yanked him close and kissed him back even more deeply.

Then she spun on her heel and walked away, looking far too proud of what she'd done. He'd get even later, but at least the fear was long gone from her eyes. Seconds later, she was back with his rifle. She looked worriedly toward the woods.

"Any sign of them?"

"No, so far it's quiet. I don't know how bad off the old man was, but they may have their hands full trying to get him taken care of. If so, there's no telling when they'll come after us." He looked past her to the trees. "If they come at all."

"I don't know their names, but I know they ride

with Ambrose." She gave Wade a guilty look. "I should have warned you sooner about the kind of man he really is."

Wade could have let her think he was shocked, but he'd promised himself to tell her the truth whenever he could without compromising his mission. "He'd told me something of the sort when he asked about the men who shot me. He recognized them from my description of their horses."

"But he didn't tell me . . ."

"He probably didn't want to worry you." That much was true, but she wasn't naive. She had to know her brother-in-law attracted the worst type of killers to ride with him. He figured he owed Ambrose something for saving his life. Keeping him in the good graces of his sister-in-law was as much as Wade was willing to do for the murdering bastard.

She nodded after a second and disappeared down the hall. More and more Lottie reminded him of his own sister-in-law. When his older brother died, Lily had taken up the reins on their ranch and kept it going. When troubles piled up, she shouldered the burden. He'd done his best to fill his brother's shoes, but she'd really been the one to rise to the occasion. And when she'd looked for a man to fill his brother's place in her life, it hadn't been Wade that she'd chosen.

Now, for the first time since then, he'd found a woman who might just fill the hole Lily had left in his own life when she married a gambler, willing to believe that Cal would put aside his wandering ways for her. Would Lottie ever trust Wade enough to give him the same sort of chance?

* * *

After the sun had been down for some time, Wade figured there wasn't much point in staring out into the darkness. He set his rifle down on the kitchen table and went looking for Lottie. She was in his room, still trying to peer out the window.

"Let's try to get some rest. If they haven't come by now, chances are they won't, leastwise until morning."

She nodded but still looked worried.

"I'll sit up for a spell if that would make you feel safer." He held out his hand to help her up off the bed. She hesitated only briefly before shaking her head.

"No, we both need to sleep while we can." She trudged down the hallway toward her room.

Wade followed behind her. "I'm going to bring in some extra water and wood. Can you stay awake long enough to let me back in?"

"I'll help. It'll take less time if we both work at it."

He wanted to argue, but as soon as he opened his mouth to say something, her chin came up.

"Fine. You do the water. I'll handle the wood." She nodded and reached for the bucket.

Although she could find her way to the water pump easily enough without a lantern, he took one with him. Woodpiles were a favorite hiding spot for snakes of all kinds. He didn't mind the occasional blacksnake, but he was in no mood to deal with a copperhead.

Lottie was already back inside when he made his final trip with an armload of kindling and wood for the stove. Chances were that Ambrose's men had gone to ground, but if not, he and Lottie had enough supplies to wait them out. He'd sleep better knowing that.

"Well, I'll say goodnight, then."

She looked as if she had something else to say but wasn't sure how to go about it.

"Is there something else you want me to do?"

Her chin quivered and tears welled up in her eyes. He had her wrapped in his arms before the first tear could fall. She pulled him close as she rested her head on his shoulder.

"Could you just hold me?"

Since he already was, she had to be talking about something else.

"Lottie, honey, I love having you in my arms, but you need your sleep." He did, too, but the feel of her so close up against him had its own way of giving him new energy. At least in certain parts of his body. He tried to shift a bit so that she wouldn't notice how he was reacting to her touch. To his surprised delight, she moved with him, seeking to fit her body to his.

She whispered, "I mean all night." Then she sought his mouth with hers.

He couldn't have strung two words together at that point, but it didn't matter. She was already leading him right back to where he'd wanted to be earlier. When she saw that her bed still bore the signs of their previous encounter, she blushed but set about straightening up the bedding.

That done, she shyly reached for the first button on her dress. He put his hand out to stop her. If she wanted him to hold her and nothing else, he'd do it. As much as he wanted to do more than that, now wasn't the time. He had to choose his words carefully, though. If he said the wrong thing, she'd be back to thinking that he didn't want her.

"Why don't you get yourself all tucked in? After I get washed up, I'll come back in and lay on top of the blankets and cuddle you." Before she could question him or protest, he added, "I'll need my wits about me if Bardell's men do come back. If I crawl under the covers with you, I'll only be able to think of one thing: you."

He ended his explanation with a quick kiss on her forehead and hustled out of the room before his shaky resolve disappeared altogether. Using some of the fresh water they'd brought in, he washed his face and hands. That done, he gave himself a stern lecture on honor and decent women.

Determined to do the right thing, he slung his gun belt over his shoulder and headed back into Lottie's room. She had done as he suggested, as far as it went. It didn't help that he knew in great detail how it felt to slide in between the sheets with her. When he entered the room, she turned on her side to face him. His wayward eyes slid down the curves and valleys of her body and back up to her face.

Then, before he'd gone two steps into the room, she gave him a woman's smile, all knowing and full of temptation. With a flip of her wrist, she turned back the covers on the empty side of the bed in blatant invitation. It was about then that he noticed her nightgown was still hanging on the peg on the wall, right next to the dress she'd been wearing.

The battle was over before the first shot was fired. His intentions were good—even honorable—but in the face of a superior force, he surrendered.

Lottie knew she was risking another dose of the hurt she'd experienced earlier. Some kind of demon was riding Wade hard, making him blow hot and cold when it came to the attraction between them. But he couldn't hide the truth that he wanted her, not when those eyes of his swirled and darkened with such heat every time he looked in her direction.

Her own motives for wanting him back in her bed were unclear. Partly, she was still frightened by what almost happened at the river. Without Wade's timely arrival, there was no telling what those men would have done to her. But that was only a small part of what was driving her. Wade's obvious regrets after they'd made love didn't dim the memories of how incredible the whole experience had been for her. When he'd taken her, filled her, he'd claimed part of her in a way no other man would. She was woman enough to know that he'd given her more than mere passion.

What she felt for him, drifter or not, was powerfully close to love. And if he didn't care for her strongly on some level, he wouldn't worry so much about hurting her.

But she was thinking way too hard. It had taken all her courage to crawl into bed naked and wait for Wade to walk back into her room. She had him hooked as soon as she turned back the covers and patted the pillow beside her. His quick eyes knew instantly that this time there would be no barriers between them, unless he chose to leave his own clothes on.

As soon as he reached for the buttons on his shirt, she knew she'd won. Relaxing back onto her own pillow, she took pure pleasure in watching him strip off his clothes as fast as his fingers could work. Her body ached in readiness for him.

"Hurry, please."

He didn't need to be asked twice. Luckily, he must have taken his boots off out in the kitchen, so he didn't have them to deal with. His shirt hit the floor,

followed by his trousers. Her breath quickened at
the blatant evidence that he wanted her as much as
she wanted him.

Finally, he was completely and gloriously naked.
He knelt on the edge of the bed with one knee and
leaned across to kiss her. She opened her mouth at
the first touch of his tongue and moaned in pure
pleasure at the sudden invasion. He propped himself up with one hand, but the other one immediately slipped under the sheets to find her breasts.
He palmed first one and then the other into hard
peaks.

Feeling bold with the success of her seduction,
she did some exploring of her own. Without asking
permission, she encircled his manhood with her fingers and squeezed gently. His pleasure was evident
by the way he thrust more firmly into her grasp.

He punctuated his gratitude with short kisses.
"Honey, you . . . have no . . . idea . . . how good
that . . . feels."

When she increased the tempo of her caresses,
he grabbed her wrist and made her stop.

She immediately let go. "Did I hurt you?"

"Lord, no, but if you keep that up, it will all be
over with before we really get started."

"We wouldn't want that to happen, would we?"
She pulled him down on top of her. "I want this to
go on forever."

She felt the vibration of his answering chuckle
through the muscles of his chest.

"I'll do my best to please, but forever might be a
bit more than I can handle."

She cupped the side of his face with her hand.
"Whatever you can give me will be enough."

If he understood that she was talking about far
more than the time they'd spend together in her

bed, he didn't let on. But now wasn't the time for serious thoughts or plans for the future.

Giving herself over to the wondrous sensations he was creating with his lips and hands and tongue, all coherent thoughts flew out the window. And when he rose over her, ready to take her, she opened her legs, her arms, and her heart in welcome.

Ten

Lottie took her time waking up. She hadn't gotten much sleep during the night, but fresh energy had her heart pumping and her face smiling. She all but purred as she snuggled a bit closer to the long, hard body next to hers.

"Sleepyhead, chores aren't going to do themselves."

She pried one eye open and looked up at Wade. His beard had darkened overnight. Wondering how it would feel to the touch, she ran her fingertips over the enticing roughness. She liked it.

"Kiss me."

He obliged her. Her legs stirred restlessly, tangling with his.

"Lottie, we can't."

Her hand trailed down, caressing the proof that he was lying. When once again he stopped her, she giggled.

"You want to; you know you do."

He immediately pinned her hands over her head. "Yes, I do, but now is not the time."

Unfortunately for him, the blankets had slipped down while they were tussling, revealing her breasts. Instantly, his eyes darkened as his head dipped down to nuzzle between them. The rasp of his beard about drove her crazy.

Abruptly he pulled back and didn't stop until he was standing beside the bed.

"Damn it, woman, you'd tempt a saint. Now, I'm going to get dressed and take care of the animals. You can get breakfast ready while I'm doing that."

"And if food isn't what I'm hungry for right now?" She couldn't believe how daring she was being.

"That's all you're going to get," he told her as he walked out of the room. Then he ducked his head back in the doorway long enough to say, "For now."

For the first time in ages, Lottie faced the day with renewed excitement. She drew off enough hot water to wash up with and put on a clean dress. Tying her apron over her skirt, she got breakfast started. Biscuits were in the oven, and bacon and eggs were fried up just the way Wade liked them before he came back in from the barn.

His hair was damp and his face once again clean shaven when he came in from outside. He set his rifle down just inside the door, keeping it handy in case trouble showed up. She hated no longer feeling safe in her home.

She'd be having words with Ambrose the minute he came riding back in with the children. How he wanted to live his life was his business. But when it followed him to her door, well, that was an entirely different matter.

Wade looked tired as he pulled out a chair and sat down. He hadn't got any more sleep than she had. The memory of what they'd spent the dark hours of the night doing had her blushing. He happened to look up right at that moment. A smile tugged at the corner of his mouth, telling her that some of the same memories were dancing through his mind.

She forced her attention back to the matter at hand. He'd never let her live it down if she burned the biscuits daydreaming over him. In short order, she handed him a plateful of eggs, bacon, and her best biscuits. After serving up her own portion, she poured them each a cup of coffee and joined him at the table.

For several minutes, they enjoyed the companionable silence. Knowing full well that she was playing with fire, she let herself imagine a future of such meals. Wade's rugged good looks would only improve with age.

"Don't."

She thought about pretending not to understand, but he'd recognize the lie.

"I was just . . ." Dreaming? Lying to herself?

"I can't promise more than this, Lottie." He took a quick swallow of his coffee, as if giving himself time to think through what he wanted to say. "I'm not the man you think I am."

She already knew. She answered for him. "I didn't ask for more than this, did I? In fact, I never asked for you to be here at all. I'm fully aware that the time's coming when you'll be moving on." She started clearing the table. "And when you leave, things will go back to being the way they always were."

There. The words had been said. Everything was laid out nice and clear so there wouldn't be any misunderstanding. No expectations. No promises. Wade didn't look any happier about it than she felt. She thought about asking him why, but she had her pride. He of all people knew for a fact she'd never been with another man. There was nothing she could say to convince him that she took such things casually.

But she'd made her decision, and while she might have some painful times ahead, she refused to have regrets as well. With that thought, she was able to offer him a more genuine smile.

"The stage isn't due in until tomorrow, so we don't have anything special that needs doing today. Why don't we pack a picnic lunch and eat down by the river this afternoon?"

Before he could answer, she remembered what had happened the last time she went there. "Do you think they'll be back?"

Wade shrugged. "No way of telling for sure, but if we haven't seen them by now, chances are they've gone to ground for a while. Remember, they didn't know for certain that Ambrose wasn't around. They might be hiding from him. Either way, I think we should wait a day or two before we risk going down to the river."

Wade carried his own plate to the sink. "Do we know for certain when Ambrose is coming back?"

"He thought they'd be gone for over a week, but he didn't know for certain."

She shook her head as she drew some hot water to wash the dishes with. "Most times, I can't wait for him to leave. This is the first time that I wish he'd hurry up and get back here. Somebody has to do something about his men."

"I'll be outside, looking around some." Wade poured himself another cup of coffee. "But you're right: somebody does."

Lottie watched him leave, puzzled not so much at what he had said, but how he said it. Maybe he just needed some time to himself.

* * *

The week had flown by. During the day, they worked side by side to get the chores done. Nights were spent in Lottie's bed learning new ways to find pleasure in each other's arms. Knowing that their time alone was coming to an end had Wade feeling edgy. With Jack and Rose back in the house, he and Lottie would have to be more circumspect about spending time together. He didn't even want to think about Ambrose.

Wade had been working his frustrations out by grooming every damn mule that Lottie had. Once he had their coats shining, he got out the shears and started roaching their manes. Buck would be dazzled by how fine his team looked when Lottie harnessed them to the stage.

Not that the driver couldn't use some grooming himself. Wade knew that Lottie was fond of the old coot, but he had to laugh at the way she opened all the doors and windows to air the house out every time Buck came through. The old man had told Wade himself about the time she'd taken a broom to him for spitting chewing tobacco on her kitchen floor.

"What has you smiling?"

He hadn't heard Lottie's approach. He wondered how long she'd been watching him. He straightened up and looked at her over the back of the mule he was working on.

"I was thinking it was a shame that I couldn't hog-tie Buck when he comes through and give him a good haircut and polish him up some."

Lottie laughed. "Many's the time I've had the same thought myself. I even hinted that some of the passengers had complained, but Buck couldn't understand what they were upset about. After all, he took a bath last year."

It felt good to see the good humor back in her blue eyes. Earlier, despite her brave words, he knew she was already hurting over the thought of his leaving. That pain would be nothing compared to the betrayal she'd feel when she found out what he was really up to.

She was right about one thing though: someone had to do something about Bardell and his men. She just didn't expect it to be Wade. He noticed that she had a basket sitting on the ground by her feet.

"I thought we'd better have our picnic today." She sounded wistful. He knew she'd been missing the children, but she wasn't ready to have Wade go back to sleeping in the back room.

He looked up at the sky. The sun was directly overhead.

"I lost all track of time. Let me wash up some, and we'll go have that picnic you promised."

"No need to apologize, especially when you're doing my work for me."

He opened the gate and slipped out of the corral. After giving the pump handle a few good strokes, he ducked his head under the flow of cold water. He washed off the morning's collection of dust and sweat. That done, he used his bandanna as a towel and dried off his hands and face.

Lottie stood nearby, clearly anxious to be on their way. He took the basket from her and then offered her his arm. He could tell the gesture pleased her. He liked the feel of her hand on him as they walked down the path to the river.

The past few days hadn't been quite as hot, but in the depths of the woods there was little air moving. By contrast, the river seemed to cool everything several degrees. It felt good to his skin.

Lottie picked a place on the gravel bar that jutted out into the river to have their meal. A convenient log made a good seat for both of them. She opened the basket and began spreading out the feast she'd prepared.

He could have served himself, but she seemed to want to fuss over him a bit. He liked her doing for him, so he didn't interfere. At breakfast a few days earlier, he'd recognized the dreams she was having about the two of them, because he'd had some of the same ideas himself. He just wished that there were a chance in hell of any of those dreams coming true.

"Can I ask you something? You don't have to answer if you don't want to."

Lottie's hesitance made Wade realize that despite everything that had happened between them, she'd never before asked him any personal questions.

"I'll try to answer," he offered, fully aware that he was hedging his bets. He hoped he could keep the promise he'd made to himself not to lie anymore to her.

"Where did you grow up?"

"West of here. My brother and I started a small ranch in eastern Colorado."

"That explains how you know so much about horses and mules."

He hadn't realized she'd wondered about that. "When there's only three of you, you learn to do what needs doing."

"Three of you?"

"My brother was married. When he was killed, his widow and I tried to keep things going. When things got tough, we, uhm, took on a partner named

Cal Preston." How to explain Cal? He could just imagine what her reaction would be if he told her about losing his half of the ranch to Cal in a game of poker. "Lily ended up marrying him."

He stared at the river, fully aware of Lottie's scrutiny. When he glanced in her direction, there was a frown line between her eyebrows.

"Spit it out, Lottie. I said you could ask questions."

"Did you love her very much?" She stared down at her hands folded in her lap.

Now, how had she leapt to that conclusion with the little he'd said? Sometimes the truth hurt more in the telling than a harmless lie would.

"Yes, I did. He's made her happy, though. They've been together for about seven years. She's expecting a baby soon."

"Do you ever go home?"

"The ranch stopped being home for me a long time ago." The bitter taste of that truth never faded.

"I bet they don't feel that way."

"No, they don't. Last time I stopped in for a visit, Lily tore a strip off my hide for staying away so long." He smiled at the memory. "She's a little bit of a thing, but tough as they come."

"I bet she's pretty." There was more than a touch of insecurity in Lottie's words.

"Yes, she is. Dark hair, dark eyes." He slid closer to Lottie, knocking the last of the fried chicken onto the ground. "But I find I prefer a woman with bright blue eyes and hair that looks like spun silver and gold."

He let his kiss reassure her. After the past few nights, there should be no doubt in her mind how much he wanted her. Hell, his body was back to clamoring for hers at the first touch of their lips.

Lottie met his embrace eagerly, kissing him back with the same enthusiasm she'd shown last night in her bed.

And damned if he didn't wish they were there right now. He needed to cool down. He broke off the kiss slowly. It took him a minute to catch his breath.

"I think I'll take a quick swim."

She gave him a considering look. "You do that. I'll pack up the dishes."

"Turn your back," he ordered as he started unbuttoning his shirt.

She giggled. "I've already seen you naked."

"It doesn't matter. A man needs some dignity. Turn around."

She did as he ordered, but as soon as he had his pants halfway down, she peeked. When he complained, she stuck her tongue out at him. He turned his back to her, but not before he returned the gesture.

When he'd dispatched the last stitch of his clothing, he waded into the river. The cool water felt like heaven to his overheated skin. He took a deep breath and pushed off the bottom to swim across the deepest end of the pool. On his third trip across, something grabbed at his leg.

He came up sputtering to find Lottie treading water a few feet away. Before he could respond, she splashed water in his face and took off swimming. She might be sneaky, but he was stronger and caught up with her before she'd got too far.

Much to his pleased surprise, he realized that she was as bare-naked as he was. As soon as he touched her, she turned into his arms. Her water-slicked skin slid over his. His body's reaction was both predictable and profound.

"Are you looking for trouble?" he growled in her ear.

She wrapped her legs around him, pressing her breasts against his chest. "Yes, I think I am."

He thrust against her. "I think you've found it."

Her eyes dropped half closed, and her lips parted as she stilled in his arms. "Lord, I hope so."

She rocked against him in blatant invitation. He gave in to her demands. The coolness of the river water contrasted with the sweet heat of her body as he eased inside her. She arched back, her eyes closed as he worked hard at pleasuring her.

Tomorrow or the next day, Wade knew they would have to rein in their passion. However, that made what they were sharing in the river all the more precious.

The stage had come and gone. The day was hot enough to sap the last bit of energy she had. Poor old Buck had been bitterly disappointed that there wasn't a pie cooling in the window when he pulled in, but even he had to admit that it was too hot to do much baking.

He'd generously accepted her promise to make things up to him come fall, but he still grumbled about it when he climbed back up on his seat and flicked the reins. Lottie refused to feel guilty. She knew for a fact that none of the other station managers Buck dealt with ever made him special treats, and he knew it, too.

The majority of her work done for the day, she sank down on the front step to catch her breath. A drink of cool water sounded wonderful, but at that moment she couldn't muster enough energy to walk as far as the pump. It dawned on her that she hadn't seen Wade since before the stage pulled out. He'd done his usual fine job of bringing out the mules as she'd needed them, but he'd disappeared shortly after she finished harnessing the last pair.

He wasn't in the house, because she'd just come from there. She couldn't imagine him working in the barn, because it was like an oven on days like those. The river was a definite possibility, but it seemed unlikely that he'd go swimming without inviting her. After the other evening, she doubted that she'd ever look at the swimming hole in quite the same way. The memories had her blushing still.

She was about to go looking for him when she caught sight of him coming down the hill on the road. He had his rifle with him, but resting back over his shoulder, so he didn't seem overly concerned about anything.

Even knowing it wasn't polite to stare, she took advantage of the opportunity to study her lover as he approached. He had his hat slouched forward, shading his face from the sun. Even so, she could feel the power of his gaze from under the shadowed brim.

He moved well, his build rangy and strong. Although well acquainted with every inch of his body, she wished she knew more about what went on inside his head. He was a puzzle, that was for sure. Sometimes she could feel him drawing away from her, as if he were already on the road to somewhere else. Other times, it was easy to forget that his presence was only temporary, because he fit so smoothly into their lives.

And into her heart, not to mention her bed.

Drat, she promised herself not to think that way because she'd promised Wade that she wouldn't ask him for more than he could give. To that end, she mustered up a welcoming smile, knowing that if he caught her pining after him, he'd feel bad. Maybe she was fooling herself, but maybe he wouldn't be in too much of a hurry to leave if she made it easy for him to stay.

He crossed the last little distance to sit down beside her. Before she could ask him where he'd been, he laid his rifle down and drew her close for a kiss. If there was a hint of desperation in his embrace, she ignored it.

The heat generated by his kiss made the day's temperature feel cool and temperate. When at last he let her go, she tried to catch her breath and gather her scattered thoughts.

"It's nice to see you, too." She picked up his hat, which had fallen off while they were kissing. "See anything interesting from up on the hill?"

"Yeah, we're about to get company."

He pointed back up the road. Three familiar figures were just coming into sight.

Lottie jumped to her feet and started out to meet them. "Jack and Rose! Welcome home."

They probably couldn't hear her yet, but she was so happy to see them that it didn't matter. Wade came up behind her, keeping his distance in front of the children and Ambrose. She felt the loss even as she celebrated the return of her family. It seemed to take forever for the horses to carry their precious burdens the final distance back to Lottie.

She held the reins to Jack's horse as he dismounted. At the same time, Wade held his arms up to lift Rose down from her saddle. Both children ran directly to Lottie and let her gather them into her arms. All too quickly, they squirmed to get free, so she let them run to the house.

No doubt, they'd been in the saddle most of the

day. It probably felt good to them to be able to run around for a while. There would be plenty of time in the coming days to find out all the details of their adventure.

Wade led their two horses away toward the barn. Normally, she expected Jack to care for his own mount, but this time she'd let Wade do it as long as he was willing.

The two children were at the pump, drinking their fill of cool water and splashing not a little on each other. It felt good to hear their giggling and young voices again.

Ambrose finally dismounted and led his horse over to where Lottie was standing.

"Thank you for bringing them back."

He draped a companionable arm around her shoulders. "I told you I would."

"I know, but thank you anyway. I've missed them."

"How about me?"

She stiffened, remembering the fear his men had caused her. He didn't protest when she stepped away from him. One look at her face had him frowning.

"What happened?"

"I was down at the river when three of your men came calling." She shivered in the day's heat. "One of them said that he wanted me to show him some of the same hospitality that I show you."

"Son of a bitch!" Ambrose kicked an innocent rock as far as he could send it. "Who was it? Describe them if you don't know names."

She rarely saw the killer in Ambrose, but it was all too evident at the moment. She didn't let it stop her from pointing fingers at the guilty parties. "Two of them were the men who shot Wade. He said he recognized their horses—a paint and a blood red bay. Neither of us knew the third one."

Ambrose looked toward Wade, who was still unsaddling the kids' horses. "Where was he while all this was going on?"

"I'd gone down to the river to be by myself. Luckily, he came looking for me. If they'd left peaceably, he would have let them go. But when they came at me, he shot the older one."

Her brother-in-law let loose with a string of curses that would have done Buck proud. Normally, she would have chided him for talking like that in front of her, but under the circumstances she felt it was justifiable.

"I'm sorry, Lottie. I'll make sure those three never bother you again." He reached out to touch her arm, but she ducked away.

"That's not going to fix the problem." It was time to make her feelings known. "Ambrose, you know I care about you, and Jack and Rose love you as much as any children could love their father. But I don't want to live scared anymore." She gestured toward Wade. "I hate to think what would have happened to me if he hadn't been here. And we both know, he's not the type to stay here forever. Once he's gone, I don't know how I'll sleep nights worrying over who might show up next."

Ambrose started to protest but stopped. He took his hat off and ran his fingers through his hair. "Listen. I'm tired and I'm dirty. All I've been looking forward to all day is one of your home-cooked meals and a long, leisurely swim in the river before turning in for the night."

He offered one of his boyish smiles. "Let me get through the evening, and you can start chewing on me first thing tomorrow morning."

She wanted to have it out right then, but every inch of him spoke of weariness. "All right, I'll get some dinner ready for you, but first thing in the morning I'll have a lot to say about things."

Her eyes wandered back in the direction of the barn. Ambrose quirked an eyebrow and smiled.

"So, dear sister-in-law, how long did it take you to get McCord in your bed? Or did he put aside his noble feelings long enough to seduce you?"

"Don't, Ambrose." She met his all-too-knowing gaze. "Please."

He frowned. "I warned him before I left. Did he do something to hurt you?" The killer glint was back in his eyes.

"No, he didn't." And to herself, she added, "Not yet."

"And Mr. Wade, we saw the ships going up the big river."

Jack rolled his eyes at his sister. "I told you, Rose, they weren't ships. They were boats—riverboats. And the river's name is the Mississippi." After giving his sister a thoroughly disgusted look, Jack turned back to Wade. "Did you know a river could be a mile wide, Mr. Wade?"

Wade stopped eating long enough to shake his head with honest wonder. "Doesn't seem possible, but I guess if you've seen it, I'll have to believe it."

"Well, it's true. And those boats go up and down the river carrying people and stuff." Jack's eyes grew huge. "They have gambling on those boats. Is that where you played cards?"

"Shush, Jack! You ask too many questions."

To further distract her nephew, Lottie dumped a serving of mashed potatoes on his plate that Wade figured would have been enough for three boys Jack's size. He wondered what had her all riled up. Perhaps he'd find out if he answered Jack's question.

"No, Jack. I've never played on the boats. Most of my gambling has been in saloons and the like."

That did it. Lottie's lips pursed as she glared across the table at him. "Mr. McCord, gambling is not proper table conversation for children."

That was a good one. The children needed protecting from card games but not from their father, who robbed and killed for a living. He wouldn't risk hurting Jack and Rose by pointing that out to Lottie, but it rankled.

He answered Jack anyway. "This is about as far east as I've been."

"You've gotta go to St. Louis," Jack advised him. "You'd like it."

"What else did you do while you were there?"

So far, Ambrose had been pretty tight-lipped about the purpose for their trip. Even though he'd told Lottie that he had business there, Wade needed to know what that business was. He kept hoping that if he asked the children enough questions, one of them would give him a clue.

Ambrose was sitting across from him; his smile made it clear that he knew exactly what Wade was up to.

"We saw my lawyer."

There were a hundred things Wade could say to that; none of them were appropriate in front of the children. He strove to put only casual interest in his voice.

"Who is he? I might know him."

Jack frowned. "But Mr. Wade, you just said you've

never been to St. Louis. How could you know someone who lives there?'

No one ever said that these two weren't bright.
"You're right, Jack. I wasn't thinking."

Ambrose leaned over and ruffled his son's hair.
"Quick thinking there, son. Wade probably hasn't
met Mr. Benchly, nor does he know that his office
is near Laclede's Landing."

Now what was the bastard up to? The outlaw had
said his attorney's name looking straight at Wade,
as if it was important that he make note of it.

"No, I'm sure I've never made his acquaintance."
But he'd remember him, just as it seemed Ambrose
wanted him to.

"Time for you two children to finish your evening
chores and then get to bed. If you hurry, I'll read
to you before you go to sleep."

Rose immediately scrambled down from her
chair. Jack was right behind her as she disappeared
outside. Their father watched them with an odd
look on his face.

"I enjoy my children, but they surely do wear me
out, Lottie. I don't know how you manage most of
the time." Ambrose winked at her. "You do a fine
job, though."

She blushed. "Thank you, but they're easy to have
around. It was probably harder for you because
around here they have chores to do and things to
keep them busy. On a trip, you'd have to entertain
them every minute."

"True enough." Ambrose pushed his chair back
from the table. "If you don't need me for anything,
Lottie, I'll take a walk around and then head on out
to the barn for the night." He glanced in Wade's
direction. "You look like you could use some fresh
air."

Wade could take a hint with the best of them. "Sure." Out of habit, he picked up his rifle and followed Ambrose out the door. The two of them walked in companionable silence for a short time. It didn't surprise Wade when Ambrose headed for the river. If he had something to say, it was best to do so out of the children's hearing.

Ambrose waited until they reached the river before stopping. He pulled the makings for a smoke out of his shirt pocket and rolled himself a cigarette. When he was done, he blew a cloud of smoke before offering the sack to Wade, who shook his head.

"No, thanks. When I'm in the mood to smoke, I prefer a good cigar." He took a seat on the same log that he and Lottie had used for their picnic, and waited for Ambrose to speak his piece. He didn't know what he was expecting, but the outlaw's opening statement didn't tell him anything new.

"I've never had any use at all for lawmen, McCord. None at all." Whatever was riding Ambrose had him pacing back and forth. "But I trust Lottie, and for some reason, she trusts you." He abruptly stopped at the edge of the river, staring at the water as it rippled by.

A minute, maybe two, passed before he sighed and turned back to face Wade. "If something happens to me, I want you to see that Lottie and the children are looked after."

Wade started to protest, but Ambrose stopped him. "Hellfire, man, I know I've got no right to ask. The very idea of depending on a lawman for something makes me want to hit something. On top of it all, I know that you're still intent on taking me in yourself. It's a hell of a mess."

He laughed, but it wasn't happy-sounding at all. "But you aren't even close to the top of the list of men who want me dead. I figure that damn sense of honor of yours means you'll give me fair warning that you're coming after me. Those three that were here the other night sure as hell wouldn't. I suspect one of them was named McNulty. He's been doing his damnedest to push me out of the way for some time."

"Who are the other two?"

"Names don't matter. I'll see to them myself."

The last glow of the evening sun had faded behind the hills to the west, leaving Wade and Ambrose shrouded in darkness. The black shadows fit the nature of their discussion.

"You know I've got my own reasons to want them arrested and tried." Wade massaged the ache left by his chest wound almost without thinking about it.

Ambrose saw what he was doing and smiled, his teeth gleaming white in the moonlight. "If they come sniffing around here again, have at it. But I won't let you trail them back to the valley again."

Wade rose to his feet. It was time to meet Ambrose eye to eye. "You have no say in the matter, Bardell. I'll do my job as I see fit."

"Like you did the day they damned near killed you? Try it and I'll shoot you myself."

"Not likely, Bardell. Bastards like you are the reason I wear a badge. Most folks have a hard enough time of it just keeping food on the table. They shouldn't have to worry that some greedy son of a bitch is going to steal it from them at gunpoint."

Ambrose clapped his hands. "Brave speech, marshal. Hell, if you were running for office, I'd vote for you myself."

"Go to hell."

"Now, that's one order of yours that I'll be sure to carry out."

For several moments, they let the murmuring of the river and the call of the whippoorwill fill the silence of the night. Wade wished like hell he'd never taken this assignment. He didn't regret meeting Lottie and the children, but he hated like hell knowing that time was running out for him to do his job. And there was no way to accomplish his goals without destroying the beauty of what he and Lottie had found in each other's arms.

"I'm leaving after sunup. Don't follow me this time." Ambrose startled him out his reverie. "I won't be gone long, and I'm not going anywhere near the men you're looking for. I'd take you with me if it didn't mean leaving my family alone and unprotected."

The man had him over a barrel. "All right, this time. But get your affairs settled, Bardell."

"Remember the name I gave you at dinner."

"Yeah. Benchly in St. Louis, near Laclede's Landing."

"And one more thing. There's a boy who's been riding with me, name of Jeb. He's not like the others—he wouldn't be riding with me at all if his pa hadn't been killed awhile back. He's only been on a couple of jobs, holding horses and the like." Ambrose lit up another cigarette. "Do what you can for him."

Wade had to admire the sheer gall of the man. "Is there anything else?"

"Yeah, when everything blows up and goes to hell, be careful with Lottie. She's got a temper, but she gets over things if you handle her right." Ambrose gave Wade another of his irritating grins. "I figure you did a fair amount of handling her while we were gone, so you should know how to do it well enough."

Wade lunged for him, intent on doing him serious harm, but his barely healed leg betrayed him. By the time he caught his balance on the rocky ground, Ambrose had danced back out of his reach and taken off back toward the station. Wade limped slowly after him, cursing the man's very existence each step of the way.

Eleven

Something had Wade all riled up, but so far Lottie hadn't been able to figure out what it was exactly. For the past three days, he'd been taking out his frustrations on the woodpile. If he kept up the pace he might kill himself, but she'd have enough logs split to last through the winter.

When he wasn't swinging an ax, he was banging on something with the hammer. There wasn't a loose shingle or board left within hollering distance. And she figured that if he brushed the mules any harder, they wouldn't have any hide left.

He'd even helped scrub the clothes yesterday when she dragged out the tubs to do the laundry. If she weren't so scared that it was his way of saying goodbye, she'd be more grateful. Instead, each chore he started and finished worried her just that much more.

Especially when he stopped what he was doing and stared off down the road, as if watching for someone. As far as she knew, the only person he knew in the area was Ambrose. Why would he care where her brother-in-law had got himself off to?

Of course, she was feeling edgy herself. It hadn't taken her all that long to get used to having a man in her bed every night, and she missed it. She didn't regret one minute of the time that she and Wade had spent together, but she couldn't bring herself to take up with him again now that the children were home.

How could she explain it to them if Wade moved his things into her room?

She stepped back from the window and looked across at her bedroom door. Maybe it didn't have to be an all-or-nothing situation. The idea had come to her that if she waited until Jack and Rose were asleep, she might just pay Wade a visit in his room. Of course, his narrow bed wouldn't be as comfortable as her larger one, but at this point, she simply didn't care.

If only he weren't acting so strange. She was leery of approaching him, so she looked around for an excuse to talk to him. Maybe he'd like a glass of water to cool his parched throat.

She patted her head to make sure that her hair was still neatly coiled in braids at the back of her neck. Her dress was plain, but at least it was clean. Figuring he hadn't complained about her looks yet, she walked outside and pumped a pitcher full of water fresh from the well.

Picking up the ladle she kept by the pump, she cautiously walked across the yard. Wade caught sight of her and stopped. He leaned the ax against the stump he was using to hold the logs and waited for her.

"Thought you might like a drink." It was a flimsy excuse and she knew it. He was perfectly capable of pumping water for himself, but he accepted the ladle with a quick nod. Some of the water splashed out of the ladle and trickled down his throat. She wanted to lick it off. Lordy, she had it bad!

"Thanks, that tasted good."

"You're welcome." She cast around for something else to talk about. "The wood box is overflowing."

"Then I'll stack the rest out here."

Realizing that she sounded ungrateful, she blushed. "What I meant was that you've cut plenty already. You shouldn't wear yourself out. It hasn't been all that long since you were flat on your back in bed."

That remark evidently didn't go over well either, because he immediately reached for the ax.

"Damn it, Lottie, don't go treating me like an invalid. If you don't want me cutting wood, just say so." He glared at her for a few seconds before turning his back to her. "Get back out of the way."

Now her own temper stirred.

"Wade McCord, put down that ax."

He swung it two more times before he responded. "Now what?"

"I was cutting my own wood before you came, and I'll be doing it when you're gone. Just like harnessing the mules and fixing fences and everything else around here."

She drew herself up to her full height and met him glare for glare. "If somewhere along the line you decided that I should be grateful for what you do around here, you better get that idea right out of your head. I can take care of myself and the children just fine without you or any other man, for that matter."

"Like you did the other night at the river? Maybe you think you'd like to take up with the likes of them next."

Lottie gasped with outrage. How dare he? "Wade McCord, I don't know what's wrong with you, but you'd better get yourself straightened out. I'm not paying you to act like this."

"And how do you want me to act? Like I'm nothing more than the hired hand around here? Or was bedding you part of my duties? Something I do when you run out of mules for me to brush or wood to cut?"

She would not cry. She absolutely would not. "You, sir, can get your things packed and go straight to Springfield or to hell or wherever you want. I don't need this."

His eyes were stormy, glittering with temper and maybe something else. She backed away, not sure at all that she'd been wise in prodding Wade when he was in this mood.

"You're right, Lottie. That's not what you need." He reached out and grabbed her. "This is."

His mouth crushed down on hers, the violence simmering in him boiling up and over. The kiss was anything but gentle, but she had her own temper and met him on equal footing. Lord, he felt like a fire out of control. She grabbed onto his shoulders and held on for dear life as she told him without words how much she'd missed this between them.

He groaned her name as his mouth journeyed down her throat to the pulse point at the base of her neck. She arched back, giving him better access. The thrill of his need made her burn, wishing they dared slip into the barn and finish what they'd started.

"Where are the children?" Evidently Wade had the same idea.

"Inside playing."

She hate to feel him pulling back as he banked the fire that had his eyes all dark and smoky. He didn't let her go, but he did allow some breathing room between them.

"I miss this."

She rose up and brushed a kiss across his lips. Her own felt swollen and achy. "Me, too."

He leaned his forehead against hers as he settled his hands around her waist. "I'm sorry I was such a bastard a few minutes ago."

"I wasn't much nicer."

This time he cupped her face with the palms of his hands. "I want you to know this: No matter what happens, this was real."

When he kissed her again, a hint of desperation colored the embrace, making her heart hurt. She accepted what he was giving while at the same time she wanted so much more. He'd never even hinted that he was anything more than a gambler whose life centered around a poker table. If she'd let herself hope for more, it was her own foolishness.

He even talked about luck as if it were a woman, as real to him as Lottie would ever be. Knowing she couldn't compete with such a thrilling mistress, she walked away, trying to gather up the broken pieces of her heart. Inside the house, she checked on Jack and Rose, who were squabbling good-naturedly over the rules to checkers. Rose caught her trying to slip into her bedroom unnoticed.

"Are you all right?"

Rose always did see more than she should. Lottie forced a pleasant smile as she turned back to face the children.

"I have a headache and thought I'd lie down for an hour or so before cooking dinner."

"Let me feel your head."

Rose climbed down from her chair and marched right over to where Lottie stood and held up her small hand. The little minx did her best to look like a worried parent as Lottie leaned down far enough so Rose could reach her face.

"You don't feel warm. I think a nap sounds like a good idea. Let me know if you don't feel any better after you sleep."

"Yes, ma'am."

Jack had been watching the whole encounter. "I hope you feel better."

"I'm sure I will. I probably got a little too much sun."

As the children turned their attention back to the checkerboard, Lottie hurried into her room and closed the door. She hadn't been lying, for her head was pounding. To dim the light in the room, she pulled the curtains closed, and then stretched out on the bed.

Even if she didn't manage to fall asleep, it felt good to be alone. Part of the problem was that she was sick to death of pretending all the time. Over the years, she'd perfected the attitude that she could do anything a man could. Although true to a certain extent, that didn't mean that she enjoyed all the hard physical labor that went along with running a stage station.

She'd lied to everyone, including herself, about not needing anyone to depend on. Even though she'd known better from the start, she'd allowed Wade to become part of the small circle of people she trusted to be there for her.

Then there was the lie she was living about being Jack and Rose's mother instead of their aunt. No one could have loved the two of them more, but she had worked hard to bury the need to have a child of her own. A man of her own.

And now, worst of all, she had to pretend that it

didn't matter that Wade would soon ride out, leaving her alone. One tear burned its way down the side of her face, followed by another and then another.

Finally, the dam burst. No longer able to hold back the pain, she buried her face in a pillow and let the tears pour out. When the last one had fallen, she closed her swollen eyes and prayed for sleep to come.

Ambrose pulled up just before cresting the last hill overlooking the station and dismounted. He wasn't quite ready to face Lottie and her demands, much less that damn lawman. Leading his horse forward, he took cover behind a line of trees and stared down at the station below.

He'd been only moderately successful in his mission. Out of the core of men who rode with him, he'd managed to catch only three of them doing what they should be doing. One was dealing cards in a saloon in Springfield; the second was drinking himself to death in his cabin along the Arkansas border.

And then there was Jeb. It sure as hell didn't pay to expect loyalty from the kind of men who rode with him, but young Jeb was an exception. How he could still have such an innocence about him after all he'd seen and done was a constant source of amazement. He'd been genuinely pleased to see Ambrose, as if they were real friends instead of merely outlaws who happened to ride together.

As far as he knew, Jeb had given every penny of his share of their take to his mother. Incredible.

On the other hand, he doubted that he himself had ever been that naive or unselfish. Hell, he was lucky to have grown up at all, considering the drunken bastard he'd had for a father. The old man had drunk up every last cent of the money they'd had. Once Ambrose had grown up enough to be on his own, he'd sworn never to be that dirt poor again, even if it meant stealing every last dime in the state of Missouri.

He grinned to himself. He'd done his best to do just that. Unfortunately, the law took a dim view of his pursuits, which brought him back to the problem waiting for him down below. Wade McCord wasn't going to back down on his plan to bring Ambrose and his men to justice.

To a hanging was more like it. The very idea had his collar feeling a might tight, even with the first button of his shirt undone. He wasn't all that worried. McCord had a streak of honor running right through him; the kind that meant he'd give Ambrose fair warning when his time had run out. The man was a damn fool. Did he really think that he was going to take Ambrose back for trial without a fight—let alone a fair one?

Taking note that the sun was rapidly going down, he decided that it was time to start down the hillside. The children would be happy to see him even if no one else was. He'd get a good night's sleep and then roust McCord out at first light to do some hunting. Their prey would be the two-legged sort, the kind that threatened innocent women and children. Those three had made a fatal mistake when they'd come after his woman, his children.

He led his horse slowly down the rocky slope, smiling to himself. Unless he missed his guess, Lottie was no longer as innocent as she used to be. That was something else he owed the lawman for. He just wasn't sure whether he should shake the man's hand or shoot the bastard for touching her.

He guessed it would all depend on how the hand

played out for all of them. For now, if he hurried, he might just make it home in time for dinner, and with luck, there'd be a piece of Lottie's pie waiting for him.

Lottie grudgingly set another place at the table. Her headache, although not as intense as it had been, had left her in no mood to cook dinner. Of necessity, she'd kept it simple—beans and bacon would have to suffice with some cornbread on the side.

"I was hoping for pie."

Ambrose looked over her shoulder to see what she was stirring. She elbowed him in the stomach to make him back away.

"Bake one yourself."

"What's got you all riled up?"

This time he made sure he was out of reach or she would have been tempted to hit him with the skillet, beans and all.

"She has a headache." Rose had come into the room, carrying her rag doll in her arms. "I made her take a nap, but it didn't help."

Lottie managed a smile for the little girl. "No, it helped a lot, Rose. It's almost gone now."

Ambrose pulled out a chair and sat down. As soon as he did, Rose climbed up in his lap and rested her head against his chest. Lottie turned her attention back to dinner, but cast an occasional glance over her shoulder to watch the two of them talking quietly between themselves.

No doubt, Rose was telling her father all about her day. He might have his shortcomings, all right. But even she had to admit that when he was home, he spent his time with his children. If only he didn't spend the rest of his time on the wrong side of the law.

A few minutes later, the door opened and the other man of the house came in. Her heartbeat speeded up at the sight of him, but she schooled her features to hide her reaction. She could only be glad that she hadn't mentioned her plan to slip into his room after the children had gone to sleep. With Ambrose in the house, there was no telling when she'd find the opportunity to carry out her idea. There was no use in both of them being disappointed if she couldn't work something out.

"Dinner is about ready, so everybody should wash up that needs to." She checked on the cornbread. It was just starting to brown. "Would one of you call Jack in?"

Wade gave her a puzzled look. "I didn't see him outside. I figured he was in here with you."

"He was here earlier when I lay down, but he was gone when I got up. I thought he was with you."

Now Ambrose was looking worried. "Come to think of it, I haven't seen him at all since I got home." He set Rose back on her feet and stood up. "Before we all start to panic, I'll check his room."

That took all of fifteen seconds. "No sign of him there or in McCord's room." He threw open the door to Lottie's bedroom. It was empty, too.

Wade was already heading outside before Ambrose finished talking. Lottie picked up Rose in her arms and followed the two men. Her heart felt as if it was skipping every other beat while she watched the two of them run from one outbuilding to the next, looking for Jack.

When Ambrose checked the outhouse for the second time in as many minutes, terror started clawing at her stomach.

"Where could he be?" Her question sounded shrill to her own ears. That was all it took to convince Rose that something was very, very wrong. Her thumb slid right into her mouth as she clutched her doll to her chest and tried to burrow into Lottie's shoulder.

Lottie squeezed her tight, offering what comfort she could. In the fading light, she watched as Wade and Ambrose met outside the barn. After exchanging a few words, both men came at a run right for her.

Her brother-in-law, his mouth set in a grim line, walked right past her without a word. Wade stopped on the bottom step of the porch, looking every bit as worried as Ambrose had. He met Lottie's gaze over Rose's head.

"He's nowhere to be found. We're going down to check the river."

Her imagination filled her mind with all the frightening possibilities, leaving her shaken to the core. She had to maintain some semblance of calm for her niece's sake, but her control was shaky at best.

"He knows better than to go that far without telling me. I've told him and told him."

Wade joined her on the porch and slipped his arm around her. "We'll find him."

"Damn straight, we will." Those words came from Ambrose as he came out of the house. He tossed Wade his rifle and gun belt on the way by. He had his own gun in his other hand, as well as a couple of lanterns.

"I'll help you look." Lottie started to follow him, but Wade caught her arm and held her back.

"It would be better if you waited here in case Jack

comes back on his own. It would scare him pretty bad to find the house empty and everyone gone."

She had to admit that there was sense in his suggestion, but she didn't like it one bit. Even so, her protest died on her lips. Rose needed her, too. Running like a madwoman through the woods wouldn't help Jack and would serve only to frighten Rose even more than she already was.

"I'll stay, but hurry."

"We will find him. I promise."

Wade gave her another quick squeeze and then took off into the gathering darkness after Ambrose. The woods swallowed him up almost immediately, leaving her staring at nothing but shadows. There was nothing left to be done outside, so she carried Rose back into the kitchen and set her down at the table.

The room reeked with the smell of something burning.

"The cornbread!" she wailed and grabbed a couple of towels. When she threw open the oven door, smoked roiled up in her face, all but blinding her. She managed to locate the pan in the thick fog and yanked it out of the oven.

"Open the door for me, Rose."

The little girl scrambled to do as she asked and then stood out of the way while Lottie carried the charred bread outside. Figuring somebody should get the benefit of her efforts, she tossed it out in the woods for the animals to eat. That done, she went back inside and started gathering all the same ingredients again. Making a new batch would keep her hands busy until the men returned with Jack.

And if they couldn't find him, they'd need something to eat to keep up their strength for searching.

* * *

Neither man did much in the way of talking as they all but ran through the trees to the river. Once the woods thinned out, Ambrose started calling his son's name.

"Jack, where are you? Jack!"

Wade came up beside him. "I'll go left and you head right. We'll cover twice as much territory that way."

Ambrose only nodded and shoved a lantern toward him. Wade grabbed it by the handle and started upriver. He'd use the extra light if need be, but for the moment he was still able to make out enough detail to do without it.

"Jack! Holler if you can hear me!" He listened several seconds before calling out again. The only answer he got was from a bullfrog and a couple of crickets.

He could hear Ambrose calling his son's name, sounding more worried than he had a few minutes before. Wade didn't blame him. He'd had a bad feeling about this. Jack was too conscientious to go wandering off by himself. The farthest the boy had ever gone on his own was the top of the hill overlooking the station. Even then, he'd been careful to stay in sight the whole time.

Wade stopped calling Jack's name altogether and concentrated on studying the gravel bar along the river. When he reached the point where Ambrose's men had confronted Lottie, he set the lantern down on a nearby boulder and lit it. Keeping the circle of light low, he slowly walked back and forth along the riverbank.

It didn't take long to find what he'd been looking for. Several of the rocks were disturbed and turned over. There weren't many animals in the Ozark woods big enough to leave such an obvious trail.

No, the most likely culprit was a horse, and more likely, a couple of them.

He held the lantern up as high as he could reach, trying to shed light on the far side of the river. Finally, he gave up and yanked his boots off and rolled up his pant legs and waded into the water. It felt cold against his skin, but he ignored the minor discomfort it caused.

He stopped just short of the shoreline and swung the lantern around in an arc in front of him. He'd been right. The rocks showed the same signs of recent disturbance. He waded on out and took a few steps into the woods. The gravel bar gave way to soft sand and mud. This time the hoofprints were all too clear.

Jack hadn't disappeared on his own. Someone had taken the boy. Wade turned and backtracked across the narrow river. Once he was on the other side, he debated how best to bring Ambrose at a run. Figuring gunshots would carry farther in the night air than a shout, he pulled out his revolver and aimed at a convenient tree. After firing three times in rapid succession, he sat down and started to put his boots and socks back on.

He could hear Ambrose scrambling along in the loose gravel in no time at all. The outlaw skidded to a halt just inside the circle of light cast by the lantern.

"Where is he? Did you find him?"

"No, he's not here." Wade stood up and forced himself to face Ambrose eye to eye when he gave him the news. "I think your men have taken him."

"The hell they have!" Even as he denied it, he looked straight across the river, where their trail disappeared into the woods. "What did you find?"

Wade pointed to the ground. "If we'd been half an hour later even, we might not have found their trail. But if you look closely"—he pointed toward the rocks—"you can see where at least one horse, and more likely two, crossed right here. Maybe in daylight we could see where they came from on this side, but for sure we can follow their trail on the other side."

"Let's get the horses." Ambrose looked and sounded grim. Wade caught him by the arm before he could go two steps. The outlaw tried to shake him off, but not before Wade planted himself right in front of him.

"I can only guess how you feel right now, and I don't blame you one damn bit. If Jack were my son, I'd want to go charging off and kill the sons of bitches myself. But we need to have a plan before we ride out after them, not to mention supplies and ammunition. We won't do the boy a damn bit of good if we aren't prepared to follow the trail for as long as it takes."

"I leave in an hour, whether you're ready to ride or not." The man wasn't listening.

"And what about Lottie and Rose? Do you think it's safe to leave them alone? That is, if Lottie will sit still for being left behind in the first place."

By this time, he had Ambrose's full attention. "When does the stage come through again?"

Wade counted his fingers. "Tomorrow, I think. Maybe the day after."

"We'll make her promise to take Rose and ride the stage into Springfield," said Ambrose. "She should be safe enough there until we get back."

"And if she won't go?"

"Then you'll have to stay with her while I go after Jack."

Wade stood toe to with him, refusing to take orders or give an inch. "Like hell. I'm the marshal here. It's my job. You'll stay."

Ambrose snagged Wade by the shirtfront and tried to yank him off balance. "He's my son. They are—or were—my men. I'll handle it."

Wade yanked himself free of the other man's grasp. "How?"

"I'll know when I find them. If they've hurt Jack, I'll shoot them where they stand. If he's all right, I'll get him out of there, and then I'll shoot them where they stand."

Wade managed a grin. "Sounds like the same plan I had in mind." He patted Ambrose on the arm. "Tell you what. Let's go break the news to Lottie. While she gets some supplies together for us, we'll saddle up and get ready to ride out. I'll go with you. They can't have that much of a head start. With luck, we'll catch up with them some time tomorrow or the day after. If it takes longer, I'll come back to stay with Lottie and Rose."

Ambrose didn't bother to answer other than with a quick nod. By the time Wade picked up his lantern, Ambrose was already well on his way back to the house. Wade followed along behind him, hoping that Lottie would listen to reason and knowing she wouldn't.

Lottie had somehow gotten Rose to go to bed before they made it back to the house. Before she'd stay still long enough to listen, Lottie insisted that Wade and Ambrose sit down at the table and eat the dinner they'd both forgotten about. While they ate, she threw together enough supplies to last two men and a small boy several days on the trail. Between bites, they told her what they'd found.

"Why? Why would they take him?"

Ambrose washed a mouthful of cornbread down with a glass of milk. "They want me."

She put a small sack of flour into Wade's saddlebag and reached for a small skillet next.

"Who wants you?"

"My men. Those three that accosted you not long ago and maybe a couple of others."

Ambrose tossed down his fork and pushed away from the table. "They haven't been happy with how I've been running things lately, so they want me out."

"What's their problem with you?" She gave up all pretense of packing.

Wade would love to hear the answer to that one. He met Ambrose's gaze across the table. Just as he expected, Ambrose tried to avoid the issue.

"That's not important," he said as he took another mouthful of the beans.

Lottie waited with little patience for him to swallow. "And that's not an answer. I want the truth."

"Damn it, Lottie. I don't want to talk about it with him here." He gestured in Wade's direction.

"Why? What difference does it make that Wade is here? He already knows what you do for a living."

The tension in the room was already high, but now the air crackled with it. Wade held his breath, waiting to see how Bardell was going to answer that one. Slowly, the outlaw turned to face Wade. One look and Wade knew all hell was about to break loose.

"Because I have enough problems right now with my men without them finding out that I've got a damn lawman living in my hip pocket."

"But you don't have . . ." Lottie started to say, but then she looked in Wade's direction. "He's not a lawman. He's a gambler—you know that." She grabbed on to the back of a chair as if her legs would no longer support her.

"Tell him, Wade. Tell him what you are." Her eyes pleaded with him to deny the truth of Ambrose's words.

Damn, he'd meant all along to tell Lottie the truth. He should have a long time ago, but now it was too late. Without a word he watched Ambrose pull Wade's badge out of his pocket and toss it on the table in front of her.

Her hand shook as she picked it up. Her face went white as she read the inscription. When she looked up, twin red spots stained her cheeks.

"Deputy U.S. Marshal McCord? Or is that even your name?"

"Lottie, I'm sorry." He tried to put his hand over hers, but she jerked her hand clear.

"I don't want apologies. I want the truth. Who are you? Why are you here?"

"I didn't lie about my name."

"But you did lie about everything else!"

"Not everything, not about you."

She took a step toward him and then slapped him across the face with all the fury that blazed in her eyes. "Get out."

"Now is not the time for this."

"No? Then when would it be convenient? After you've finished with me?"

They'd both forgotten about Ambrose. He pushed between the two of them. "Lottie, we have more important things to deal with right now."

"What?" Then it hit her. "Oh, lord—Jack." She seemed to shrink in on herself as her shoulders slumped in defeat. "Ambrose, bring him back. Please, God, bring him back."

Both men reached out to her at the same time, but she managed to avoid their touch. She picked up the burlap bag that she'd been filling with supplies and tossed it on the floor at Ambrose's feet.

"Get out of here and don't come back unless you have Jack with you." She ignored Wade completely.

Ambrose picked up the sack along with his rifle. "I know you don't want to hear this, but I am sorry."

When she turned her back without saying a word, he walked out of the house and into the night. Wade had no choice but to follow him. He paused in the doorway, wishing like hell that there was something he could do or something he could say that would make it all better.

Knowing full well that she wasn't ready to forgive him and perhaps never would be, he had to try. "I admit that I lied about how I make my living, but I didn't lie about anything that was important. No matter what you think of me now, just remember that what happened between us was as honest and real as anything I've ever known."

He reached out to touch her but then let his hand drop to his side. "Buck is coming through tomorrow. Take Rose and go to Springfield. You'll be safe there."

"No."

"That's what I figured." He pulled a piece of paper from his pocket and laid it on the table. "We're going to need help. Send this to the marshal in Springfield."

One heartbeat and then another passed without her uttering a single sound. He would have settled for as little as a look in his direction, but Lottie could have been a statue for all the response she showed. Cursing himself for a fool, he walked out and closed the door behind him.

Twelve

"I told you to stay out of this."

The outlaw had made the same comment about once every fifteen minutes since they'd left the station. Wade always gave the same response. "Go to hell, Bardell."

When the trail widened slightly, Wade urged his horse to pull even with his companion. "This isn't the usual way to your valley."

Bardell was almost as good at ignoring him as Lottie was. Wade let another few minutes of silence go by before he tried again.

"I know you're not happy having me along, but I seem to be the only one you can trust to back your play on this. Now, we can go on as we are, with me tagging along for the ride, or you can tell me what your plans are so that I don't accidentally shoot you instead of one of your men."

Bardell grunted, but then he slowed down and stopped. Wade reined in his horse and waited. The outlaw took a long draw off his canteen and then stared off into the distance.

"There's a back way into the valley that only a few of us know about. Even if they have someone watching, there's better cover for us there than if we rode straight in the other way."

Although they'd lost the trail over an hour ago, it was clear the riders had been heading more or less directly for the hideout. Wade had been hoping that they'd catch up with Jack and his captors. He'd feel a hell of a lot better just knowing that the boy was unharmed. These men knew the area every bit as well as Ambrose did and far better than Wade. They'd managed to travel over the hardest ground in the area, leaving only the faintest traces of their passing.

"Stay back."

Ambrose urged his horse into a trot, leaving Wade behind. He thought about arguing but realized that something up ahead had caught the outlaw's attention. A lone rider sat outlined against the skyline at the top of a bald knob hill. Either the man wanted to be seen or else he was a fool. Wade wasn't willing to trust his luck to the second notion, so he hung back and waited to see what played out.

Ambrose rode straight for the stranger. While he didn't actually draw his gun, Wade noticed that his gun hand was resting on the grip of his revolver. When the other rider made no hostile move, Ambrose reined in his horse to stand beside the man. Wade would have given a lot to hear the brief conversation between the two, but figured he might do more harm than good by interfering.

He didn't have to wait long. Abruptly, the stranger wheeled his horse around and rode off into the trees, leaving Ambrose alone on the hilltop. Before he'd gone ten yards, Ambrose casually pulled his revolver and shot him in the back. When his horse screamed in fear and ran off through the trees, the rider fell to the ground and lay staring sightlessly up at the sky.

Wade cursed and cantered the last distance to

join Ambrose, who stood over his former accomplice with casual disregard. The lawman in Wade wanted to protest. On the other hand, it meant one less gun to face when it came time to rescue Jack. But if he still needed proof that Ambrose well deserved his reputation as a cold-blooded killer, he had it in spades. There wasn't anything Wade could do for the dead man except add his death to the list of crimes Ambrose would stand trial for.

"Who was that?" He didn't expect an answer and didn't get one. His stomach clenched and churned at the pungent smell of death. He wondered briefly if someone was waiting in vain for the dead man to return home—a wife, a mother, anyone at all.

"I assume you'll tell me what he had to say."

"They're holding Jack about a mile that way." Bardell gestured toward the west. "My, uh, friend was kind enough to give me their message. I'm supposed to walk into camp unarmed. They'll trade my son for me."

"Stupid bastards. Do they really think that's going to happen? A man would have to be crazy to do that."

Ambrose shook his head. "Or a father. I'd do exactly what they ordered if I thought they'd actually let the boy go."

"You got any friends down there?"

"Not any that I'd trust with Jack's life."

Wade met the other man's gaze. "Then I guess that leaves the two of us."

Ambrose laughed and dismounted. "It's a poor day when the only man I can depend on is the one who's hell-bent on delivering me up to the hangman."

There wasn't much Wade could say to that, since

it was all too true. Still, he would have backed the play of Satan himself to save Jack's life.

He had to ask, "Why did you shoot him?"

"He needed killing." With that, Ambrose led his horse off the narrow path and into the shelter of a stand of pines.

Not for the first time, Wade wondered how he'd come to be riding partners with such a cold-blooded bastard. For now, he had no choice, so he followed in Ambrose's footsteps. Once in the shade, he checked his revolver and rifle for readiness. That done, he pulled extra ammunition out of his saddlebags and filled his pockets.

"What's our plan?"

"Didn't know we had one," Ambrose answered as he rooted through their small stash of supplies.

It was midmorning, and they hadn't stopped to eat or rest since riding out the night before. Ambrose pulled out some cornbread left over from dinner. He broke off a piece and handed the rest over to Wade, following it up with an apple. It wasn't much of a meal, but there would be time for more deluxe vittles after the shooting was done.

Either that, or they'd both be dead and it wouldn't matter. Wade washed the last of the cornbread down with water from his canteen. After wiping his mouth on the back of his sleeve, he put everything back and waited for Ambrose to get ready. Out of habit, he rechecked his guns one more time and then pinned his badge onto his shirt.

When Ambrose saw what he'd done, he shook his head. "That thing will make a nice, shiny target for somebody."

"Won't be the first time." Wade shrugged his indifference. "So far, I've been lucky."

"Even though you're not really a gambler, you're

still willing to trust your life to Lady Luck. That makes a lot of sense." Ambrose spun the cylinder on his gun and then shoved it back in its holster.

"She's as trustworthy as any woman can be." If he sounded bitter, Wade didn't give a damn. First Lily and then Lottie had thrown his love back in his face. At least the lady made no pretense of being anything other than fickle. He changed the subject. "Do we have a plan now?"

Ambrose squinted up toward the sun. "About the time we reach the valley, the sun should be directly in their eyes. It's not much of an advantage, but it might help some. I'll walk straight in like they want. You'll come in from behind."

"And if they're right up against one of the bluffs?"

"Then we'll improvise."

Since he had no better suggestion, Wade followed Ambrose as he led the way down the other side of the hill and around the side of the next one. It was hotter than hell in among the hills as they paralleled the course of the trail. Walking was miserable, but it would save some of the horses' strength for making a run later on.

He figured they'd gone about half the distance when Ambrose stopped again. He handed his reins to Wade and pulled a knife out of his boot.

"If they have a sentry, he'll be up ahead on the other side of that cluster of boulders on the right. Wait here."

"I'll go after him." Wade tried to hand the reins back.

"Like hell. This is my fight."

"And it's my job to see that these bastards live long enough to stand trial."

"That's rich. You don't want me to kill them, just

so some judge can have the pleasure. Either way, they end up dead. Believe me, given their druthers, they'd rather go out in a hail of bullets than dance at the end of a lawman's rope so upstanding, law-abiding citizens can stand by and cheer."

He walked away before Wade could say another word. They'd been arguing in quiet whispers. If he called after Ambrose, he'd reveal their presence for certain. He followed him down the slope.

At the bottom of the next hill, Ambrose tied his horse's reins to a low branch and waited as Wade did the same. That done, they both picked up their rifles and started angling their way up the next slope. Near the top, Ambrose motioned for Wade to drop down beside him. Together they approached the crest of the hill, careful to keep their heads below the ridge.

At the top, Ambrose pointed off to the left. "See him?"

The sun glinted off something shiny, most likely a rifle barrel. Whoever was standing sentry was careless—a surefire way to get himself killed.

"I'll take care of him. Wait here."

Wade slipped back down the way they'd come and worked his way through the undergrowth to the far side of the stand of trees that provided cover for the sentry. From where Wade stood crouched in the shadows, he could see that the man had his eyes fixed on the trail below. Just as Ambrose had thought, they figured he'd come riding in bold as hell.

That mistake would cost them.

He waited until the man took out his fixings for a cigarette. While his attention was on that, Wade ran around the edge of a small clearing. After that, the good cover disappeared, leaving him no choice but to cross the last distance out in the open.

He brought his rifle to bear on his target, determined to shoot only if absolutely necessary. There was a small chance that the sound of Ambrose's earlier shot hadn't carried this far, but the outlaws below couldn't help but hear one at this distance.

He came damn close to making it undetected when he stumbled over a patch of tall weeds and scared up a covey of quail. The sudden explosion of wings and feathers startled Wade almost as much as it did the unsuspecting outlaw. The look on the man's face would have been funny as he whirled around, sending his tobacco scattering to the winds, if he hadn't immediately caught sight of Wade.

Luckily, he realized that he stood little chance against a rifle pointed right at his gut.

Wade pitched his voice only loud enough to be heard by the sentry. "Slowly drop your guns with your left hand. Keep your right hand in the air. Make one move toward your rifle and you won't live long enough to regret it."

The man reached for his gun belt and fumbled awkwardly with the buckle. Finally, he pulled it free and let the belt swing free from his waist. That done, he lowered it slowly to the ground. Wade kept his distance until Ambrose joined them.

He wasn't about to take any chances with his prisoner. "They'll hear a shot."

Ambrose nodded but didn't look happy about it. Wade used the man's own rope to tie him to the tree. No sooner had he gagged the man than Ambrose shoved Wade to one side and kicked the helpless prisoner in the stomach. Before he could land a second blow, Wade jerked him by the back of his collar and flung him to the side. When he fought to get past him, Wade grabbed Ambrose by the shirt-front and got right in his face.

"Damn it, Ambrose, we don't have time for this." To add emphasis to his words, Wade drew his pistol and pressed the barrel against Bardell's throat. "This man is my prisoner. I won't let you hurt him."

Bardell's blue eyes glittered with a light that wasn't quite sane. "Don't tell me what to do, law-man. I've killed better men than you."

Wade cocked his gun, knowing that in his present state of mind, Ambrose might just force him to pull the trigger. "That may be, outlaw, but right now I'm the only hope you have of getting your son back alive."

Ambrose tried again to push past Wade without success. Although they were similar in size and strength, Wade had been pushed as far as he would go. Stubbornly he maintained his position until the other man faltered. Finally, just as quickly as it had come, the killer light dimmed in Ambrose's eyes. When the tension went out of his muscles, Wade allowed him to step back.

"We're not done with this, McCord."

Wade had a temper of his own. He also had the advantage of already having his gun drawn, and right now it was aimed straight at his enemy. "I never thought we were. I told you before: I came here with a job to do. When it's time to finish it, you'll be the first to know."

Ambrose didn't even flinch. "Don't think saving Jack will keep me from using that star for target practice."

"I wouldn't want you to make it easy for me." Wade holstered his pistol. "Now let's get on with it. We wouldn't want to disappoint those men down there."

Before they'd gone more than a dozen steps, Wade asked the one question that had been plaguing him since the trouble had started. "What the hell did you do that has them all this riled up?"

Ambrose's steps faltered to a stop. "They thought I should be planning more jobs than I thought was reasonable."

Wade was willing to bet a month's salary that there was more to it than that. Even though these men might have followed Ambrose, they'd proven themselves capable of robbing banks on their own.

"What else?"

"I steal money for a living. Somewhere along the line they forgot that."

This time it was Wade who came to a stop. "You stole money from your own men?"

"I don't see it that way, but they do. Up until they pulled a couple of jobs on their own, they had no idea how much money we were taking. If anyone questioned it, I reminded them how much the newspapers liked to exaggerate things. Anyway, I kept a fair percentage for doing all the planning. Otherwise, everyone got an equal share."

Wade wasn't sure that he wanted to know the answer to the question he was about to ask. "And what did you consider fair?"

Ambrose grinned. "Half."

"Shit, no wonder they want your hide. Damn it, you know what kind of men you ride with. Did you think they wouldn't come after you?"

"Hell, yes, I thought they'd come after me, and there isn't one of them who can outdraw me." He shook his head. "My mistake was in thinking they'd never come after my family."

They were getting too close to the outlaw camp to risk talking anymore. When Ambrose figured they were directly above the end of the trail that led into the camp, he split off to the left, leaving Wade to circle around to the right. Before they separated, they checked their pocket watches.

Ambrose looked grim. "No matter what happens to me, you take the boy and get the hell out of here. Don't risk him trying to help me get away."

"But . . ."

"Damn it, McCord, don't argue. You'll stand a better chance getting him free of this mess if I'm drawing their fire. Besides, they'll have a harder time trailing us if they don't know exactly who they're after."

Wade didn't like it one damn bit, but there was no arguing with the man. And if it were his son, he'd feel the same way.

"Don't make a target of yourself," said Wade. "Jack won't thank you for it and neither will Lottie." He checked his watch again. "Give me twenty minutes to get into position."

Wade waited for Ambrose to acknowledge his order and then slipped into the dappled shadows of the trees. Not knowing the exact location of the outlaw camp hampered his movement. It wouldn't do at all to go blundering into a hornet's nest. After only a couple of minutes of rapid walking, he slowed his steps to reconnoiter.

There was a faint whiff of smoke in the air. The slight breeze was coming from his left, so he angled in that direction. Another twenty feet into the woods, he could hear voices. They were far enough away to make it impossible to determine exactly how many men were involved, but he'd guess at least three.

He checked his watch. Time was running out, because he didn't trust Ambrose to wait the full twenty minutes before acting. Weighing caution against the need to be ready, he took off at a slow lope. Finally, as the trees began to thin out, he slowed to a stop to listen again.

The voices were clearer this time. He could see movement through the trees, which had him running toward a large sycamore. When he reached it, he took time to catch his breath, all the while being careful to keep the bulk of the trunk between him and the outlaws.

The stupid bastards must be feeling pretty damn confident, because they weren't bothering to keep their voices down or to hide their campsite. He could only hope that their carelessness would play into his hands.

Once again, he checked his weapons before slipping even closer to the campsite. When he'd positioned himself to have a clear shot at most of the outlaws, he glanced at his watch. If Ambrose kept his word, he still had about five minutes left to wait. And think.

He wondered how Lottie was holding up. About now, she should be harnessing the mules for Buck. He had no doubt that she could do it on her own, but he wished like hell that he were there to help her. But unless there was a miracle of some sort, his days of being part of her makeshift family were over.

The very idea left him hurting and cold inside. Perhaps he could have handled things differently, but damned if he knew how. No matter when she found out that he was a marshal intent on hunting down her worthless brother-in-law, she would have thrown him out. While he didn't regret a single second that he'd spent in her life and in her bed, it made him furious to know that she did.

She should have trusted the truth of what they'd

shared; the lies he'd told didn't change the man he was or the way he felt. Under other circumstances, he might have even convinced her of that, but not now. By the time he got back to the station, she would have had plenty of time to turn her pain into hate for him.

The seconds ticked by, each one putting that much more time and distance between him and Lottie. His nerves stretched tighter and tighter as he waited for Ambrose to make his move. If things went as usual, as soon as the action started, a sense of calm would override his tension. He prayed that would happen soon.

In the remaining time, he risked discovery by moving even closer to the clearing ahead. It was imperative that he locate Jack before all hell broke loose. No matter what happened to Ambrose, or even Wade himself, the boy had to be kept safe.

As soon as he had a clear view of the outlaw hide-out, he did a head count. There were five men that he could see, two of whom he'd seen that day at the river. He wondered if the man sleeping by the fire was the one he'd shot. This time he might just finish the job. Since it was unlikely that they only posted one lookout, he had to figure that one, maybe two, more were within hailing distance.

That was when he noticed a small cave at the back of the clearing, not quite opposite from where Wade stood. A movement just inside the opening caught his eye. It was Jack. Relief washed over him when he realized that the boy appeared to be scared but unharmed. He only wished he could safely signal Jack that he was no longer alone.

One last glance at his watch told him that time had just run out. Right on the stroke of noon, Ambrose's voice rang out over the clearing.

"McNulty, I hear tell that you wanted to see me."

Ambrose wasn't yet in sight, but even so the men scrambled for their rifles and cover. Wade brought his gun to bear on the outlaw nearest the cave, in case he needed to clear a path to Jack.

One of the outlaws, no doubt McNulty himself, mustered up enough courage and called out, "Ambrose, come on in. Have a cup of coffee with us."

Wade eased back the hammer on his rifle and waited to see what the outlaw leader would do next.

Her body craved sleep, but her mind wouldn't rest. Hours had passed since she crawled into her bed, but she was no closer to slumber than she had been when she first lay down. Her blood thrummed in her veins, driven along by the racing pulse of her heart.

Where were Ambrose and Jack? Were they both safe and on their way home? She closed her eyes and sent yet another prayer to the heavens that they'd walk in the door any minute. Her traitorous heart sent another right along behind it that Wade was with them.

Not that she ever wanted to see him again. He'd lied to her and to the children, not to mention Ambrose. Once she'd gotten her mind around the fact that he was a marshal, it hadn't taken long for her to realize that it had been her brother-in-law's trail that led Wade to her door. And her bed.

Even in the dark of her room, her face burned hot with embarrassment. How could she have been foolish enough to think a man like him would honestly find her attractive?

Ambrose had brought the law down on his own head, so she couldn't really hold that against Wade.

But all his sweet lies and promises, whispered in her ear as he made love to her, were completely unforgivable. She'd waited her whole life for a man to make her feel the way he had; to find out it was all a lie hurt more than she could bear.

For the hundredth time, she changed positions, turning her pillow to the cool side and shifting to the middle of the bed. Nothing helped. She stared out the small window across the room. Already faint streaks of light could be seen to the east. Within the hour, the sun would clear the horizon, the start of another day in hell.

Thoroughly disgruntled, she kicked back the covers and sat up on the edge of the bed. The hours ahead would be busy with the stage coming through, and filled with endless worries about her menfolk. She wasn't accomplishing anything tossing and turning in bed. With another quick prayer, she reached for her clothing and went through all the motions of getting dressed.

If she wasn't able to sleep for worrying, maybe she could hold off the terror by keeping herself busy. With that in mind, she headed for the barn and the early morning chores.

"Please, Ambrose, bring your son home safely," she murmured under her breath as she stepped out onto the porch. Then, cursing herself for a fool, she added, *And Wade, I want to see you long enough to make sure you're all right. Then you can just ride down that road and don't look back, because I sure won't be looking after you.*

Liar! whispered the small voice inside her mind. She would look, and she would miss him. But trust, once shattered, couldn't be put back together again, not in the same way or with the same strength.

She of all people should have known better. All

along she'd tried reminding herself that men weren't to be trusted, not in any way that mattered. How could she have forgotten the lessons that first her father and then Ambrose had taught her? Had she really expected Wade to be any different? Yes, she had. Foolish woman that she was, she'd allowed herself to believe what he told her with his words, his touch, and his lovemaking. Why hadn't she wondered about the reasons behind his constant assurances that the passion between them was the truth? Was that all? Could there have been more?

She slipped inside the barn and breathed deeply of the earthy scents it contained. The familiar routine of feeding the livestock and seeing to their needs did far more to soothe her soul than anything else could. Picking up the water bucket, she took comfort in the simple honesty of caring for her animals.

With luck, by the time she had everything under control, the men would come riding back with Jack in tow. Then maybe she could start rebuilding her life.

The first shots weren't long in coming. From the way the outlaws where scattering their bullets, it was obvious that they had yet to figure out exactly where Ambrose was among the surrounding woods. Certainly they had no idea that he wasn't alone.

While they were concentrating on returning Ambrose's fire, Wade decided to risk being seen in order to signal to Jack that he was no longer alone. He stepped out of the trees long enough to wave his rifle overhead. Jack, bless him, was watching for something of the sort. He waved back but didn't call out.

Wade motioned for Jack to move to the near side of the cave, behind some boulders, while he tried to get close enough to slip the boy away from the camp. Luck was with him at first. He got within about twenty feet of the opening to the cave before one of the outlaws thought to check on their captive.

He immediately rolled over onto his back in order to shoot at Wade, but luckily Ambrose managed to wound him before he could yell out a warning. One look told Wade the man wasn't long for this world. As he continued toward the cave, he muttered a string of curses a mile long. He'd meant what he'd said to Ambrose earlier about bringing these men to justice. He wouldn't be a party to wholesale slaughter.

On the other hand, he had to admit that Ambrose was doing a fair job of keeping the rest of Jack's captors pinned down. During one burst of shots, Wade took off running for the cave, reaching it just as the gunfire died back. He dove headfirst through the entry and rolled to the side where Jack was crouched.

Careful to keep himself between Jack and the hail of bullets outside, he looked the boy over from head to toe.

"Are you all right?"

Jack's chin quivered a bit, but then he nodded. "I was scared." Wade tugged on the boy's hair and offered him a smile. "We all were. Now, son, I need you to do exactly what I tell you. I'll do my best to answer any questions when we've got you safely back at the station. Do you understand?"

"Yes, Mr. Wade."

"Good boy. Now listen: that's your pa out there stirring things up. He's trying to keep those men busy enough so they won't take notice of us. We're going to wait until he lays down some cover for us and then we're going to run like h—, ah, make that *like the wind*. You got that? Don't stop; don't look back; don't listen to anything anybody says except me or your father."

Jack was already edging back to the front of the cave. Wade placed himself directly between the boy and the remaining outlaws outside. As soon as he did, Ambrose started kicking up another ruckus, with shots throwing up dirt all over the camp.

"Now, Jack! Run!"

It was all he could do to keep up with the youngster as they tore out of the cave and immediately headed right back into the trees. Wade aimed for the thickest part of the woods before he worried at all about the direction they needed to go. If the gunmen took note of the boy's escape, they did nothing to prevent it or to recapture him.

Wade would have put it down to good luck, but considering everything that had gone wrong in the past two days, he wasn't going to depend on the lady to get them out of the situation. The two of them ran as fast as they could over the uneven ground. Downed trees and scrubby undergrowth made the going difficult, especially uphill.

Finally, they reached the edge of the clearing where they'd left the outlaw tied up. Wade stopped abruptly, yanking Jack back beside him when the boy would have kept going.

The man sat slumped over right where Wade had left him. The only difference was the bright red stain down the front of his shirt. Even from a distance, Wade could tell that someone had slit the man's throat. His life's blood had drained out quickly, pooling in his lap like an obscene blanket. Wade kept his cursing to himself, but there wasn't a doubt in his mind that Ambrose had doubled back to kill his former friend before going after the others. There was nothing that Wade could do for this man, but he hoped that Ambrose's concern for Jack would keep him from staying at the outlaw camp long enough to kill all the others.

Nudging Jack to move to the left, the two of them skirted around the clearing and kept heading directly for where Wade had left his horse tied. Before they approached the animal directly, he waited to make sure they weren't walking into a trap. Once he was reasonably sure that it was safe to do so, he and Jack ran to the horse and mounted up.

They left Ambrose's horse where he'd left it, figuring he would follow along when he got free of the camp. Wade had promised Bardell that he'd take Jack straight home, but he had other reasons for hurrying along as well.

First and foremost, he wanted to relieve Lottie's worries. If these hours had seemed an eternity to him, waiting and not knowing had to be about to kill her. But he also wanted time to get ready to face down Ambrose.

It was plain that the man wouldn't stop killing until someone stopped him.

And although it would hurt Lottie and the children, in the long run, forcing Ambrose to face justice for all his crimes would be the best thing for all of them. Lottie had already been threatened and Jack kidnapped because of who and what Bardell was. It had to stop.

Even if it cost Wade everything he'd come to care about.

Thirteen

Wade fought hard against the urge to speed up. His poor mount had been over twenty-four hours without rest or a decent meal. The same was true for him, of course, but he wasn't carrying the weight of two people on his back.

Instead, his shoulders were burdened with a heavy load of guilt that was increased with each mile crossed on the way back to Lottie. Jack snuggled against Wade's back, confident that his small part of the world was about to return to normal. But it would never be that way again, not once he realized the significance of the star pinned to Wade's shirt.

It had been almost a relief that he hadn't noticed it yet, probably because of all the other stuff that had happened to the boy in the past forty-eight hours. Once they reached the station, however, Lottie wouldn't ignore it. It hurt bad enough that Lottie hated Wade for what he was and what he'd come to do. He wasn't sure he could bear to see the same pain in Jack's eyes or Rose's.

Needing a break from his own thoughts, he stopped before crossing a small stream. Besides, he figured Lottie wouldn't appreciate it if he rode her horse to death before he managed to get Jack home. He offered his hand back to Jack to help the boy dismount. Wearily, he swung down out of the saddle himself and led the horse to drink. Needing something to wash down the trail dust, he moved upstream a few feet and lay down to scoop handfuls of water to his mouth.

When he'd drunk his fill, he splashed his face with water, trying to make himself more alert. Pushing back up off the ground, he looked around for Jack. He spied him immediately, lying curled up on his side in a patch of grass not five feet from where they'd dismounted. The dark circles under the poor little fellow's eyes made Wade's own weariness seem insignificant.

For a minute, Wade flirted with the idea of letting him stay asleep long enough to knock the edge off his exhaustion. Only the knowledge that each minute they delayed was a minute spent in hell for Lottie kept him from doing just that. Wishing he didn't have to disturb Jack, he carefully shook the boy's shoulder.

"Jack, wake up. I know you're tired, but you can sleep all you want once we reach the house. You'll be more comfortable in your own bed, anyway."

At first, Jack grunted without opening his eyes and swatted at Wade's hand. Finally, though, he pried his eyes open and managed to sit up. He blinked several times, as if trying to make sense of his surroundings.

"Come on and get a drink of water, then I'll lift you up in my lap. Maybe you can sleep some on the way home." Carrying Jack that way would make it hard for Wade to pull his gun, but this close to home he was willing to risk it.

After a couple of awkward tries, he finally got Jack situated on his lap after they mounted up. In no time at all, Jack settled back against Wade's chest, and his eyes drifted shut. Wade let the horse pick its own way along the valley for the time being, which left his hands free to hold on to his slumbering burden.

By his reckoning, they should reach the station in less than an hour. When they started up the hill, he glanced back over his shoulder, trying to determine if they were being followed. If there were riders, they were far enough back to be no danger yet. It suddenly occurred to him to wonder what had happened to Bardell. He hoped the bastard showed up soon, because Wade was in no shape to go back out to look for him.

Besides, he wouldn't willingly leave Lottie and the children alone and undefended one minute longer than he had to. No matter what she said, he was staying until the help they so desperately needed arrived. He figured on two days, three at the most, before at least half a dozen deputies descended on the station.

That is, if she'd sent his message with Buck. He knew that she saw calling in the law as a betrayal of Ambrose, but surely she understood that her safety and that of the children had to come before any misguided loyalty. Even the bastard who'd brought all this trouble to her door in the first place would agree.

Just past the top ridge, he caught sight of a stream of smoke rising above the trees to the east and breathed a sigh of relief. The two of them would be home in a matter of minutes.

Then he cursed himself for a fool for even thinking that way. Of course, Jack would be welcomed home. Lottie and Rose were already there. And with his damnable good luck, Ambrose probably had survived the day and would turn up to be greeted with open arms. Of all of them, only Wade had no right to think of the station as home, and never would.

With that cheery thought, he urged his weary horse into a slow trot. Since there was no avoiding the pain, he'd rather face it and get on with his job.

Lottie's knees hurt almost as much as her back did. The rest of the weeds would live to see another day in the garden because she'd had enough. The effort to climb back to her feet left her breathless and in need of a cool place to sit for a spell. She made it as far as the big sycamore before sinking back down onto the cool grass. Knowing she didn't have the strength to fight against it, she let her eyes drift shut of their own accord.

Damn, she was tired, allowing herself the small wickedness of cursing. Since leaving her bed before sunrise, she'd stopped only long enough to fix makeshift meals for Rose and herself. And if it hadn't been for the little girl, she wouldn't have made any effort at all. She'd choked down a few bites at each meal because it would have worried Rose if she hadn't. Now, hours later, her stomach churned unhappily.

After only a few minutes of respite, she sat up and looked around for Rose. She spied her standing on the porch and staring at something off in the woods. Knowing the little girl's constant curiosity about anything and everything, Lottie didn't immediately take much notice. But when Rose's face lit up as she flew off the porch at a dead run, whooping and hollering, Lottie knew someone was coming.

Her heart about did somersaults as she tried to see who had triggered Rose's excitement. Finally, about the time she managed to find the strength to stand, she saw a single horse trudging its way down the hill. Even at that distance, Lottie knew that horse and that rider. Despite her anger and disappointment, she couldn't help but breathe a sigh of relief that Wade McCord had survived the confrontation with Ambrose's men.

It was equally obvious that he had Jack cradled in his arms. She fought down the surge of alarm at her nephew's stillness. If he'd been hurt—or worse—Wade would have killed that poor horse getting him home to her. That he wasn't in a hurry was reassurance enough that Jack was safe and sound. She walked out to meet them. Every so often she looked past them up the hill, wondering where her brother-in-law was. Had something happened to him?

The horse stumbled to a stop just short of where she stood waiting. Wade met her gaze, obviously unsure of his welcome. She had good reason to be angry with him, but that didn't stop her from being grateful to him for bringing Jack back home safely. For the moment, her relief at their return was so profound, she couldn't force a word past the lump in her throat. Wordlessly, she reached up to take his sleepy burden.

The sudden movement woke the boy up. One look at her had him diving headlong into her waiting arms. His skinny little boy arms wrapped around her neck in a choke hold. Tears streamed down her face as she buried her face in his neck and held on for dear life. Rose, wanting to be part of the reunion, held on to Lottie's legs.

"Look at us, a bunch of watering pots!" Lottie teased.

Jack pried himself up from her shoulder and

looked at her face and at his sister's. A small smile played around his mouth, reassuring Lottie that he would recover from the trauma of the past two days. Rose, whose tears Lottie suspected were more a response to Lottie's own than to any real terror on her part, sniffled a bit and then wiped her face on Lottie's skirt.

"Rose Hammond, my dress is not a handkerchief."

That got both children to giggling. Deciding they'd all had enough of tears for a while, Lottie shifted Jack's weight to one arm and then offered her free hand to Rose. That done, she looked back over her shoulder to thank Jack's rescuer, only to realize that Wade had already left them.

She almost stumbled over her own feet as she spun around, trying to figure out where he'd gone. Surely, as tired as he'd been, he hadn't been so foolish as to leave again.

"Wade! Where are you?" she called, trying without success to keep the panic out of her voice.

To both her relief and profound embarrassment, he came charging out of the barn, gun drawn and looking around for a threat to her and the children.

She hastened to reassure him. "I'm sorry I alarmed you. I was afraid that you'd left us."

"Why would you care?" Without waiting for her to answer, he disappeared back into the shadowy interior of the barn.

For some reason, she didn't want him to have the last word. "I'm taking the children inside for a light supper. I'll expect you to join us."

When she reached the porch, Jack wiggled to get down. Evidently, he'd had enough of her fussing over him for the moment. Rose tagged along behind when he ran inside the house. Lottie took advantage of their absence to watch for any sign of what Wade was up to.

When she saw him turn the gelding loose in the corral, she breathed a sigh of relief to see he was in no hurry to leave them yet. Although her main concern had been for her nephew, she hadn't missed seeing that Wade's face was gray with exhaustion, his eyes dull and lifeless. She wouldn't turn a complete stranger out in that condition.

And truth be told, Wade was far more than a stranger to her. In fact, she knew him far too well; the scent of his skin, the sweetness of his kiss, the strength in his arms.

Content that he would be along presently, she walked inside, all the time wondering how she'd ever manage to forget how much those things meant to her.

Wade stepped up on the porch and wished he were anywhere else. He hadn't missed the way Lottie had gathered only the children to her side. Hell, he'd been in the barn for damn near ten minutes before her screeching had sent him charging out like a fool.

Up until then, she hadn't even said a word to him. He hadn't known what to expect from her, but complete silence hadn't been it. The woman sure as hell ran hot and cold. One minute she acted as if he didn't exist, and the next she panicked because he was out of sight. He'd like to think that she was concerned about him, but it was more likely she was worried about her precious bloodthirsty bastard of a brother-in-law.

Dallying on the porch wouldn't make things any easier, but another few minutes outside to gather his wits wouldn't hurt. He glanced up at the sky and was surprised to see storm clouds rolling in over the valley. Judging by their color, all hell would break loose some time in the next few hours. As if to confirm his suspicions, a jagged tear of lightning flashed over the most distant hills, followed by a faint rumble of thunder.

It suited his mood perfectly.

The door opened behind him. Without looking, he knew it wasn't Lottie.

"Mr. Wade, aren't you coming in for dinner?"

"I'll be in shortly."

Rose joined him at the railing to see what he was looking at. She jumped about a foot when another crack of thunder rolled over them. Immediately her small hand found his.

"I like storms." The slight trembling in her fingers gave proof to the small lie.

"Do you, now?" He squeezed her hand.

She nodded bravely. "Yes, 'cause it's God's way of doing his laundry."

Now, that was one he'd never heard before. "I've never heard tell of God having dirty clothes."

The little girl giggled at his foolishness. "He washes the whole world with rain, not his clothes. After the storm, everything will smell clean and new again. He makes a lot of noise because it's such a big job."

Leave it to Lottie to comfort her child's fear with such a story. He had dim recollections of his own mother telling him similar tales to ward off a small boy's fears. The memories made him smile.

"We'd better go inside and leave God to his chores."

Rose led the way in, heading right for the kitchen table. Jack was nowhere to be seen, but Lottie was standing at the stove waiting for them. She motioned for them to take their seats. She shot a questioning look at the rifle in his hand. He made a point of setting it down within easy reach of the table. Lottie was still trying to shield Rose from the hard reality of their situation, but safety had to come first. Although Lottie frowned, she said nothing about the gun.

"Jack went straight to bed."

"Doesn't surprise me. He was pretty worn out after all the excitement."

Lottie looked pointedly at her niece, another hint that they should take care with their words. With her usual efficiency, Lottie set dinner on the table. The simple fare of soup and biscuits smelled like heaven.

"Rose, would you like to say grace tonight since Jack is in bed?"

Wade watched as the two bowed their heads. Out of respect, he followed suit.

"God, thank you for this food and Mr. Wade and Lottie and please bring my pa home safe."

When she stopped, both adults started to raise their heads. Rose, however, wasn't quite done.

"And I know you're washing your laundry, but please don't make too much noise because it keeps me awake." Then with a resounding "Amen!" she picked up her spoon and started eating.

Wade managed to choke back a laugh. He looked to see how Lottie was reacting to Rose's comment. Her blue eyes sparkled with suppressed amusement, and for a brief time they shared the moment. But then reality crept back.

"Mr. Wade, when will my pa be back? Did those bad men get him, too?"

Keeping his eyes pinned on Lottie's, he chose his words carefully.

"Well, I don't rightly know how soon he'll be here. Jack and I came on ahead because it was getting to be your brother's bedtime."

That satisfied Rose, but from the way Lottie frowned, it definitely raised a few more questions in her mind. He had some for her as well, but knew they would have to wait until after Rose was safely tucked in bed.

For the remainder of the meal, Lottie seemed content to let Rose control the conversation. That was fine with Wade. He was so tired he hurt. He wasn't sure he could string more than ten words together and make much sense.

When he'd taken the last bite of his soup, he asked, "Where do you want me to sleep tonight?"

He was betting on the barn. But with a storm threatening, he hoped that Lottie would take pity on him and not send him out to sleep with the mules. To his relief, Lottie seemed confused by his question.

"You must be tired if you can't remember where your room is."

Somehow, he doubted that she'd forgotten her previous orders. Just yesterday she'd told him to plan on leaving as soon as Jack was safely returned home. Had something changed her mind? Well, he wasn't about to be the one to remind her. Perhaps she didn't want to be left alone with the children until Ambrose returned to the station.

Lottie shooed Rose out of the room. "You get your nightgown on and say your prayers. I'll be along shortly to tuck you in."

Rose climbed down off her chair and came

around to stand at Wade's side. "Good night, Mr. Wade. I'm glad you're back."

When she held up her arms for a hug, Wade obliged her. If he squeezed her extra tight, she didn't protest. He was glad to be back and wished he wasn't going to have to leave. He watched as Rose scampered down the hall and out of sight, his heart heavy with knowing he was going to miss watching her grow up. There was some comfort in knowing that his wasn't the only heart she'd win in her life.

"I'm going to take a look around outside and then turn in for the night." He shuffled to his feet and reached for the rifle.

Lottie was nervously twisting a towel in her hands. "Should I try to stay up and stand guard?"

Wade knew she'd had no more sleep in the past twenty-four hours than he had. He considered the matter, but a flash of lightning that brightened the whole room decided it for him.

"I don't think that's necessary. With that storm coming in, anyone in their right mind is going to find someplace dry to wait it out."

"Then I'll finish up the kitchen and head to bed myself after I check on the children."

When Wade started out the door, Lottie reached out and placed her hand on his arm. Despite his weariness, his unruly body responded to even that fleeting touch.

"I know I didn't say much earlier, but thank you for all you did to bring Jack home."

"It was my job."

The light in her eyes dimmed at his words. He would have apologized, but he'd told her the truth, or at least part of it. He would have gone after any child because he was a marshal and because that was the kind of man he wanted to be. But the truth was, he went after Jack because it was his duty as a member of the family, even if he was the only one who saw him in that role.

"If there isn't anything else, I'll see you in the morning." He studied her face, hoping for even the smallest sign that she would offer him more than a lonely bed to sleep in. When she turned away to clear the dinner dishes, he walked away feeling more alone than he had in years.

Wade would leave. He had to go for more reasons than she could count, so there was no question about it. And when he rode away, either with Ambrose as his prisoner or without, Lottie would never see him again. The very thought hurt because she hadn't stored up nearly enough memories to savor in the lonely years to come.

The rain rattled against the windows as the wind rampaged through the trees outside. Every so often, a limb would give up the battle and snap off, crashing to ground in the woods. A couple had only narrowly missed hitting the house. One part of her mind decided that she could keep Rose and Jack busy tomorrow dragging the windfall branches around to the woodpile. Once the wood dried out some, it would make good kindling.

But somewhere in her mind, her thoughts were of a different nature. Earlier, when Wade had disappeared down the hall to his room, she'd been reminded of her earlier plan to join him there to build up a few more of those memories. Of course, that was before she'd found out that he'd lied to her about who and what he was.

The irony of the situation didn't escape her. From the beginning, she'd tried to guard her heart from a man who freely admitted to being a drifter and a gambler. Though she didn't want to tie her life to such a man, she could at least be grateful that he was honest about his wandering tendencies. Unlike her father and Ambrose, Wade had made sure she knew exactly what he was.

Except that he'd lied to her from the first minute they'd met. How could she forgive him for that? Sighing, she stared out into the violence of the night. Most women fell for a man and then found out he was far less than he'd promised. Wade, on the other hand, was a U.S. marshal with a strong sense of family and honor. He'd even tried to warn her in his own way by telling her that the passion that they'd shared had been honest and real.

The house shivered in the onslaught of wind and rain. The weather fit her mood perfectly. The wild power behind the storm seemed to replenish her own energy, making her restless and hungry for the shared heat of a woman and a man.

And what she needed—or rather, who—was only a short distance down the hallway.

Tomorrow would bring its own problems, but maybe tonight there was a way she could find some peace, if only for a few hours. Quickly, before her courage faltered, she took determined steps toward her bedroom door. On the way, she reached for her wrapper but changed her mind. Her nightgown, soft with years of wear and washing, felt heavy against her skin. Another layer would only be one more thing she needed to shed besides her second thoughts and conscience.

Barefoot, she slipped down the hallway, pausing long enough to make sure the storm wasn't disturbing the children, especially Rose. After tucking their blankets up around their chins and pressing a kiss to their cheeks, Lottie drew a calming breath and walked toward that last door on the hall.

The doorknob felt cold to the touch, sending a shiver coursing through her of something that wasn't quite desire and wasn't quite fear, but a heady mixture of both. It wasn't too late to back away and run back to her own lonely bed, but she'd have enough nights in her life to sleep alone. This didn't have to be one of them.

With new resolve, she turned the handle and swung the door open. As she took the first step, lightning lit up the room. Her breathing stopped. Wade wasn't asleep. He wasn't even lying down.

In a heartbeat, he was on his feet and standing right in front of her. When he started to speak, she put her hand across his lips.

"No questions, no promises."

He pressed a gentle kiss against her fingertips, sending a jolt through her that made the lightning pale by comparison. She reached out with her hands and her heart. He met her, touch for touch, need for need.

"Lottie . . ." He made her name a prayer in the heavy night air.

She closed the last little distance between them, lifting her hands to rest on his shoulders. His welcoming smile gave her the last bit of courage she needed to offer herself up as a woman to this particular man. His lips teased at hers as he brushed his mouth across hers with feather-light kisses.

When his mouth wandered on to trace the line of her jaw to her ear and back, she arched her neck to ease his way. To her delight, his shirt had already been open. It was a simple thing to slip her hands inside to touch his skin, enjoying the contrasts of smooth muscles and the light dusting of crisp hair on his chest.

Feeling more daring, she tugged his shirt down his arms, reveling in the groan of approval that rumbled through him. His hands began to match hers move for move. He tugged at the ribbon that held her gown closed. That done, he eased it away from her neck as he nibbled along her collarbone, making her ache for more.

He backed toward his narrow bed; she followed him willingly. It was only a matter of a few feet, but it seemed to take forever to reach their goal. Wade immediately sat down and then pulled her astride his lap. She whimpered with pleasure at the sudden pressure of his need against the center of her own heat. No doubt such a position was scandalous, but she was beyond caring.

He bunched her gown in his hands and lifted it over her head, leaving nothing between them but his drawers, which offered little protection. She rocked against him, slowly at first, glorying in the power it gave her over this man. He cupped her bottom and thrust up against her, matching his movements to hers. Then, as he molded her breasts to fit his palms, she could feel the crest coming, but she didn't want to ride it out without him surging inside her.

"Take me!" she begged. "Now, please, oh Lord, please, Wade."

He lifted her to the side as he shed the last of his clothes, leaving them skin to skin, wet heat against silken steel. He eased her back down onto his lap, fitting himself to her, becoming part of her for the time their passion built. Her body stretched, learning the shape and fit of him as she took him deep inside.

He stilled her rocking, slowing the tempo as he suckled one breast and then the other. When both were pebble hard, he palmed them and squeezed. It felt like heaven and fanned the flames until her body felt as if it were no longer hers alone, but one with his.

Finally, she panted out his name as he moved her beneath him, wresting control of the moment. He knelt on the bed, positioning her legs over his shoulders. He thrust once, twice, then times too numerous to count, pounding his passion into the heart of her. Then, with one last move, she flew over the edge and took him with her.

He didn't know why she'd made the trip down the hallway to find him, but he was damn glad that she had. He'd been on the verge of seeking her out, unsure of his welcome. At first he'd thought the sound at the door had just been the storm making itself felt. Then she'd stepped across the threshold, and his world had felt right for the first time in days.

As the last tremors of passion faded, he looked down into the mysteries in her eyes and wondered what she was thinking. He wasn't sure he wanted to know. Now wasn't the time for questions or even explanations. Here in the darkness, he would accept what she could offer and give whatever she'd take in return from him.

With that in mind, he eased his body away from hers and stretched out beside her. This bed wasn't all that comfortable, but with her in it, it felt like heaven itself. He rose up on one elbow and then leaned down to kiss her already swollen lips. She brushed her fingertips along the side of his face and then tangled them in his hair, tugging him closer yet.

She immediately teased him back with the tip of her tongue, and once again he was lost in the wonder of her kiss. It was too soon for both of them to stir the embers of passion back into raging flames. Instead, it was enough to draw warmth from the sweetness of the moment.

"Lottie . . ."

She shushed him. "Don't talk."

"But . . ."

"Please, let it be for now. Just hold me."

He had questions and things he needed to tell her. Such as how sorry he was about lying to her and that he wasn't the man she'd wanted him to be. Maybe, if he'd been daring enough, he might even have told her that he loved her. But right now, he wasn't that brave, nor did he want to be. Any wrong move on his part might send her fleeing back down that hallway to her own bed behind a closed door.

So he held back his words, cursing himself for both a coward and a fool. Tucking Lottie's head under his chin, he gave himself over to sleep, his last memory the scent of her hair teasing his senses.

Just as he feared, Lottie was already gone from his bed when he woke up. He supposed that the fact that he slept through her leaving was testimony to how exhausted he'd really been. On the other hand, he wasn't doing all that well at guarding the house if he couldn't even keep track of his lover.

He dragged himself upright and sat on the edge of the bed until he cleared out some of the cobwebs cluttering up his mind. Finally, he shuffled to his feet and stood over the basin on the bedside table and splashed water on his face. That done, he pulled on the cleanest clothes he could find and wandered out into the kitchen.

Lottie and the children were nowhere to be seen, but she'd left him a plate warming on the stove. He picked it up and carried it out onto the porch. Just as he'd suspected, all three of them were already hard at work around the station.

If he knew more of what Lottie's expectations for him were for the day, he'd be more willing to gulp down his food and pitch in to help. But if all she was going to do was hand him marching orders, well, then, he'd dawdle over breakfast as long as possible.

He was just finishing up his eggs when Rose saw him and jabbed Lottie with her elbow. Lottie, who'd been helping Rose water the garden, immediately started for him. He braced himself for the worst.

"Do you think we should go looking for Ambrose?" She shaded her eyes from the sun as she looked out toward the woods. "I would have thought he'd be back by now."

Wade set his plate down on the edge of the porch. "I plan on going after him."

With the children out of hearing, she let all of her worry show. "Do you think he's all right?"

Determined to lie to her no longer, Wade shook his head. "I honestly don't know. He told me to take Jack and run, so I did. It didn't set right with me to leave him behind, but neither of us was willing to risk the boy."

"Do you know where to look for him?"

"I'll backtrack the way we went before. If I don't find him there, I will work my way back around their camp and try trailing him from that direction."

He had to tell her the rest.

"Lottie, you have to know that if I do find your brother-in-law, I'm bound to take him back to stand trial for his crimes."

Lottie's face blanched, making her eyes appear huge and frightened. She immediately looked over her shoulder toward Jack and Rose. "He's their father. You care about them; I know you do. How can you take him back to stand trial when you know they'll hang him?"

Wade slowly rose to his feet, feeling the full weight of his oath as a law officer. "It's my job, Lottie. It will damn near kill me to hurt those two, but I'll still do it."

"He's been a decent father to them. You know he has. Don't do this." Her hands knotted into white-knuckled fists.

His stomach hurt just seeing the pain in her eyes. "That doesn't change what else he's done. People have died at his hands—not only his gang members, but good, decent people whose only crime was to stand between him and the money he wanted to steal."

That was when the light died in her eyes. She stepped back, giving him a wide berth as she walked past him into the house. He debated whether or not to follow her, but before he could decide, she was back out. She had his few belongings in her hands.

"Do what you want to, but don't come back here again." Her voice cracked and a single tear rolled down her cheek. Before she turned her back on him again, she threw his saddlebags into the dirt at his feet.

"Lottie . . ."

"Go."

"I love you."

Her back stiffened, as if his words were a physical blow meant to do her harm. "Strange way you have of showing it, Marshal." She somehow made his title sound like the worst curse word she could think of.

Feeling far older than his years, he picked up his belongings. "If the others come riding in, will you at least point them in the right direction?"

Her only answer was to slam the door as she disappeared into the house. He wanted to go after her, but he'd promised himself that he'd never be less than honest with her again. If he walked away from this without bringing Bardell and his men to justice, he'd be lying about all that he held dear. If she couldn't accept him for who he was, then there was no hope for them anyway.

Knowing that it was for the best no matter how much it hurt, he headed for the barn. One way or the other, he was going to finish what he came to do.

Fourteen

Instead of leaving everything fresh and cool, the storm had only made the air feel heavy, damp, and hotter than hell. Sweat poured off Wade's face as he rode through the woods, watching both the trail and the woods for some sign that Ambrose had passed that way. The mosquitoes were out early, hanging in the air like patches of gray fog. Their constant buzzing around his face wasn't helping his mood at all.

So far, he hadn't seen another living being except one white-tailed deer. An eight-point buck, biggest damn deer he'd ever seen, had been dozing in the shadows when it came bolting out of the underbrush right in front of Wade's gelding. The horse had taken offense at the animal's sudden appearance and decided to rear and buck. Grim determination had kept Wade in the saddle, but not before he'd been slapped in the face by a couple of low branches and had his knee pinned against a sapling. He guessed it was lucky it wasn't the leg he'd been shot in, but then, he wasn't quite sure how to limp with both legs at the same time.

All too aware of time passing, he was growing more worried about Ambrose. It would be ironic if the wily bastard had managed to elude every lawman who'd come after him, only to be brought down by his own men.

Wade dismounted at a small spring long enough to water his horse and to make sure he was still following the same route that he and Ambrose had used to find Jack. If he didn't find Bardell along the trail, he'd circle around the outlaw camp and then try to find the other way out into the valley. The rain the night before would have wiped out all sign of someone's passing, making tracking all but impossible.

It was always possible that Ambrose had made sure that Jack had gotten away safely and then taken off himself. He had to know that Wade would come looking for him, not as a friend but as a deputy marshal. The man was surely a puzzle. He had a way about him that kept Wade guessing. One minute he was a caring father; the next he'd slit his own man's throat without a second's remorse.

But at no time did Wade think the man would surrender without a fight. For the hundredth time since he'd left the station behind, Lottie's face flashed through his mind. He'd hurt her. Nothing he could say or do would ever wash away the guilt he felt, but he had no choice in the matter. Sure, he could ride away and not look back. But his conscience wouldn't allow him to sleep nights knowing he'd let a cold-blooded killer slip through his grasp.

Even if it meant that Lottie would allow him back into her life. He wouldn't buy his own happiness at the cost of other innocent folks losing their money or, worse yet, their lives.

He refilled his canteen and soaked his bandanna with cool water. He wiped his face clean of sticky sweat and then tied the scarf around his neck. It would help keep him cool for a few minutes anyway.

Giving his horse a break, he walked along the faint trail for a short distance before mounting up.

About halfway up the hillside, something caught his attention. He froze in his tracks, tilting his head to the side to see if he could pick up the faint sound again. The jingle of a bridle came from off to his left. Drawing his gun, he made his way toward a clump of gray boulders about thirty feet away. Before he'd gone even ten feet, he heard it again, louder this time.

Even from a distance, he could see a horse standing head-down and exhausted. And unless he was mistaken, it was the same roan that Ambrose had been riding.

He hurried his steps, figuring whoever was hiding in the rocks was likely to be of little danger to Wade or anyone else. That didn't mean he was going to go rushing in like a damn fool. He circled around, his gun cocked and ready, until he could see inside the rough circle.

"Ambrose, is that you?"

"McCord? About time you came looking for me."

Wade holstered his gun and hurried his steps, relieved that the outlaw felt good enough to be complaining. He swung his legs over a down log and came up against the business end of Bardell's rifle. Wade shoved it aside, deciding that if the outlaw had wanted to shoot him, he'd already be dead.

"Where the hell have you been?"

Bardell laughed weakly and leaned back against a boulder for support. His right sleeve was crusted with blood, and there was a nasty gash along his face.

"Well, I managed to lead the bastards on a merry chase before they almost caught up with me. Luckily, that storm hit and gave them second thoughts about being out. No doubt, they holed up somewhere warm and dry. I don't know why they haven't come after me today, but I'm not complaining."

He tried to stand up but almost fell flat on his face. Wade caught him before he hit the ground and helped him over to a log to sit down. That done, he fetched his own horse, figuring the rocks offered pretty good cover should trouble come riding by.

"Have you had anything to eat?"

The outlaw shook his head. "Not since yesterday some time. My canteen's empty, too."

Wade offered him his water to drink and then pulled some bread out of his saddlebags. It wasn't much, but it would tide the weary man over until he could get him back to the station.

"Can you ride?"

"Hell, yes."

But when Bardell tried to sit up straighter, it was a poor effort at best. A quick glance a the sky told Wade that they had little time to rest and still make it back to the station before nightfall. That is, if Bardell's men didn't come charging over the ridge in the meantime.

"When do you think they'll be back?"

Bardell closed his eyes to give the matter some thought. He was silent so long, Wade was beginning to think he'd actually fallen asleep.

"Counting the two I took care of before we reached the camp, I managed to account for about four of them for sure. That leaves another three or four that were already in the valley. I think they might round up some more help before they come after me again."

"Do you think they'll go after the family again?"

"They did once; no reason to think they'd wouldn't do it again to get at me."

"There's a small spring down the hill. You wait here while I water your horse. Then we'll see about getting you back up in the saddle. You can ride my horse, and I'll lead yours to give it a rest."

When Bardell didn't argue, Wade led the weary beast down the hillside. He let it drink its fill slowly, making sure the water wouldn't do more harm than good. Finally, he left the horse tethered in a small patch of grass and trudged back up the hill after Bardell. His own legs were protesting the time spent on the rough ground, especially the knee that he'd hit on the tree. He shook his head. He and Bardell made a fine pair: one of them shot up, and the other still healing from the last time he'd come up against Bardell's men.

It took a couple of tries to get Bardell up in the saddle, but once he was settled, he looked as if he'd be able to make the trip back without too much trouble. Wade decided it would be easier just to lead both horses for as long as his legs would support him.

The effort left him too breathless to do much talking, and Bardell was more asleep than awake at the moment. When the trail opened up a bit, he decided to risk riding Bardell's roan for a while. Even though there'd been no sign of the outlaw gang, he felt time was running out. There wasn't much chance that the outlaws would give up and move on. For sure, they wouldn't think one wounded outlaw and a lone marshal would be much of a threat if they were determined to get their money out of Bardell any time soon.

He was certain that several deputies would be sent in response to his call for help, but there was no telling how far they'd have to come. At the worst, it could take a week or more for them to arrive, depending on how quickly Buck delivered the message.

He urged the exhausted roan into a faster pace, apologizing to the poor animal. Once they got back to the station, he'd give it a good rub-down and an extra ration of oats.

He glanced at his companion. He hadn't bothered asking Ambrose how badly he was hurt. Since he was holding the reins with his bloody arm, the wound couldn't be all that serious if he still had use of it. The cut on his face looked bad, but it wasn't a deep cut, just a bloody one.

If there was time, he'd stop at a creek along the way and clean Bardell up some to keep from upsetting Lottie more than she already was. Without knowing more about what they were up against, though, they couldn't risk it. Once again, the sense that time was running out kept driving him along, leaving him no choice but to keep pushing Bardell, himself, and even the horses harder than he liked. Since there was no time to disguise their tracks, anyone with eyes could follow their trail.

With luck, the two of them would reach the station soon and find everything was quiet and peaceful. But the back of his neck was itching something fierce, as if someone was following every move he made. And maybe someone was.

That thought had him asking his poor horse to pick up the pace once again. The poor animal shuffled its feet along faster for a few feet and then tried to slip back into a plodding walk again. Wade immediately kicked the roan lightly in the ribs, ordering it to speed up again.

Bardell spoke for the first time. "If I'm not mistaken, we should be able to see the station from the top of that next rise."

Wade, who had been concentrating on the horses, looked up and saw that Ambrose was right. Even the horses seemed to sense that the long trip was about over, because he no longer had to fight to keep them moving along at a good clip.

In fact, he was probably the only one who was in no hurry to reach the end of the trail. Lottie had already made it abundantly clear that he was no longer welcome at her home. And then there was the small matter of arresting Bardell and taking him back to stand trial.

Only the belief that danger still lurked around Lottie and her family kept him from bypassing the station altogether and taking his prisoner straight through to Springfield. But even if he did that, he'd still have to come back to face Lottie and the children. The same sense of duty that had him on the outlaw's trail would prevent him from sneaking off without letting them know what happened to Ambrose.

Besides, no matter what crimes Bardell had committed, he still deserved the chance to say good-bye to his children. The whole damn mess made Wade sick to his stomach.

Just as Ambrose predicted, Wade could see the station nestled in the clearing below. Despite all his problems, it still felt like coming home. Cursing himself for a fool, he spurred his horse into a bone-jarring trot. Nothing was going to get any easier by delaying the inevitable confrontation waiting for him ahead.

A loud crack snapped a branch right over Wade's head just as he started down the hillside. His first thought was that another storm was stirring up trouble in the area, but the sky was blue with only the occasional cloud to be seen.

Another crack sent a shower of leaves flying off the tree to the left. This time there was no mistaking the sound of a rifle shot. His horse needed no urging on his part to take off at a run, dragging Ambrose and his horse right along behind them.

"Hold on!" Wade shouted back over his shoulder. "We'll head straight for the house."

He tried to spot Lottie and the children, hoping that they would have the sense to barricade themselves in the house as soon as they heard the first shot. There sure as hell wouldn't be much time to go searching for them with Bardell's men hot on their trail.

Another volley of bullets kicked up a streak of dust too close for comfort. He could only hope their luck held out long enough to get to cover. As they neared the station, he debated settling for the closer haven of the barn, but he wasn't about to let the outlaws get between him and Bardell's family.

He kept the horses in the dubious cover of the trees as long as possible, breaking for the porch when they were within thirty yards of the house. He didn't need to tell Ambrose to keep his damn head down. Besides, the bastard had survived enough chases by angry, armed men to know how to live through it. Hell, he was an expert in the matter.

Evidently, Lottie had seen them coming, because the front door of the house swung open as Wade reined in the two exhausted horses. He hit the ground in one breath and pulled Ambrose down out of his saddle in the next. Together, the two men stumbled up the steps. Wade shoved Bardell into Lottie's waiting arms and spun back to the horses to retrieve the rifles and saddlebags. He took the time to uncinch the saddles, letting them drop to the ground. There was no time to do more for the poor beasts.

"Git!" he shouted and slapped the roan on the rump.

Tired of being abused, the two horses trotted off into the woods. Wade felt a fleeting bout of guilt for mistreating them, but there was nothing he could do about it right now. If he managed to survive the next few hours, he'd make it up to them with oats and the promised rub-down.

He picked up his saddle and tossed it on the porch, all too aware that he was making a fine target of himself. When he reached for the second one, he heard the door open again. Lottie had already dragged the first one in the door along with his saddlebags. He followed her in, kicking the door shut behind him.

"Throw the bar," he ordered as he rushed to the window to see if the unknown rifleman had come into sight.

The heavy beam sounded reassuringly solid as Lottie slid it into place. He studied the trees, watching for some telltale sign that Ambrose's men were moving into position. He thought he saw a flicker of movement not far from where he and Ambrose had left the woods. Several seconds later, he saw it again, a little closer in.

Right then, he'd give almost anything to know how many of the bastards were out there. He and Bardell should be able to hold off a few men until help arrived. But if they'd managed to round up a lot of help, they'd be able to wear the two of them down.

A hand touched his shoulder, causing him to jump about a mile straight up. On some level, he recognized the feel of Lottie's hand, because he didn't immediately turn and fire.

"What's happening?" she asked.

"Someone is shooting at us."

"Who?"

"Damn it, woman, how the hell should I know? Do you want me to go outside and ask?"

Lottie gasped and jerked her hand back, stepping away. Wade immediately regretted the sharpness of his words.

"I'm sorry. No sleep, a long trail, and being shot at has left me with the temper of a bear." He offered her an apologetic smile and then turned back to the window.

"I'll see to Ambrose."

Wade nodded. "Make sure you keep away from the windows and keep the children down on the floor."

"I will. When I get Ambrose's arm and face taken care of, I'll bring you a cup of coffee and something to eat."

"Bless you, woman."

Damn, now someone was moving around from the other direction. That there wasn't a back door was a mixed blessing. It meant that no one could come charging in from behind, but it also meant that there wasn't another way out if they needed to make a run for it.

A string of curses from behind him told him that Lottie wasn't being any too gentle in dressing her brother-in-law's wounds. She scolded him for it.

"Don't talk like that in front of me or the children!"

"Then don't pull on my sleeve. Soak it off."

Wade glanced over his should just in time to see

her give the cloth another yank. Ambrose let out another yelp.

"Don't be such a baby. Wade's wounds were worse and you didn't hear him whining like that."

"He was unconscious!"

"Keep arguing with me, and I'll knock you senseless myself."

One more tug and the rest of the sleeve pulled free from the crusted blood on his arm. She immediate started sopping up the fresh flow of blood. She left the wound uncovered for a short time, no doubt trying to make sure it bled itself clean. That done, she washed his arm and then began to wrap a strip of clean cloth around the upper arm.

Wade smothered a smile when he saw that she wasn't being any gentler with the face wound. Ambrose glared at her but had the good sense to keep his mouth shut. It was obvious that Lottie was seriously out of sorts with her brother-in-law at the moment. She'd no doubt figured out right away that the reason for their current predicament could be laid right at his feet.

She dabbed at the open wound with a cloth soaked in pure whiskey. It had to sting like hell, but Wade had to give it to Ambrose for keeping his mouth shut. His knuckles were white with the effort of holding back any complaints. The children were scared enough without their father upsetting them more.

As soon as Lottie was finished torturing him, Ambrose pushed himself to his feet and picked up his rifle. He joined Wade at the window.

"See anything?"

Wade kept his voice low. "They've been working their way around the house. I've only seen two so far, but they wouldn't be attacking without backup."

"I'd guess that not all of them are here yet. They sent a couple ahead to keep us penned in while they round up all their cousins and uncles and whoever else they can convince to join in the fun."

That said, Ambrose leaned against the wall for support. He looked more tired than badly hurt. Even so, the pinched look around his mouth made Wade wonder how long he'd hold up if his men decided to attack in force.

"Go lie down."

Ambrose started to protest, but Wade shook his head. "I need to know I can depend on you. Right now you couldn't pull that trigger, much less hit anything you aim at."

Wearily the outlaw nodded. "Call me when you need me."

"Don't worry, I will."

Lottie was still bustling around the stove. "Go lie down in my room. I have the children playing on the floor in the hall."

Ambrose snitched a piece of bread off a plate. Lottie slapped at his fingers, but then handed him another slice.

"Thanks." Ambrose lowered his voice, but not enough. "No matter what, wake me in a couple of hours. Your lawman boyfriend isn't much better off than I am."

Wade pretended not to hear that particular comment, but he took some pleasure in the realization that Lottie hadn't corrected Ambrose. He continued to watch the trees, grateful for the few minutes of peace no matter what the reason behind it.

Lottie interrupted his reverie. "Come sit down and eat. I can stand watch for a bit."

Wade handed her his rifle and gratefully sat down at the table. The bowl of leftover stew smelled heavenly. Hell, he couldn't remember the last time he'd eaten. He made short work of the meal, sopping up the last of the gravy with a hunk of bread. It wasn't the same as a full night's sleep, but he felt a hell of a lot better than he had.

Lottie had all her attention trained on the limited view outside the small front window. If he had to gauge her mood, he'd guess she was furious. Not that he blamed her.

All she wanted out of life was to raise her small family in peace and quiet. One by one, all the men in her life had betrayed her, himself included. There wasn't much he could do to fix things for her except make sure that this particular bunch of desperadoes didn't bother her again.

It was a sign of how damn tired he was that it just now occurred to him to ask, "Did Buck take my message back to Springfield?"

She looked back at him and nodded, her sad eyes reflecting the hurt caused by his betrayal. "He said he'd take it directly to the sheriff." After glancing toward her bedroom door, she had a question of her own. "What will happen to Ambrose if they come?"

A sudden burst of gunfire saved him from the necessity of answering. He lurched to his feet and took the rifle back from Lottie. A sole rider approached the house, waving a white rag tied to the barrel of his rifle. Smart man. If Wade refused to accept the sign of truce, he only had to lower the rifle to fire back.

"Hey, you in the house!"

Wade didn't hesitate. He used the butt of his rifle to break out the glass before answering. The loud crash startled the man's horse, but he fought it back under control with the ease of an expert horseman.

"I'm listening." Wade kept his gun trained right on the man's midsection.

"What was that noise?" Jack came running into the room. Rose was right behind him.

To Lottie, he whispered, "Get Ambrose. Take him his rifle and tell him what's going on out here. He needs to make sure that this one isn't keeping me busy while his friends come at us from behind."

He nodded toward the children. "Then take them in the hallway and lie flat on the floor until I say otherwise."

The rider was talking again. "We've got no problem with the woman and her children. Send them out and we'll give them safe passage."

"Like you did with the boy?" Wade taunted. "If that's your idea of safe passage, then I wouldn't trust you with a dead dog."

"Listen, mister, you don't know what you've got yourself into here. We've got you surrounded. It's not going to go easy for you or that bastard you're harboring. Give yourselves up now and I promise to watch out for the woman."

Wade would give five years' salary to know how far away help was. He and Ambrose could hold the outlaws off as long as the ammunition held out, unless the bastards decided to burn them out. It was time to lay his cards on the table and trust to the lady to get the posse here in time.

"You're talking to Deputy U.S. Marshal Wade McCord, mister, and I'll tell you what *you've* gotten yourself into," Wade hollered back, echoing the man's own words. "Ambrose Bardell is my prisoner. Be damn sure you understand that you'll have to go through me to get to him."

He punctuated his threat with a shot in the dirt right in front of the man's horse. Once again, the man struggled to bring the animal back under control.

"Well, lawman, the only place you'll be taking your prisoner is straight to hell."

With that, he spurred his horse into a gallop and disappeared into the trees. Another volley of shots peppered the ground outside right up to the porch. Silence hung heavily, building up tension as if lightning were about to explode over the valley. After a minute, maybe two, had passed, Ambrose stuck his head out Lottie's door.

"Nothing moving out here. Anything on your side?"

"Not so far." Wade backed away from the shattered remains of the window. "I'm going to check out the back."

Ambrose took Wade's place in the front. With only two of them, it was going to be damn near impossible to keep up a constant vigil. Lottie was sitting in the short hallway, reading a book to the children. He wanted to order her to lie down beside them, but he knew she'd only wait until he was out of sight to do what she damn well felt like.

As he stepped over Jack and then Rose, he could feel Lottie's eyes following him. No doubt, she wanted very much to know what had occurred outside, but neither adult would discuss it in front of the children. He just wished there were some way to get the three of them out of the house and out of harm's way.

That clearly wasn't possible, so that left setting up a line of defense to keep the only innocents in this battle safe and sound until help arrived. He checked out the back window but couldn't see anything. Feeling frustrated, he resisted the urge to break something, even another window. He headed back to where Ambrose was waiting.

"See anything?"

Ambrose edged back from his vantage point. "I think I've counted about four of them. They don't seem to be in much of a hurry."

Wade poured himself and Ambrose each a cup of coffee. "Could be they're waiting for sundown. They'd be less of a target that way."

Ambrose set his rifle down and accepted the cup. He wrapped his hands around it, as if to absorb its heat. He couldn't have got more than a few minutes of sleep, but his color had improved considerably.

He cocked his head and looked at Wade. "So I'm your prisoner, am I?"

Wade was in no mood to be baited, so he ignored the question and asked one of his own. "Any suggestions on how to get Lottie and the children the hell out of here?"

For the first time, Ambrose looked worried. "No. If the woods were closer to the house, I'd say take them and run for it before their reinforcements show up. But the way things stand, you'd be an easy target no matter how many of them are out there."

He took another long drink of the coffee before speaking again. "Besides, they're smart enough to realize that was you who helped get Jack back. Now that they know you're a lawman, they want your hide as much as they want mine. That hideout has been our secret for a long time; they won't let you live long enough to tell anyone else about it."

"I already did."

"The hell you did! You haven't had time."

"Lottie sent word to Springfield with Buck when the stage went through. I'm expecting about half a dozen deputies to come riding in anytime now."

That was enough to make Ambrose collapse on the nearest chair. He shook his head in bafflement. "Well, that beats all. I don't rightly know which is worse: knowing my own men want to kill me or knowing your friends will want to do the same thing, only legal like."

"That's not funny."

Neither of them had heard Lottie walk back into the kitchen. She glared at both of them. "What if I'd been Jack or Rose hearing you talk like that? I swear, I'd be surprised if either one of you has as much sense as those mules out there. To tell the truth, I know they have you both beat. They do an honest day's work without complaining. That's more than I can say about you two."

Ambrose stood up and pulled her into his arms. "I'm sorry, Lottie, about everything. We'll get through this somehow."

Wade watched as she accepted her brother-in-law's offer of comfort. When she realized that he was watching her, she very deliberately turned her head in the other direction. It made him sick to know she preferred the company of a notorious criminal to his, but he couldn't blame her. No matter what crimes Bardell had committed, he was family.

Wade wasn't. It was that simple.

Turning away from the scene before he did something rash, he picked up his rifle and made the rounds again. All was clear outside the front window. Next he checked the side window in Lottie's room. He very deliberately averted his eyes from her unmade bed. It stirred up memories and needs he couldn't afford to think about right then.

Nothing was moving out in the woods as far as he could see. That left the back of the house. To get there he had to go past the children again. So far, the two of them had been pretty quiet, but they had to be wondering what was going on. He was relieved to see them hovering over the checkerboard, more concerned about their next move than the trouble he and their father had brought down on their heads.

They barely looked up as he stepped over the board and made his way back to his little room. This time he was more successful. If the sun hadn't been on its way down, he'd have never spotted them. But two of Bardell's former gang members were smoking cigarettes about twenty feet back into the trees. If they'd been his, he'd have called them on the carpet for such stupidity.

Instead, he took aim and made sure one of them wouldn't live long enough to know better. The other one took a couple of wild shots back at Wade before retreating farther back into the shadows. This time, Wade aimed farther back and squeezed off another round. He didn't stand much chance of hitting anything, but he figured it was about time those bastards realized that he wasn't simply going to wait for them to come charging in.

Ambrose and Lottie ran into the room just as he fired the second time. When the two of them both tried to fit through the door at the same time, he almost laughed but thought better of it.

The outlaw was no doubt disappointed to have missed the action, but Lottie definitely felt otherwise.

"Are they coming?" She succeeded in pushing past her brother-in-law to plant herself in front of Wade.

"One of them won't be going anywhere again. I'm not sure about the second one."

"There were only two of them?" She made as if

to look out the window, but Wade stepped in front of her.

"On this side of the house. Now there's only one."

Lottie stood up on her toes to see over his shoulder. Even at that distance, she could see the dead man's legs and boots. She eased back down and closed her eyes. When Wade saw her lips moving, he realized she was praying.

The thought disgusted him. Right that minute she cared more about the soul of a murdering bank robber than she did about him. Well, if she was asking God to forgive him, she shouldn't bother. He didn't regret gunning the scum down in cold blood. If it meant keeping her and the children safe, he'd do it again. And again. And again, until every one of Ambrose's men was dead or running for his life.

If Lottie Hammond didn't approve, that was too damn bad. He was tired of feeling guilty about a situation that Ambrose Bardell had caused. Rather than point that out to her again, he pushed past her and her beloved brother-in-law. Out in the kitchen, he poured himself another cup of coffee, knowing it was a damn poor substitute for a good night's sleep. Unfortunately, he couldn't risk sleeping until he knew how the men outside were going to react to the situation.

He got his answer when he made the mistake of walking directly in front of the broken window. The wood around the missing window exploded, sending shards of glass and splinters of wood flying. He ignored the sudden pain from a couple that hit his arm and stung his face. Trying to conserve ammunition, he held off returning fire until he could figure out what direction the shots had come from.

A second shot buried itself in the wall behind him.

To hit where it did, the gunman had to be almost straight out from the window, possibly alongside the barn. He risked a quick peek out the window. Sure enough, he could see the faint shadow of someone standing along the far side of the barn. Unfortunately, he'd pulled back far enough that Wade couldn't get off a clear shot. Figuring it wouldn't hurt to let him know he'd been spotted anyway, Wade fired a couple of quick shots right at the corner of the barn and then dropped to the floor.

Rose and Jack came running into the room, crying in fear. Wade charged across the room to gather them into his arms. He dragged them back out of the kitchen. Despite the limited space in the hallway, it offered the best protection from flying bullets.

"You two stay here and stay down." There wasn't time for him to be polite or to coax them into obeying him.

He started to yell for Lottie, but before he could say a word, she came out of his room. "Keep these two right here."

"Don't order me around," she snapped even as she sank down onto the floor and held her arms out to the children.

"Don't argue with me now, Lottie. I've got more important things to do than to waste time trying to be polite." He softened his next words with a quick wink at Rose and a pat on Jack's shoulder. "I know this is all pretty scary, but you know your father and I won't let anyone harm either of you. Still, it's important that you do exactly what we say."

Jack gave him a shaky smile. "We will, Mr. Wade."

Rose looked worried and stuck her thumb in her mouth. She crawled up onto Lottie's lap and buried her face against her. Wade wanted to comfort her himself, but now wasn't the time.

Ambrose stuck his head out of the back room. "They're moving again. I can't see how many there are, but they're going try something damn soon."

Wade ran for the window and looked out. Bardell was right. The bastards were working themselves up to another attack. And, unless he was mistaken, the reinforcements they were waiting for had arrived.

"Lottie! Bring me all the ammunition you can find! Split it between me and Ambrose."

He fished around in his saddlebags for his own supplies. He hoped she had better luck than he did, because otherwise the pickings were pretty slim. She came crawling into the room about the time he'd reloaded both his handguns and his rifle.

That's when he noticed that she had her own rifle with her. Instead of handing it to him, she was heading into her bedroom with it.

"Where the hell are you going?"

"I'll take the window in my room."

"Like hell you will. Get back in the hallway with Jack and Rose."

She shot him a look that would melt paint. "I've told you before that you work for me. That puts me in charge. I won't cower in the hallway and leave a window uncovered. What's to keep one of them from coming in that way while his friends keep you busy on this side?"

He hated to admit that her argument made sense, but the truth was, he needed her and her gun.

"Keep your head down, damn it."

"Yes, sir." She gave him a mocking salute and crawled out of sight.

Right then all hell broke loose outside, and he was too busy returning fire to worry about more than keeping Bardell's men from charging the house.

Fifteen

The gunfire finally slacked off. She sank down to the floor and leaned back against the wall. Lordy, she was tired. The two men must be almost dead on their feet. Poor choice of words, but close to the truth, anyway. She could hear Wade cursing a blue streak, but he sounded mad rather than hurt. At least she hoped that was the case. Ambrose hadn't stuck his nose out of the back room since the shooting had begun, but since she could hear shots coming from that direction occasionally, he had to be holding his own.

She just wished she could be out in the hallway with the children. The poor babes had to be terrified by now. She could only be grateful that they were doing as they'd been told. None of the three adults had time to hold their hands through this. If they got through it all—no, make that *when* they got through it—some fancy talking would be needed to help the children understand what had happened.

And why.

She'd never wanted them to know what kind of man their father was, but maybe she hadn't done them any favors by protecting them from the truth. They'd grown up thinking that the only thing different about Ambrose was that his job involved traveling. How was she going to explain to them why Wade was going to drag him off to stand trial?

Then there was Wade himself. In a single instant, he'd changed from a poorly paid hired hand into a bona fide deputy U.S. marshal, complete with badge and orders to follow. Once again she berated herself for not seeing through him sooner. That the man had too much character to be a down-on-his-luck gambler should have been obvious to even the casual observer.

And her feelings about him had been anything but casual. Even now, when he made her furious and his betrayal hurt. Despite it all, she still hungered for the comfort of his arms and the sweetness of his touch.

Her eyes burned with exhaustion and grief. There was no way anybody was going to end up happy when the last shot was fired. According to Wade, help should be on its way. But even if the marshals arrived in time to save them all, there was the little matter of Ambrose being Wade's prisoner.

She swiped her apron across her eyes, wiping away the few tears that managed to escape. This was no time for feeling sorry for herself or even the children. Realizing that she wasn't accomplishing anything by wallowing in self-pity, she pushed herself back up onto her knees and looked through the window.

Outside, night was at most only minutes away. Until the moon rose directly overhead, she wouldn't be able to see more than a few feet beyond the house. As long as they didn't light any lamps inside, then their attackers were as blind as she was.

Perhaps she could risk leaving her post long enough to check on Rose and Jack. She crept across the room, carrying her rifle with her. As soon as she slipped out of the room, both of them came flying to her. She laid her rifle down within reach and let the children crawl into her lap. Truth was, she needed their comfort as much as they needed hers.

Wade and Ambrose must have had the same idea, because all of a sudden everyone was in the hallway. Ambrose held his arms out to his daughter. She went willingly, while Jack reached out for Wade. Lottie would have felt abandoned, but she knew on some level that the men needed the same reassurance that everyone was safe and sound—for now.

That didn't mean that she wanted to watch the two of them acting as if nothing was wrong other than the house's being under siege. How could they smile at the children when the two of them were about to tear Jack and Rose's world apart?

"You all stay here. I'll fix some bacon and eggs." She was on her feet and around the corner into the kitchen before anyone could say a word. Rather than stumble around in the dark, she lit a single lamp and turned the wick as low as it would go.

By the time she had her skillet on the stove and the fire stoked up, she was no longer alone. Silently Wade took the slab of bacon from her hands and sliced it just the way she liked it. Even that small gesture was upsetting. Maybe he was only trying to help, but she didn't need any reminders of how much he'd come to know her in the weeks he'd shared her home.

"I said I'd fix us something to eat." She kept her back toward him as she started breaking eggs into a bowl.

"I know, but you're every bit as tired as the rest of us." He kept his voice low and calm, which only served to irritate her more.

"It's my kitchen."

From the sound of the knife hitting the plate, he was now whacking off chunks of bacon instead of slicing it. He wasn't as cool-headed as he wanted her to think.

Another loud whack was followed by a muttered obscenity. "No one said it wasn't." *Whack, whack, mutter.*

Suddenly, she felt like smiling. "If you're having trouble with that, why don't you get out and let me do my job?"

"That does it!"

Wade slammed the knife down on the table and came at her. He caught her arm and spun her around to face him. His eyes swirled with shades of green and fury.

"Now listen here, Lottie Hammond! Damn it, this is not all my fault. Some of it, maybe, but not all of it. Right now I'm working on no sleep and precious little to eat. You've made it abundantly clear that you don't want me here, but neither of us has any choice in the matter. Even if I could get out of here without getting shot full of holes, I wouldn't leave."

He never raised his voice much above a harsh whisper. He paused to take a breath and then started in on her again. "Up until the other deputies show up to help out, you and those children need me or at least my gun."

That last part sent a flash of pain across his face. She wished she could deny the truth of his words, but she wasn't that much of a liar. At the very least, she owed him an apology.

"I'm sorry. I do appreciate your help." Almost against her wishes, her fingers found their way up to trace the shape of his jaw. After the briefest of touches, she yanked her wayward hand back down to her side. "I may not like everything you've done,

Wade, but you're much more than that gun or even that star."

Afraid that she'd do something really foolish, such as try to kiss him, she turned back to the eggs. He stood beside her for another few seconds before walking away, leaving the badly butchered bacon lying in a greasy heap on the table.

Dinner was an uncomfortable meal. They all huddled in the narrow hallway in almost complete darkness. Ambrose had wanted to light another lamp, but Wade argued against it. In the end, they'd settled on one small candle, its light muted by setting it inside an upended crate. The narrow circle of light didn't do much for their spirits, but it was a step above eating in complete darkness.

The children had long since given in to the need for rest. Rose was curled up against her father on one side while Jack was on the other. Ambrose finished off the last of his meager meal and set his plate down on the floor. That done, he leaned back against the wall and closed his eyes. The dark shadows under his eyes weren't entirely due to the poor lighting.

Wade watched as Lottie gently spread a quilt over her brother-in-law as he slept. The jealousy he felt was a familiar companion. He'd fought the same pain years ago watching Lily with Cal. The only difference was that this time it was so much worse. Looking back, he realized he'd loved Lily with all the passion of youth and inexperience. With Lottie, though, he knew damn well what he stood to lose if she insisted on casting him out of her life.

All because of her misguided feelings of loyalty to a man who'd brought nothing but trouble right to her door. Unable to watch any longer, he closed his own eyes and let sleep overtake him. With luck, by the time daylight woke them all up, help would be at hand.

It seemed that no sooner did he manage to find a comfortable way to sit and sleep, when pandemonium erupted outside again. In one fluid motion he was on his feet, running for the front window with Lottie and Ambrose right behind him. When he realized that she was trying to force her way between the two men in order to look out, he shoved her back.

"Damn it, Lottie, are you trying to get yourself shot? Get back in the hallway with Jack and Rose."

Ambrose blocked her when she tried to get back between them. "If you have to do something, go check the other windows. Call one of us if you see anything."

Since all the shots seem to be coming from their side of the house, it seemed a safe enough suggestion. The new day was at best only an hour or two old. Shapes were still vague in the early morning light. That didn't prevent them from picking out a few likely targets to shoot at. They realized their mistake when they heard Lottie scream.

"Get back or I'll shoot."

The two men crossed the kitchen in less time than it took to think about it. The hall, which had seemed so crowded and small only moments before, suddenly stretched out forever to where Lottie stood, her rifle aimed at someone only she could see.

"I mean it. You take one more step and you're a dead man."

Ambrose and Wade froze midstep, not wanting

to startle their unwanted guest into doing something rash. Rose and Jack were wide awake, staring at their aunt with fear in their eyes.

Ambrose knelt down and placed his finger over his lips, warning them to stay quiet. He motioned toward the kitchen, shooing the two of them back out of the way. Wade had to admire the way they instantly responded to their father's unspoken orders. With the two of them around the corner and out of sight, he and their father had more maneuvering room in which to help Lottie.

Each passing second increased his fear for Lottie tenfold. He could have faced a dozen armed men without flinching, but the thought of Lottie facing even one was unacceptable. He drew his gun as he inched his way down the hallway. Ambrose kept pace with him on the opposite wall. Neither of them knew exactly what to expect.

Had someone actually squeezed through the narrow window without their hearing? It was unlikely, but not impossible. *Damn*, he hated not knowing. Ambrose stopped short of the doorway. Wade couldn't go quite that far—not without risking being seen. He considered jumping forward in hopes of drawing the unknown gunman's fire.

Ambrose beat him to it.

"Drop, Lottie!" Ambrose shouted as he spun away from the wall and right into the doorway, already firing.

Hoping like hell that Lottie had the good sense to follow orders for once, Wade started in after Ambrose. The early morning sun had yet to do much more than lighten the shadows in the bedroom, but each detail as he dove in the doorway seemed to stand out in stark relief.

Lottie was crouched on the floor over a body. She

was covered with blood as she tried to stop the bleeding with nothing more than her hands. Ambrose stood over her, staring down at the wounded man as if he were looking straight at hell. Something had gone very, very wrong.

Wade holstered his gun and dropped down beside Lottie. It was all too obvious that she fought a losing battle for the man's life. On closer look, he realized that the victim was little more than a boy, certainly no older than Wade had been when he'd lost the ranch and left home. Judging from the reactions of both Lottie and Ambrose, the youth was no stranger to either of them.

"Who is he?"

"Jeb." Ambrose leaned against the wall as if saying the name had drained the last of his energy.

The name sounded familiar, but it took a second or two before it came back to him. "He's the one you wanted me to look after."

The outlaw didn't answer, but his obvious pain said enough.

"Lottie?" The boy's words gurgled as blood trickled out of his mouth with the effort it took him to talk.

Lottie lifted his head into her lap. "I'm right here, Jeb. Don't talk."

He struggled to focus but relaxed a little when he found her face. "I heard what they were planning. Wanted to help. Not right for them to come after the boy that way."

She stroked his hair back from his forehead with a mother's touch. Mustering up a smile, she tried to shush him again. "You need to rest. Jack's all right. He's safe now."

"Tell my ma that . . ." his voice faded away as he struggled to form the words.

"You're going to tell her yourself, Jeb, once you get your strength back. Now let me get you up on the bed."

The boy shook his head and smiled slightly. "Never thought you'd lie, Miss Lottie. Promise me you'll tell her I loved her, but don't let on about what I've been doing. It would only upset her."

Tears streamed down Lottie's face, and Wade felt his own eyes burning. No one moved, knowing that Jeb's last breath was at best seconds away.

"Ambrose?"

At first, Wade thought Ambrose wouldn't answer, but he was wrong. He watched the outlaw squat down and pick up his friend's cold-looking hand in his own.

"Check on my family when you can."

"Sure thing, boy."

"Thanks. Knew I could trust you."

With a final rattling gasp, it was over. Her hands shaking, Lottie closed Jeb's eyes as she eased him back down onto the floor. Wade reached past her to pull the blanket off the bed. He covered the still form and then tried to help Lottie to her feet.

She didn't seem able to pull her eyes away from the boy. "I didn't recognize him. If he'd said something, anything, I would have known."

"You didn't shoot him. I did." Ambrose stood up. "I killed him."

Wade didn't know which one of them was in worse shape, but right now there wasn't time to mourn the boy. There was still the matter of the rest of Ambrose's men. With no one returning fire, they could be right on top of the house by now.

"Bardell, get back in the kitchen and check on the children. Call me if you need help." He shoved the stunned man in the direction of the door, hop-

ing the abrupt orders and movement would snap
him out of his daze.

Once Ambrose was gone, he turned his attention
back to Lottie. He hefted the pitcher on the bedside
table to see if there was any water left it. It was only
about half full, but it would do. He poured it into
the bowl and then grabbed the small towel that Lottie kept beside it.

That done, he pulled Lottie closer and began to
wipe Jeb's blood from her hands and arms. It took
several tries, but finally the worst of it was gone. He
rinsed out the towel and wrung out most of the
water. He used a clean cloth to wash Lottie's face.
Her lack of response was worrisome, but he didn't
know what else to do for her.

Finally, she looked up at him.

"He didn't have to die. He was just a boy."

Wade wasn't sure if she would accept comfort
from him, but he had to offer it. He wrapped his
arms around her shoulders and pulled her close.
All he could offer was the truth.

"He knew he risked being killed every time he
rode with Ambrose and his men."

He felt the first shudders of tears and tightened
his embrace. Between sobs, she choked out her
words.

"All he wanted to do was help his mother and
his family. Now who is she going to turn to?"

There was no easy answer to that one. Children
were orphaned every day. The pain of his own parents' deaths was one of his clearest memories, but
he and his brother had struggled together to survive. It had been hard, but they'd done it.

"She'll make it. Look at the kind of son she
raised. If the others are anything like him, they'll
do fine."

Evidently, she believed him, because Lottie's tears gradually dried up. When she pushed against his chest to get free, he reluctantly let her go.

"You go in with the others. I'll see to things in here and then be right out."

"Do you want me to help?"

"No, go on. Jack and Rose will be needing you."

Just as he had expected, the mention of their names was enough to send her flying from the room. Once she was gone, he bent down and grasped Jeb's shoulders and pulled him out of the direct path to the window. He hated to disturb the body even that much, but if they needed to ward off an attack from this side of the house, he didn't want to go tripping over it.

Before he left the room, though, he looked back toward the boy who could have been him at that age.

"I'll look in on your ma for you, boy. And I'll make sure she knows you died trying to help a friend."

"We're almost out of water."

Wade rubbed his eyes, wishing like hell he were anywhere else but pinned down in an Ozark stage station with two frightened children and their outlaw father, not to mention one extremely angry woman.

"Then we'll do without." He knew immediately that wasn't the right answer, but under the circumstances it was the best he could do.

"That's fine for you, but what about them?"

He didn't have to guess who Lottie was talking about. Hell, he was worried about the children, too, but there wasn't a hell of a lot he could do about that, either.

Bardell's men were currently taking a break from shooting up the house, but it was only a matter of time before they started up again. He understood their game because he'd do the same thing himself. Hit hard and then back off, doing the most damage with the lowest number of casualties. There'd been no more attempts to parley since the first one.

No doubt, they'd realized the futility in trying to negotiate. Ambrose wasn't about to give himself up, even if Wade had been willing to let him go. He wished like hell that there were a way to get Lottie and the children to safety, but even if the outlaws offered them safe passage, Wade didn't trust them to hold to any agreement.

He looked around the room. Jack sat listlessly looking at a book while his sister huddled in a corner with her thumb firmly stuck in her mouth. Lottie was dividing her time equally between fussing over the children and glaring at the two men.

And he'd bet his last dollar that Ambrose was planning something. Several times Wade had caught him counting bullets as he stared out the window. Each time he realized that Wade was watching, he had immediately backed away and pretended to be doing something else.

Lottie crawled over to where Wade was sitting. "What time is it?"

"Does it matter?" he asked even as he reached for his watch.

"I want to know if it's time to start dinner."

Something in her voice made him look at her more closely. Water wasn't the only thing they were low on, and her past few attempts at preparing a meal had been pretty sad.

"It's going on five."

"Well, then I'd better get busy." Her voice dropped to a low whisper. "I think Ambrose is up to something."

"So do I."

"You've got to stop him."

"Since I have no idea what he's planning, what do you suggest that I do?"

Lottie sighed, her frustration clearly building. "He'll get himself killed if he goes charging outside."

"It isn't exactly safe in here, either."

Lottie jerked back as if he had hit her. Damn, she was right to be worried, and he had no business taking his own bad mood out on her. There were new lines carved along the side of her mouth, and dark rings circled her eyes. The past few days had taken a toll on all of them.

He pushed himself up to his feet. "I'll talk to him. You rest for a while. Dinner can wait."

He found Ambrose in Lottie's room in the process of arming himself with every conceivable weapon he could find.

"Going somewhere?"

This time Bardell didn't try to disguise his actions. He kept loading bullets into a spare pistol. That done, he checked to make sure that his knife slid easily into the top of his boot.

"One of us has got to make a move. If I can fight my way free, they'll come after me and leave my family alone."

"That's bullshit, and you know it. You run and that leaves us one less gun to defend ourselves with. You've made it abundantly clear to them that your family means something to you. Even if you make it to the horses and get out, they know that all they have to do is hold Lottie and the children hostage. Besides, now that they know who I am, they're not about to ride out without killing me first." He placed himself firmly between Ambrose and the window.

"Help is on the way. We just need to wait them out."

Ambrose muttered a few curse words of his own. "Some help. Either I get killed in the crossfire or your friends will haul me and anyone left alive outside back to Springfield to dance at the end of a rope. I'd rather take my chances out there."

Before he could say another word, Wade had his pistol pointed right in Ambrose's face. "I never figured you for a damn coward! I can't believe you'd go looking for the easy way out and leave your family to fend for themselves." He pulled back on the hammer. "On second thought, I don't know why it would surprise me. It's what you've been doing all along."

Ambrose didn't back up an inch. He knew damn good and well that Wade wouldn't shoot him. Not here and not now.

"Either shoot or get out of my way."

Both men froze at the sound of a rifle being cocked. They both turned slowly to face Lottie. She vibrated with barely controlled fury.

She stepped into the room, taking dead aim at her brother-in-law. "Stop it, both of you. Neither one of you is going anywhere until that help you promised gets here. After that, I don't give a damn where you go or what you do. But for now, shut up and keep an eye on things. Something is going on outside."

Now that she pointed it out, Wade could hear

some sort of ruckus going on outside. "Stay with the children in the hall."

Lottie nodded and ducked back out into the hall-way.

Their fight temporarily forgotten, both men rushed to the window to look out. Nothing was stirring outside Lottie's room, so they headed back into the kitchen. Wade shouldered Ambrose out of his way to get there first. One look outside told him Lottie was right. Ambrose's men were slowly gathering out behind the barn.

Unable to see any more than just that, he ran back to his room and looked out that way. Nothing. Carefully avoiding looking at the shrouded form on the floor, he rushed back to the kitchen.

"I don't like the look of this at all. Whatever they're planning, this could be their final rush."

"They've got torches." Ambrose eased away from the window. "What did you see out back?"

"If there's anyone out that way now, he's far enough back that we can't see him."

The situation, already grim, had taken a decided turn for the desperate. They'd just run out of options.

"We've got to risk it."

One look at Bardell's eyes told Wade exactly what he was thinking. Although he tried to come up with another alternative, he couldn't, because Bardell was right. If his men charged the house with torches, the building would burn like kindling. If the outlaws managed to get even one or two torches on the roof or underneath the house, it would be only a matter of time before Lottie and the children had to run or be burned alive. They had no choice at all.

"They're your family. Take them out the back while I keep your men busy."

"Damn noble of you, lawman, but I don't think so. It's me they want the most. As long as they know I'm in the house, there's a chance they'll stay right here. You and Lottie can take the children out through the window while I give you cover fire. Once you make it as far as the woods, head for the river. When you've had time to get clear, I'll follow."

Wade wanted to argue, but there wasn't time. Besides, their choices had narrowed down considerably in the past few minutes to almost none. There wasn't much he could say except "Keep your head down."

Once in the hallway, he motioned for Lottie to follow him into her bedroom.

The second Wade pulled her aside, Lottie knew something was dreadfully wrong. She fought down the cold taste of fear. Considering all that had gone on over the past few days, if it was bad enough to scare Wade, whatever he was about to tell her must be horrific indeed.

"We've got to make a run for the river."

"But you said help was on its way," she protested.

"That was before they decided to burn us out."

The floor below her came rushing up at her. Wade caught her before she hit the floor, and dragged her to the edge of the bed and forced her to sit down.

"Damn it, Lottie, breathe. We don't have time for this." The roughness of his words were in direct contrast to the gentleness with which he held her.

She fought for each breath until at last she could fill her lungs. Wade kept his arm draped around her shoulder, offering her what comfort he could. It was little enough, but it helped.

The rifle in her hands suddenly felt as if it weighed a ton. She set it down gently.

"Who would do such a thing?"

Wade's look reminded her that the answer was obvious: the type of men who followed her brother-in-law. Ambrose had much to answer for.

"Grab whatever food you can carry. We'll head for the river, so water won't be a problem."

"How can you be so calm about this?"

"Because someone has to be. If it makes you feel any better, I'll have a fit of vapors when we reach safety." He fanned himself and batted his eyes at her for effect.

She smiled, as he had intended. Knowing there was no time to be wasted, she pushed herself up off the bed and retrieved her rifle from the floor. "I'll get the food. You and Ambrose get the children ready."

For the second time in a very few minutes, Wade was giving her that look that warned her that she was about to hear more bad news.

"He won't be coming with us, at least not right away."

"But the house . . ." she started to say, but then she knew. "He's going to try to buy us time."

"That's the idea. Once I get you and the children down to the river, I'll come back for him."

"Then let's hurry."

Once in the kitchen, she headed straight for her brother-in-law. Despite all his shortcomings, he was family and she loved him. He saw her coming and held out his arms.

"You be careful," she mumbled against the hard wall of his chest.

Wade was waiting when she stepped back. For

once, he didn't seem to resent seeing her hug Ambrose.

"I'll watch the windows. I thought you might have something you wanted to say to Jack and Rose."

"Thanks."

Ambrose ran to the hallway. Lottie followed a few steps behind. He already had both children gathered into his arms.

"Now listen, you two. Mr. Wade and Lottie are going to get you to safety. I'm going to wait here for the other marshals to come." He kissed both of them on the forehead. "Do what you're told and make me proud."

Jack only looked confused by the intense expression on his father's face. Rose, with that almost adultlike wisdom of hers, picked up on the undercurrents right away. She burrowed in closer to her father and held on for dear life.

"I love you," she whispered when Ambrose moved to set her down.

Lottie thought her heart would break. Her brother-in-law, the outlaw, gently shoved his daughter toward her. His eyes had a suspicious sheen to them, but his expression dared her to say anything.

She herded the children toward the back bedroom, wishing they didn't have to pass by Jeb's body. Wade was right on their heels. He did his best to shield Jack and Rose from the grim spectacle.

"I'll climb out the window first, so I can take a quick look around."

And draw any fire if someone was watching the back of the house. She heard the words just as if he'd actually spoken them.

"On my signal, hand out Rose and then Jack. I'll stand guard while you climb down."

It wasn't much of a plan, but she couldn't come

up with anything better. He pulled the sheet off the bed and laid it across the windowsill to blunt the jagged edges of the broken glass. That done, he worked his way through the narrow opening. Once he was outside on the ground, she handed him his rifle and the meager sack of supplies she'd gathered.

He ducked out of sight for several long seconds before returning to the window. She didn't realize that she was holding her breath until he poked his head back through the window to tell Rose to get ready. The trusting little girl handed him her doll to hold until Lottie could help her climb out into Wade's waiting arms.

Jack immediately held up his arms so Lottie could lift him. "You're getting to be almost too much for me to lift anymore."

That idea pleased him, bringing the first smile to his face in days. "I'm going to be as tall as my father."

She silently prayed that Ambrose would live long enough to see that come true. Reminding herself that the sooner they got away, the sooner Wade could come back for him, she began the awkward climb out the window herself. She landed hard on her right foot, sending a jolt of pain shooting up her leg. Wade did his best to catch her again, but he had his hands full with the two rifles.

"Are you all right?"

"I'll have to be," she assured him. Taking back her rifle, she held out her hand to Jack and prepared to follow Wade.

"On a count of three, I want all of us to run as fast as we can go to that stand of trees over there. We need to be as quiet as we can. Got that?"

Jack nodded. Rose grabbed Lottie's hand and

held on for dear life. Silently, Wade held up one finger, then two, and then three. Despite her exhaustion, it felt almost exhilarating to be outside in the fresh air. The four of them ran as fast as the children could move, ignoring the sudden commotion coming from the other side of the house.

She prayed long and hard for her brother-in-law but didn't let her worry for him hamper her need to get the children to safety. The trees didn't seem to be getting any closer as she struggled to keep up with Wade. She'd pay for the abuse to her injured ankle later, but she couldn't afford to favor it now. When the racket from the outlaws seemed to be getting louder—*please God, not closer*—she picked Rose up in her arms and put on a final burst of speed. Wade didn't even break stride when he scooped up Jack.

When they reached the first scattering of saplings, she slowed only slightly to allow for the rougher ground ahead. Each step they took put them that much farther out of harm's way. Finally, she risked a look back over her shoulder. They'd gone far enough into the woods that the house was almost obscured from sight.

Wade slowed almost to a stop. "Can you make it to the river with your ankle?"

She managed to drag up a smile, more to reassure the children than Wade. "I'll make it."

"Are you sure?"

Lottie glared at him. "I said I would."

Since there weren't any options other than to keep moving, Wade started out again, but a little slower than before. Since Rose seemed to be getting heavier with each passing moment, Lottie wasn't about to complain. Finally, when she was convinced that somehow they'd lost their way in the confusion, she caught sight of the river through the trees ahead.

Wade turned off to the left and then stopped. He set Jack back down on his feet and waited for Lottie to catch up.

"Stay here until I come back for you."

"But . . ."

"Damn it, woman, don't argue."

"I wasn't going to; I just wanted to know what I should do if . . ."

"I'll be back." Wade planted a quick kiss on her mouth before moving away. He looked back over his shoulder before he disappeared into the trees. "I promise."

She wanted to shout after him that she knew very well what most men's promises were worth: nothing. But he was already almost out of sight. Sighing with weariness, she drew what comfort she could from the possibility that this man took his oaths more seriously than most. Looking around for a convenient log to sit on, she pulled the children closer to her side and sat down to wait.

Sixteen

He could smell oily smoke long before he could see the station through the trees. He slowed his steps, trying to judge the best way to approach the unknown situation ahead. If they'd already set the house aflame, then there wasn't much he could do except to make sure that Ambrose escaped the fire.

If they were still only making threats, then he might have a few more options. He paused for a moment to get his bearings and to make sure he was still alone on this side of the house. No such luck—a pair of men came running around the back corner of the house. The two of them passed underneath the window he and Lottie had used for their escape only minutes before. His debt to Lady Luck was piling up.

For men on the attack, they sure as hell weren't being too damn careful. He debated whether to teach them a lesson the hard way, but he didn't want to alert them to the fact that most of their prey was no longer inside the trap. He pressed back against a large tree and waited for them to pass by. Instead, they stopped.

He peeked around the tree trunk to see what had brought them to a halt. His temper, already short, exploded into action when he saw what they were doing. He hadn't noticed the roughly made torches in their hands. It looked as if they'd soaked rags in oil of some kind and wrapped them around the end of a stick of wood. While he watched, one of them struck a match and held it to the rag.

His gun was in his hand and blazing before the torch did more than smolder. He hit the closest rider with his first shot and then turned his attention to the second one. It took two bullets to bring him down, but then who was counting?

Both men lay wounded on the ground, but from this distance he couldn't tell how badly they were hurt. He supposed he should care, but he damn well didn't. Any bastard who'd willingly set fire to a house with children inside deserved to die.

Having reduced the enemy by two more, he figured his luck would hold long enough for him to reach the window. He ran straight for the house. After dropping his guns through the opening, he grabbed the sill and pulled himself up. He could only hope that Ambrose wouldn't hear him and shoot before checking to see who he was.

A small sliver of glass sliced into his palm when he tried to lift himself up. It hurt like a son of a bitch, but he ignored the pain. Lottie had tossed the sheet they'd used for padding back inside, rightly figuring it would have been a clear signal to their captors that someone had escaped. With a final twist of his shoulders, he pulled himself through the window and tumbled down onto the floor.

Breathing hard, he picked up his guns and reached for the doorknob. Easing the door open slowly, he peered out into the hallway. The way was clear, so he stepped out of the bedroom.

"Ambrose!" he called softly.

No answer.

"Bardell!" His second try was met with silence.

With his back to the wall, he sidestepped down the hall to the kitchen. His gun cocked and ready, he paused at the corner before risking a look. One glance had him running. The kitchen was empty, and the door to the porch was wide open.

Where had the bastard gone to ground this time?

That was when he noticed that the only noise he was hearing was the sound of his own breathing. He ran back to the kitchen window. One look outside and his stomach lurched.

He didn't know how Ambrose came to be outside, but he was facing down half a dozen men, all with their guns pointed straight at him. Wade had to admire the courage—or maybe it was stupidity—it took to look certain death in the face with such calm.

He strained to hear what was being said.

"So, McNulty, you think you've got the brains to run this outfit?"

"Damn straight."

"I give you a month before the lot of you are either dead or waiting in jail for your turn to dance at the end of a marshal's rope."

The laughing response to Ambrose's comment echoed in the morning stillness.

"That may be, Bardell, but you sure as hell won't be around to see it happen. And that marshal friend of yours isn't going to live long enough to come after us."

Wade figured Ambrose would be able to take out one, maybe two of the others if he was lucky. He himself had a clear shot at their leader, but even if the lady was pulling for him, there wasn't a chance in hell of getting Ambrose out of there alive, much less unharmed.

For the moment, neither side had the clear advantage, but Ambrose had to know if he even blinked, the others would be on him in a heartbeat. Not for the first time, Wade wondered where the other deputies were. At least one or two of them should have had time to reach the station.

He moved around to look out toward the road, but no one was in sight. Had Buck failed to pass along the message? No, the old man would have delivered the letter to Satan himself if Lottie had asked him to.

There wasn't any use in depending on help that might not come. Once again, he stood next to the window and listened to the conversation. He was surprised that Ambrose's men were still listening to his insults.

"Damn straight I robbed the lot of you. It's not my fault that you weren't smart enough to pick up on that. Besides, you all ended up with more money than you could have earned on your own, even if you did spend it all faster than you could steal it."

The men shifted restlessly. Their newly chosen leader took a step closer to Bardell but backed away when Ambrose's rifle came up to point right at his chest.

"Back off, McNulty. I've already warned you what would happen if you got too close."

McNulty eased back slightly, but his own gun didn't waiver an inch. "We want that money back."

Ambrose laughed. "So do the people we took it from. I figure you have about the same chance as they do of seeing even a penny of it again."

"What did you do with it all?"

"That doesn't concern you."

As if he could feel Wade's gaze on him, Ambrose glanced right at the kitchen window. Then he very deliberately looked toward the barn and back again.

Wade followed Ambrose's line of sight. At first he didn't see anything, but then he caught a small movement in the brush behind the corral. The mules stirred restlessly.

Now that he knew where to look, he saw two or three others working their way around behind Ambrose's captors. The posse had arrived. Soon they'd have the whole bunch in a deadly crossfire. Considering who Bardell was, they wouldn't be all that concerned about keeping him safe. If he was killed, it would mean one less trial and one less hanging. Rough justice, perhaps, but not undeserved.

Once again, Wade fought with his own conscience. There wasn't a doubt in his mind that Bardell deserved whatever happened to him, but his children and his sister-in-law didn't. Hell, against his own better judgment, he liked the man.

He needed to get outside. There wasn't time to use the back window again, which left the front door. If he could draw the outlaws' attention, the other marshals could come up from behind. He checked his ammunition before stepping through the door. As long as he stayed close to the wall, no one could see him. Even if he made it as far as the edge of the porch, he wouldn't have a clean shot at anyone except Bardell himself.

Instead, he decided to circle around the back. If he came up behind, he'd stand a better chance of helping Ambrose survive the morning. He stepped off the far side of the porch onto the ground and ran along the length of the house. The two wounded outlaws had either crawled away on their own or someone had helped them. It had to have been one of Wade's men, or else Wade would be getting a hotter reception right now.

He looked around for some sign of where they'd

gone. The grass was matted down as if something heavy had been dragged off into the woods. He followed the trail with his eyes. Sure enough, someone was waving his rifle over his head to get Wade's attention. He recognized him as a deputy by the name of Carter, with whom he'd worked before. A new surge of energy rushed through him now that he knew for sure he wasn't alone in this mess.

As he watched, the lawman took off through the woods at a lope, no doubt to spread the word that Wade had been found. It was time to bring this mess to a conclusion. Wade braced himself for the worst and marched across the end of the house. He turned the final corner.

"Drop your guns," he said. "We have you surrounded."

To emphasize his point, several of the other deputies stepped out of their hiding spots long enough to make sure that no one made the mistake of thinking Wade was only bluffing. At first the outlaws froze, but then two made the mistake of trying to fight their way clear of the ambush. They were dead before they'd gone two steps.

Maybe McNulty was smarter than his companions, because he immediately dropped his rifle and threw his hands up in the air. The others, including Ambrose, followed suit.

Wade slowly started forward, watching to make sure that no one decided to try something stupid. When he got within spitting distance of Bardell, the outlaw leader slowly dropped his hands. One of the other deputies barked out an order for him to stop.

Instead, Bardell lunged forward and grabbed McNulty's pistol out of his holster. In the space of a single breath, he gut-shot his former companion and then turned to face Wade. His shots and those of the deputies blended into one loud roar. First McNulty, then two of his men, and finally Ambrose himself jerked and twitched in a twisted dance of death as they were cut down in the bright sunshine.

It was all over in a matter of seconds. Wade dropped his still smoking gun to rush to where Ambrose lay bleeding into the rocky Missouri soil. He didn't know if his bullet was the one that brought the outlaw down, and didn't want to. Ambrose's eyes sought out Wade's face in the crowd gathering around him. A faint smile played around his lips.

"Damn you, Ambrose," Wade muttered. "Lottie and your children deserve better than this." He fought the urge to punch the already dying man. How was he supposed to explain to Lottie that he was most likely the one who had killed her beloved brother-in-law?

One of the other deputies demanded to know, "What the hell made him do something like that?"

Wade gave the only answer they'd understand. He motioned toward McNulty's bloody corpse. "The bastard threatened his family."

He pointed in the general direction of the river. "He held them off while I got his children and sister-in-law out of the house. Her name is Lottie Hammond, and she's the station master here. A couple of you head that way through the woods. Make sure she sees your badges, because she has a rifle and isn't afraid to use it." He glanced back down at Ambrose. "Better tell her to hurry. The rest of you, clean up this mess."

Ambrose stirred restlessly. "McCord . . ."

"Save your breath for your family."

The outlaw struggled to say something else, but then he lay quiet. Wade knelt down in the bloody dust and lifted Ambrose up over his shoulder. Later there'd be time to explain his actions to the others, but for now he wanted to get Ambrose inside. Jack and Rose didn't need to live the rest of their lives remembering their father as a bloody corpse.

When he reached the porch, he braced himself against the railing long enough to catch his breath. That done, he eased through the doorway and headed directly for Lottie's room. He deposited his heavy burden on the bed. She might not appreciate bloodstains on her quilt, but considering the circumstances, he didn't care.

He pulled the other side of the bedding over Ambrose and then propped the dying man up on the pillows.

"I'll get you some water."

"Don't bother, lawman. It would just run right back out through all the holes I've got in me."

Wade let his temper boil over. The bastard was dying and still he was making jokes. "What the hell were you thinking of? You knew as soon as you made a move you were a dead man."

"Bound to happen some time. Besides, it was better than hanging."

Wade couldn't tell whether the sound Ambrose made was a laugh or a wheeze. It didn't matter much at this point.

"McCord. Remember what I told you."

"I said I would."

"Make Lottie listen. You two deserve each other." This time it was clearly laughter.

Not knowing what to make of that remark, Wade went back outside to watch for Bardell's family. The deputy was just coming into sight, leading a horse with Lottie and both children on its back. He wished he'd thought of suggesting it himself, but then he'd had other things on his mind. He'd thank the man for his thoughtfulness later. Even without Lottie's sore ankle to consider, the three of them were in no condition to walk any distance.

And they had more hard times ahead of them. He stepped forward to meet them. When the horse slowed to a stop, Lottie roused herself enough to look around. She spotted Wade first and the blood on his shirt second. Her cry of distress had him hurrying to reassure her that he was unharmed.

"It's not mine," he assured her as he reached up to help first Rose and then Jack to the ground.

When they were safely afoot, he held his arms up to Lottie, willing her to let him help her at least that much. She hesitated only slightly before accepting his aid. She grimaced in pain when she put her full weight on her ankle, but then straightened up as if determined to make it on her own. Knowing how stubborn she could be, he stepped back and let his hands drop to his side.

He wondered if she'd ever learn to accept his help without arguing. Considering everything, probably not.

"Ambrose is inside."

She met his gaze over the children's heads. The questions didn't need to be spoken out loud. He answered with a simple shake of his head.

"Rose, Jack. Your father needs us."

Knowing his help was no longer wanted, he watched the three of them trudge into the house and close the door behind them. He bitterly resented being shut out of the family circle, but there wasn't much he could do about it. Lottie had made her feelings all too clear on the subject.

He forced his feet to walk away from the house, feeling some relief that he had other pressing matters to see to. As he came around to the side of the building, he almost ran headlong into Carter.

"We're about done here. What about the one inside?"

Wade looked past him to see that the other deputies already had the rest of the outlaws, dead and alive, on horseback and ready to ride out. He'd stay behind long enough to help Lottie bury her brother-in-law and then take Jeb home to his mother. It was the least he could do for the boy.

"I'll take care of him."

Carter gave him an odd look but didn't question him. "Should I tell the boss you'll be along directly?"

"Yeah. I have a few loose ends to tie up before I come in."

"He'll be happier than hell that you managed to draw this bunch out. They've been a burr under his saddle for a long time. Never could figure out where they were going to ground."

"They have"—he started to say, then corrected himself—"had themselves a sweet little hidey-hole tucked up in the end of a valley. I'll make sure everybody knows where it is in case someone else decides to take up residence there. But the other reason we could never find them was that Bardell sent them all home after every job. They were never together for more than a few days at a time."

"We always figured him for a smart son of a bitch." Carter walked toward his horse with Wade following along beside him. After he swung up in the saddle, he gave Wade a considering look.

"There's reward money on some of these bastards. Who should get it?"

Lottie would need every penny she could get to

raise Jack and Rose by herself, but he knew she'd only see it as blood money.

"I'll let you know when I get back to town."

"Good enough. See you in a few days, then."

It was with some relief that he watched the others ride out. He'd been afraid they'd want to rest overnight, but that would have only made it harder on Lottie and her small family. She didn't need any more grim reminders of the past few days than she already had. He watched until the last horse disappeared over the hill, and then headed into the barn.

There were chores that needed doing: mules to feed, stalls to clean, a grave to dig.

Repairs on the station were going slowly. It didn't matter, though. New glass and patched holes wouldn't do much toward erasing certain images from Lottie's mind. She looked out the window to where Jack and Rose were playing in the shade of the sycamore tree. As they grew up, their memories of Ambrose would fade. She could only hope that they would manage to cling to the good ones.

But he wasn't the only one she was trying to forgive and forget. Closing her eyes, she let the image of Wade McCord fill her mind. It had been three weeks and then some since she'd last seen him. The pain in her heart hadn't eased at all in that time. Sometimes it hurt so bad that she didn't think it would ever go away.

And she wasn't sure she wanted it to. Hurting was better than feeling nothing at all. Her life before Wade came walking down that dusty road seemed distant and cold. He had fit right into their lives as if he'd been custom ordered. Jack and Rose both asked about him daily. It bothered her some that they had fewer questions about their father.

But then, Ambrose had never been part of their daily routine the way Wade had been. He'd shared their chores, their meals, her bed. She turned away from the window, looking for some way to keep her hands and mind busy. It was bad enough that she tossed and turned during the night with images of Wade plaguing her dreams. She wouldn't share her daylight hours with him, too.

Anger burned in her stomach, some of it aimed at herself for ordering him to leave, and the rest at him for leaving so easily. He could have put up more of a fight.

A distant sound caught her attention. After a second, she heard it again. Jack came running through the door.

"The stage is coming in!"

Pure panic had her charging out onto the porch to make sure that Jack wasn't mistaken, and praying that he was. But no, here came Buck snapping the reins and sweet-talking his mules.

"Oh, Lordy, I forgot."

Jack's eyes about popped out of his head at that announcement. Never in his whole life had she failed to have Buck's team ready and waiting for him. There was no hiding her mistake, but if they hurried, they could minimize the delay.

"You start brushing the mules. I'll be right out."

Lifting her skirts, she ran back inside to change into a shirt and pants. It was bad enough she was late, but harnessing mules while wearing a dress was nothing short of ridiculous.

By the time she came back outside, Buck had already pulled into the yard and set the brake. He looked around for his replacement team. When he didn't see it, he climbed down from his seat, looking more worried than angry.

"Miss Lottie, are you all right?" He'd been fussing over her every time he came through ever since he'd heard about what had happened.

"Just fine, Buck. I guess my mind wandered off somewhere today." She stood by him as his passengers climbed out to stretch their legs a bit.

When the last one had stepped down from the stage, she told them, "There's hot food and fresh bread inside. Help yourselves." Several of them gave her curious looks. As usual, she put it off to their never having seen a woman in her line of work before.

As she hurried past them to the barn, she thanked whatever angel had spurred her into making a kettle of soup that morning. Maybe on some level she had remembered the stage was due in, but either way, her guests would be occupied long enough to get the mules hitched up to the stage.

Jack already had the first pair brushed up and waiting for her. Grateful for his help, she got the harnesses laid out and started fastening the endless array of buckles and straps. By time she had the second pair in place, Buck was back outside. He fell in beside her without a word. In short order, the fresh team was in place, and the tired animals were resting in the corral.

For once, Buck didn't complain about the lack of pie. Although he usually shared some of the latest gossip in town with her before leaving, this time he seemed in an unusual hurry to be on his way. It had taken her a little longer than normal to get his new team ready, but she didn't think she'd made him all that late. He practically ran into the house to hustle his passengers along.

"All right, folks. We need to be going."

She had to choke back a laugh when he helped the last fellow along by giving him a hefty shove through the door of the coach. Unless she missed her guess, the poor man landed right in someone's lap, who then shoved him off onto the floor. Buck paid no attention to the ensuing complaints as he climbed back up on top and picked up the reins.

"I'm sorry about today, Buck. It won't happen again."

"Don't you go worrying yourself about me, missy. You just take care that you don't make any other mistakes that you might regret." With that remark, he looked back over the stage toward the road behind him.

She wondered what he was looking for but didn't see anything except a pair of turkey buzzards circling high in the sky over the ridge. There was no telling what was bothering the old coot, so she went up on the porch with the children to wave good-bye as the stage rolled out.

Before it was even out of sight, she headed for the barn and the weary mules. Picking up the brushes and currycombs, she started on the first animal and worked her way through to the last one. That done she filled the water trough and carried out several pitchfork-fulls of hay. The hungry animals tore into their feed with relish.

Tired and aching from all the lifting, she stretched her back and trudged back toward the house. She realized that a good couple of hours had passed without her even once thinking of Wade McCord. She was making progress, but if she had to work this hard to get over him, she'd be dead within the year. It was a grim joke, but it still made her smile.

One look at the shambles the stage passengers had made of her kitchen had her shaking her head. By the time she got that mess cleaned up, she'd be ready to turn in even if it was well before dinnertime. Knowing that if she sat down she might not be able to get up again, she picked up her apron and started in.

"Jack, come dry dishes for me."

He came in dragging his feet a few minutes later. She wasn't surprised, knowing it wasn't exactly his favorite chore. He'd long ago figured out that the faster he worked, the sooner he would be free to play some more. So it came as a surprise when she set the last plate on the stack of dishes waiting to be dried, only to realize he'd hardly touched a thing.

"Jack, come away from that window and get busy." When he didn't immediately comply, she demanded, "What's so interesting out there?"

He gestured with the cup in his hand. "There's a man out at the well."

"I didn't hear a horse ride in."

"Doesn't have one. Looks like he walked."

Suddenly, her heart pumped a lot of energy and built excitement through her weary body. Not wanting to look for fear she was wrong, she took one step and then another toward the window.

One glance outside and she ordered, "Jack, stay inside and keep Rose with you."

"But it's . . ."

"Jack," she said in that tone of voice she saved for the occasions when she would brook no arguments.

"But . . ." he tried one more time.

She shot her nephew a look that would melt iron. "Stay. I'll deal with this."

Picking up her rifle, she marched out to the water pump, ready to do battle.

* * *

"Turn around nice and easy."

Unlike the first time, Wade wasn't surprised either by the sound of a rifle being cocked or that the station manager was a woman. A beautiful one, at that.

He raised his hands and slowly turned to face the one woman in the world who had the power to bring him to his knees even without the gun she held in her trembling hands.

"Where's your horse, mister?"

"Don't have one."

"How did you get here?"

"A friendly stage driver drove me as far as my money held out."

"I didn't know Buck charged by the mile."

"He said that ex-gamblers got special treatment on his route. There was something about maybe earning my keep, if I was lucky." His arms were starting to ache. He hoped he wasn't mistaken about the slight softening in her expression. He'd taken a big risk coming here with no way to leave if she was of a mind to send him packing again.

"He said that, did he?" The gun lowered a fraction of an inch. "You have any experience working with mules?"

"Yes, ma'am. I was taught by the best."

"I don't have much use for drifters. How long you planning on staying?"

The time for make-believe was over. He took his hat in his hands and put his heart in his eyes.

"If there's a God in heaven, I'll be here until the day I die."

She considered the matter. "What about your other job? I've had enough of men riding in and out of my life."

"I resigned." He drew a deep breath and plunged

ahead. "I didn't mean to be gone so long, Lottie. I had some business to see to that took longer than I expected."

"What business?"

Figuring she wasn't ready to hear about the money Ambrose had set aside for the children, he left that part out. "There was reward money to be collected."

The rifle barrel came back up. "I've got no use for—"

"I gave the money to Jeb's mother. Figured she'd have need of it." He hadn't planned on telling Lottie the rest of it, but decided she'd want to know. "I told her he died a hero, trying to save your lives. It's close enough to the truth."

Lottie's eyes sparkled with tears as she laid down the rifle.

"That was right decent of you, Wade. I wouldn't have thought of doing that. I'd like to think that Ambrose wouldn't have minded helping her out."

"He asked me to look after Jeb, you know, even before . . ."

That had her smiling. "About that job, I think you'd be about perfect."

Then she moved into his arms, feeling as natural there as if they'd been practicing for a lifetime. He buried his face in the silvery silk of her hair and held her tight.

"You'll have to make an honest woman of me," she murmured against his chest.

"Yes, ma'am. First thing."

"We'll go visit your friend Lily and her husband for a honeymoon."

"Yes, ma'am, that's the third thing on my list."

She leaned away to look up at him. "You skipped number two."

"That's because I can't wait any longer for this."
He captured her mouth with his.

Hours later, he wandered out onto the porch. He
thought Jack and Rose would never settle down
enough to go to bed. If he didn't get Lottie alone
soon, he feared for his sanity. Now that she'd welcomed him back into her life, he wanted to use
every means at his disposal to convince her she'd
made the right decision.

The thought of taking her to bed had kept him
hard and needy all evening long.

At last, he heard the door behind him open.
Without waiting to be asked, she slipped inside his
arm and nestled against his chest. The simple gesture filled a hole inside him that had been cold and
empty for far too long. At the moment, it was
enough to have his woman at his side, enjoying the
night sounds.

Katydids and crickets sang their hearts out as the
lightning bugs flickered in the woods. The last bit
of sunset faded as they watched the hills to the west.

"Want to go inside?" Lottie's voice sounded
husky with something more than a simple invitation.

"More than I've wanted anything in a long time."

"Look up there."

He glanced in the direction she was pointing in
time to see the final flash of a shooting star.

"What did you wish for?" Lottie asked as she took
him by the hand and led him inside.

He didn't even have to think about his answer.
"Not a blessed thing. I've already got everything I
could possibly want."

Then he stepped through the door and shut the
rest of the world outside.

If you liked LUCK OF THE DRAW and KING OF HEARTS, be sure to look for the first book in Pat Pritchard's new Ballad series, *The Luminary Society*, available March 2003 wherever books are sold.

In THE BOOK OF LOVE, store owner Lucy Thomas is determined to take her future into her own hands—and to take some of the local women with her. Now that the small town of Lee's Mill, Missouri, is being rebuilt after the destruction of the War Between the States, Lucy believes it's time for the Luminary Society, dedicated to improving the lot of the town's women. But newspaper owner Cade Mulroney begs to disagree, leading to more than a few arguments—and some very explosive sparks. . . .

COMING IN SEPTEMBER 2002 FROM
ZEBRA BALLAD ROMANCES

__AFTER THE STORM: Haven
by Jo Ann Ferguson   0-8217-7377-1 $5.99US/$7.99CAN
Cailin Rafferty will stop at nothing to find her children. Her journey
brings her to the sleepy town of Haven, Ohio, where gentle Samuel
Jennings had rescued them from the orphan train. For Cailin, wrench-
ing them from the peaceful comfort of Sam's home is hard—almost
as difficult as admitting her feelings for the quiet, warm-hearted man.

__EXPLORER: The Vikings
by Kathryn Hockett   0-8217-7259-7 $5.99US/$7.99CAN
Unaware that he is the son of a Viking jarl, Sean was raised in an
Irish monastery. But then he offers shelter to a lovely young slave—
and changes his life forever. For when Natasha is recaptured and dispatched aboard a Viking ship, Sean knows that he must rescue her.
He ventures out on the high seas—seeking his heritage, his family,
and his lady love.

__THE HEALING: Men of Honor
by Kathryn Fox   0-8217-7244-9 $5.99US/$7.99CAN
On the run after killing her violent lover in self-defense, Jenny Hanson
needs a safe haven. She heads for Dawson City—only to hitch a ride
with the very man sent to bring her to justice. Northwest Mounted
Policeman Mike Finnegan is a man who left behind a troubled past
to serve the law. He's also a man offering her protection and love . . .

__TO TOUCH THE SKY: The MacInness Legacy
by Julie Moffett   0-8217-7271-6 $5.99US/$7.99CAN
Gillian Saunders is content with her simple life, until it is turned
upside down by handsome physician Spencer Reeves, who's been
badly injured in a shipwreck. She never expects to be swept into an
irresistible passion . . . or that an ancient curse which haunts her family will soon threaten her newfound love with him.

Call toll free **1-888-345-BOOK** to order by phone or use this coupon
to order by mail. *ALL BOOKS AVAILABLE SEPTEMBER 1, 2002.*

Name _____

Address _____

City_____ State _____ Zip _____

Please send me the books that I checked above.

I am enclosing $_____
Plus postage and handling* $_____
Sales tax (in NY and TN) $_____
Total amount enclosed $_____

*Add $2.50 for the first book and $.50 for each additional book.
Send check or money order (no cash or CODs) to: **Kensington Publishing
Corp., Dept. C.O., 850 Third Avenue, New York, NY 10022**
Prices and numbers subject to change without notice. Valid only in the
U.S. All orders subject to availability. **NO ADVANCE ORDERS.**
Visit our website at **www.kensingtonbooks.com**